Even Inspector Witherspoon himself doesn't know—because his secret weapon is as ladylike as she is clever. She's Mrs. Jeffries—the charming detective who stars in this unique Victorian mystery series. Enjoy them all . . .

The Inspector and Mrs. Jeffries
A doctor is found dead in his own office—and Mrs. Jeffries must scour the premises to find the prescription for murder.

Mrs. Jeffries Dusts for Clues
One case is solved and another is opened when the Inspector finds a missing brooch—pinned to a dead woman's gown. But Mrs. Jeffries never cleans a room without dusting under the bed—and never gives up on a case before every loose end is tightly tied.

The Ghost and Mrs. Jeffries
Death is unpredictable . . . but the murder of Mrs. Hodges was foreseen at a spooky séance. The practical-minded housekeeper may not be able to see the future—but she can look into the past and put things in order to solve this haunting crime.

Mrs. Jeffries Takes Stock
A businessman has been murdered—and it could be because he cheated his stockholders. The housekeeper's interest is piqued . . . and when it comes to catching killers, the smart money's on Mrs. Jeffries.

Mrs. Jeffries on the Ball
A festive Jubilee celebration turns into a fatal affair—and Mrs. Jeffries must find the guilty party.

Mrs. Jeffries on the Trail
Why was Annie Shields out selling flowers so late on a foggy night? And more importantly, who killed her while she was doing it? It's up to Mrs. Jeffries to sniff out the clues.

continued . . .

Mrs. Jeffries Plays the Cook
Mrs. Jeffries finds herself doing double duty: cooking for the inspector's household and trying to cook a killer's goose.

Mrs. Jeffries and the Missing Alibi
When Inspector Witherspoon becomes the main suspect in a murder, Scotland Yard refuses to let him investigate. But no one said anything about Mrs. Jeffries.

Mrs. Jeffries Stands Corrected
When a local publican is murdered, and Inspector Witherspoon botches the investigation, trouble starts to brew for Mrs. Jeffries.

Mrs. Jeffries Takes the Stage
After a theatre critic is murdered, Mrs. Jeffries uncovers the victim's secret past: a real-life drama more compelling than any stage play.

Mrs. Jeffries Questions the Answer
Hannah Cameron was not well liked. But were her friends or family the sort to stab her in the back? Mrs. Jeffries must really tiptoe around this time—or it could be a matter of life and death.

Mrs. Jeffries Reveals Her Art
Mrs. Jeffries has to work double time to find a missing model *and* a killer. And she'll have to get her whole staff involved—before someone else becomes the next subject.

Mrs. Jeffries Takes the Cake
The evidence was all there: a dead body, two dessert plates, and a gun. As if Mr. Ashbury had been sharing cake with his own killer. Now Mrs. Jeffries will have to do some snooping around—to dish up clues.

Mrs. Jeffries Rocks the Boat
Mirabelle had traveled by boat all the way from Australia to visit her sister—only to wind up murdered. Now Mrs. Jeffries must solve the case—and it's sink or swim.

Mrs. Jeffries Weeds the Plot
Three attempts have been made on Annabeth Gentry's life. Is it due to her recent inheritance, or was it because her bloodhound dug up the body of a murdered thief? Mrs. Jeffries will have to sniff out some clues before the plot thickens.

Mrs. Jeffries Pinches the Post
Harrison Nye may have had some dubious business dealings, but no one expected him to be murdered. Now Mrs. Jeffries and her staff must root through the sins of his past to discover which one caught up with him.

Mrs. Jeffries Pleads Her Case
Harlan Westover's death was deemed a suicide by the magistrate. But Inspector Witherspoon is willing to risk his career to prove otherwise. Mrs. Jeffries must ensure the good inspector remains afloat.

Mrs. Jeffries Sweeps the Chimney
A dead vicar has been found propped against a church wall. And Inspector Witherspoon's only prayer is to seek the divinations of Mrs. Jeffries.

Mrs. Jeffries Stalks the Hunter
Puppy love turns to obsession, which leads to murder. Who better to get to the heart of the matter than Inspector Witherspoon's indomitable companion, Mrs. Jeffries.

Mrs. Jeffries and the Silent Knight
The yuletide murder of an elderly man is complicated by several suspects—none of whom were in the Christmas spirit.

Mrs. Jeffries Appeals the Verdict
Mrs. Jeffries and her belowstairs cohorts have their work cut out for them if they want to save an innocent man from the gallows.

Mrs. Jeffries and the Best Laid Plans
Banker Lawrence Boyd didn't waste his time making friends. With a list of enemies including just about everyone the miser's ever met, it will take Mrs. Jeffries' shrewd eye to find the killer.

continued . . .

Mrs. Jeffries and the Feast of St. Stephen
'Tis the season for sleuthing when wealthy Stephen Whitfield is murdered during his holiday dinner party. It's up to Mrs. Jeffries to solve the case in time for Christmas.

Mrs. Jeffries Holds the Trump
A very well-liked but very dead magnate is found floating down the river. Now Mrs. Jeffries and company will have to dive into a mystery that only grows more complex.

Mrs. Jeffries in the Nick of Time
Mrs. Jeffries lends her downstairs common sense to this upstairs murder mystery—and hopes that she and the inspector don't get derailed in the case of a rich uncle-cum-model-train-enthusiast.

Mrs. Jeffries and the Yuletide Weddings
Wedding bells will make this season all the more jolly. Until one humbug sings a carol of murder.

Mrs. Jeffries Speaks Her Mind
When an eccentric old woman suspects she's going to be murdered, everyone thinks she's just being peculiar—until the prediction comes true.

Mrs. Jeffries Forges Ahead
A free-spirited bride is poisoned at a society ball, and it's up to Mrs. Jeffries to discover who wanted to make the modern young woman into a postmortem.

Mrs. Jeffries and the Mistletoe Mix-Up
There's murder going on under the mistletoe as Mrs. Jeffries and Inspector Witherspoon hurry to solve the case before the eggnog is ladled out on Christmas Eve.

Mrs. Jeffries Defends Her Own
When an unwelcome visitor from her past needs help, Mrs. Jeffries steps into the fray to stop a terrible miscarriage of justice.

Mrs. Jeffries Turns the Tide
When Mrs. Jeffries doubts a suspect's guilt, she must turn the tide of the investigation to save an innocent man.

Mrs. Jeffries and the Merry Gentlemen
Days before Christmas, a successful stockbroker is murdered
and suspicion falls on three influential investors known as the
Merry Gentlemen. Now Mrs. Jeffries won't rest until justice is
served for the holidays.

Visit Emily Brightwell's website at
emilybrightwell.com

Berkley Prime Crime titles by Emily Brightwell

THE INSPECTOR AND MRS. JEFFRIES
MRS. JEFFRIES DUSTS FOR CLUES
THE GHOST AND MRS. JEFFRIES
MRS. JEFFRIES TAKES STOCK
MRS. JEFFRIES ON THE BALL
MRS. JEFFRIES ON THE TRAIL
MRS. JEFFRIES PLAYS THE COOK
MRS. JEFFRIES AND THE MISSING ALIBI
MRS. JEFFRIES STANDS CORRECTED
MRS. JEFFRIES TAKES THE STAGE
MRS. JEFFRIES QUESTIONS THE ANSWER
MRS. JEFFRIES REVEALS HER ART
MRS. JEFFRIES TAKES THE CAKE
MRS. JEFFRIES ROCKS THE BOAT
MRS. JEFFRIES WEEDS THE PLOT
MRS. JEFFRIES PINCHES THE POST
MRS. JEFFRIES PLEADS HER CASE
MRS. JEFFRIES SWEEPS THE CHIMNEY
MRS. JEFFRIES STALKS THE HUNTER
MRS. JEFFRIES AND THE SILENT KNIGHT
MRS. JEFFRIES APPEALS THE VERDICT
MRS. JEFFRIES AND THE BEST LAID PLANS
MRS. JEFFRIES AND THE FEAST OF ST. STEPHEN
MRS. JEFFRIES HOLDS THE TRUMP
MRS. JEFFRIES IN THE NICK OF TIME
MRS. JEFFRIES AND THE YULETIDE WEDDINGS
MRS. JEFFRIES SPEAKS HER MIND
MRS. JEFFRIES FORGES AHEAD
MRS. JEFFRIES AND THE MISTLETOE MIX-UP
MRS. JEFFRIES DEFENDS HER OWN
MRS. JEFFRIES TURNS THE TIDE
MRS. JEFFRIES AND THE MERRY GENTLEMEN
MRS. JEFFRIES AND THE ONE WHO GOT AWAY

Anthologies

MRS. JEFFRIES LEARNS THE TRADE
MRS. JEFFRIES TAKES A SECOND LOOK
MRS. JEFFRIES TAKES TEA AT THREE
MRS. JEFFRIES SALLIES FORTH
MRS. JEFFRIES PLEADS THE FIFTH

MRS. JEFFRIES

AND THE
ONE WHO GOT AWAY

EMILY BRIGHTWELL

BERKLEY PRIME CRIME, NEW YORK

THE BERKLEY PUBLISHING GROUP
Published by the Penguin Group
Penguin Group (USA) LLC
375 Hudson Street, New York, New York 10014

USA • Canada • UK • Ireland • Australia • New Zealand • India • South Africa • China

penguin.com

A Penguin Random House Company

MRS. JEFFRIES AND THE ONE WHO GOT AWAY

A Berkley Prime Crime Book / published by arrangement with the author

Berkley Prime Crime Books are published by The Berkley Publishing Group.
BERKLEY® PRIME CRIME and the PRIME CRIME logo are trademarks of
Penguin Group (USA) LLC.

For information, address: The Berkley Publishing Group,
a division of Penguin Group (USA) LLC,
375 Hudson Street, New York, New York 10014.

ISBN: 978-0-425-26810-0

PUBLISHING HISTORY
Berkley Prime Crime mass-market edition / February 2015

PRINTED IN THE UNITED STATES OF AMERICA

10 9 8 7 6 5 4 3 2 1

Cover illustration by Jeff Walker.

CHAPTER 1

———◆———

Alice Robinson had almost reached the entrance when she spotted Lavinia Swanson racing toward her. For a split second, she was tempted to dash across the road, but she thought better of it as Lavinia began waving at her. "Blast," Alice muttered, "I don't have time to listen to her this morning." But it wouldn't do to slight the woman in any way. She was a force to be reckoned with in the local community and Alice needed to stay in her good graces.

So she stopped and forced a smile to her lips as Lavinia, huffing and puffing as hard as a freight train, halted in front of her.

"Oh my goodness, I wasn't sure it was you. But then I saw that it was and I was afraid you'd not seen me"—Lavinia shifted her shopping basket to the other side of her considerable bulk—"and I want to tell you what Kingston did this morning. I know how you love hearing about his adventures."

"What's the clever boy done now?" Alice asked. Oh Lord, the silly cow could natter on for hours about that stupid cat of hers.

"He had a go at Mr. Ashley's bulldog. Can you believe it, a little thing like my Kingston going after that brute of a dog." She giggled and pulled the edge of her bronze-colored jacket down.

"He's always been a brave one, hasn't he." Alice forced a short laugh. The brute of a dog was a good twelve years old, blind and so stiff with age he could barely move, and Kingston was the fattest tom in the neighborhood. She edged toward the corner. "I'd so like to hear more, but I'm afraid I must be off."

Lavinia's small eyes narrowed behind her wire-framed spectacles. "But where are you going? There's nothing down there but the entrances to Highgate Cemetery."

"I'm going to the West Cemetery," Alice explained, referring to the older, more established section of the burial grounds. She struggled to keep her voice even, but in truth, she was furious. She wasn't used to explaining herself and found it especially galling that she had to put up with this nosy old woman. But she'd do what she must in order to keep Lavinia thinking that Alice Robinson was a nice, middle-class widow. "My family has a crypt," she lied. "There's a crack in the roof tiles. I'm meeting a builder to see what can be done about it."

"It'll cost you the earth to get it repaired properly." Lavinia clucked her tongue. "Now, let me know what your builder's estimate will be and I'll have a word with Coleman. We've used him for years and he's a good reputation."

"That's very kind of you." Alice glanced at the sky and

saw that heavy, low-hanging gray-black clouds had come in from the west. "I'll most certainly do that. Oh dear, I must be off now. It looks like it could rain and I need to stop by the chemists once I'm done here."

Lavinia glanced up and frowned. "Kingston hates the rain and if there's thunder, he gets in a miserable state. He goes under the maid's bed and won't come out. I'll be off then. Mind you, come see me about that estimate."

Alice kept her smile firmly in place until Lavinia disappeared around the corner in the direction of the high street. Then she hurried down the road toward the West Cemetery entrance. She went through the main entrance and past the chapel, all the while watching her surroundings to make certain she wasn't being followed. But as far as she could tell, there was no one on her trail. When she reached the Egyptian gate, she ignored the obelisks and headed deeper into the cemetery proper.

It was a beautiful place, but Alice was in no mood to enjoy the lush evergreens or the barely budding trees planted amidst the tombs and elaborate headstones lining the avenue. A gust of wind swept the area, raising the dead leaves and sending them dancing in the now cold air, but the sudden chill had no effect on her. She simply quickened her pace, determined to get to the meeting place and have this out once and for all. The pathway descended onto a circular space lined by crypts surrounding an ancient cedar tree.

She stopped three-quarters of the way down and surveyed her surroundings. Her gaze skimmed over the ornate grave monuments before moving to the arc of crypts. Squinting, she strained her eyes trying to see if anyone lurked in a darkened entryway or beneath an overhanging lintel. She moved farther down the slope and onto the wide path surrounding the crypts. The area seemed deserted, but her view of it was obscured because the wretched place was circular so she couldn't see what might be ahead of her. She slowed her pace as she moved farther around the circle and saw that several paths led down this way. Stopping, she looked over her shoulder. For once, she hoped there might be someone close by, a groundsman or a gravedigger or even a ruddy mourner bringing a bouquet of useless flowers for the dead. But she was alone. Her only company was the sound of the wind as it whistled through the trees.

A branch cracked and she whirled about, but there was no one there.

"Stop being such a ninny," she muttered as she reached into her pocket and felt for the handle of her derringer. It was safely there, and though she was sure she wouldn't need it to take care of this niggling little problem, experience had taught her to keep it close. The gun gave her courage. She was tired of dancing to someone else's tune, so instead of moving, she stood where she was. "Is anyone here?"

But there was no answer. Again, she heard a noise from behind—this time, it sounded like running footsteps. She turned again, but the pathway was empty. "If you don't answer me, I'm going to leave," she yelled. This was absurd. She'd been taken in by a silly note because that half-wit she'd caught snooping through her things had made a lucky guess. Well, she'd see who had the last laugh. Nobody made a fool of her. Nobody.

Fuming and muttering the most unladylike utterances

imaginable, she stalked farther around the circle, heading for the nearest path leading to the highest point. She was out of breath by the time she reached the top. The graves here were newer, gaudier, and more extravagant than the crypts. The headstones were topped with statues of cherubim, seraphim, and saints with hands folded in prayer. Alice stopped for a moment to get her bearings and realized to get back to the main gate she'd need to skirt around the circle again or slip through a section of raised, flat grave markers used to house entire families.

A drop of rain hit her face, and that made up her mind; she was wearing a new skirt under her cloak, and she bloody well wasn't going to ruin it because of this wild-goose chase. She plunged ahead, turning sideways to pass between two massive slabs of what looked like concrete. She came out onto another path lined with smaller mausoleums and headstones and started toward the gate. But as she went past the first one, an elaborate carving of a giant angel with a sword in one hand and a Bible in the other, a figure suddenly appeared in front of her. It stood on the raised base of the headstone. Surprised, she stopped, her eyes widening as she looked at the familiar face. "You're going to be sorry . . ."

But those were the last words she ever uttered, as a cord was looped around her throat, the two ends crossed beneath her chin and then yanked hard.

Alice tried to scream as she clawed at her killer's hands but they were encased in heavy workman's gloves. Panicking, she forgot about her derringer as she bucked and threw her body frantically every which way. Her attacker was not only strong, but had taken the precaution of bracing against the angel and had the added advantage of being above Alice by a good six inches. Her lips worked frantically as she gasped repeatedly in a vain effort to force air into her starved lungs. Her arms flailed out as she tried to hit at her attacker, but it did no good as her killer merely pulled the cord tighter and tighter around her throat.

Alice couldn't believe this was happening, not to her. But it was happening, and when the life had gone from her eyes and her knees buckled, her murderer finally let go. She flopped, rather heavily, onto the now damp pathway.

Making sure there was no one about before kneeling next to the corpse, the killer searched Alice's pockets and then put a neatly folded paper in her lifeless fingers before tucking her hand safely beneath the cloak.

Alice Robinson's expression was such that even the policemen who responded to the loud screams of the widow who'd almost stumbled over the body when she'd come to put flowers on her late husband's grave remarked that they'd never seen a corpse that looked so surprised to be dead.

Mrs. Goodge, cook to Inspector Gerald Witherspoon of the Metropolitan Police, put a bag of flour on her work-table and looked at Mrs. Jeffries, the housekeeper. "I can't believe it's already the middle of March. Where does the time go? I tell you, Mrs. Jeffries, the older I get, the faster it flies." The cook was a portly woman with gray hair neatly tucked under her white cap, and spectacles that frequently slid down her nose.

"You're not old," the housekeeper protested.

"Of course I am, but I don't mind one bit. I'm one of the lucky ones, you know."

Mrs. Jeffries looked up from the household account book she'd spread on the kitchen table and stared at the elderly cook. "What do you mean?"

"By the time you reach my age, most people are so set in their ways they're incapable of change, but thanks to you nudgin' us to do our bit for justice, I've not only done something useful, but I've completely changed how I think about this old world of ours. You remember what I used to be like. I thought everyone should kowtow to their betters, stay in their place, and be grateful for a crust of bread. But thanks to our investigatin', our workin' for the cause of justice, I've changed how I think, and that's what makes me so lucky." She leaned down and yanked her big bread-making bowl out from under the worktable. "When my time comes and my Maker asks me to account for my life, I can honestly say that I did my best to make the world a better place."

Mrs. Jeffries frowned. Mrs. Goodge was generally of a practical nature and not given to speaking at any length about the nature of life or its changes. But two days ago, Mrs. Goodge had gone to see her doctor. Was there something wrong? Was there something the cook wasn't telling? "Is everything alright? Are you ill?"

"Ill?" she repeated. She looked surprised. "What makes you say that? Is my color off?"

"No, no, you look fine, just fine. But you went to see Dr. Holt, and you didn't say much when you came home and, well, considering you've mentioned going to meet your Maker five times in the last two days, I was a bit concerned."

The cook eyed her curiously for a long moment and then burst out laughing. "Oh my gracious, I'm so sorry. I'd no idea I was wittering on about such a thing."

"So you're alright?"

"I'm fine. I saw Dr. Holt because my knees have been aching something fierce, and I was hoping he'd be able to give me something stronger for the pain. But there isn't much he can do but give me the same old prescription I've been taking for years now. Although he did recommend a nice shot of whiskey before I went to bed, saying it might help me sleep better. Unfortunately, I can't stand the taste of that stuff."

"Why don't you have a glass of sherry—you like that," Mrs. Jeffries suggested. She'd buy her friend a case of it if it would ease her misery.

"Hmm, maybe I'll try that." She smiled at the house-keeper. "But not to worry, though, there's nothing wrong with me but old age."

Relieved, Mrs. Jeffries smiled. "He actually used that phrase?"

"He was a tad more tactful. I can't remember his exact words but that was the gist of it. Our investigations are keepin' my mind young and sharp, but they're not doin' a thing for my agin' joints. But I'm not bothered, as I said. I'm grateful for the chance I've had, especially as it came so late in my life. When I first applied for a position here, I thought workin' for a policeman was almost shameful, but coming to this house was the best thing that ever happened to me. It let me spend the last years of my life doin' some-thing important."

The cook was referring to the fact that her employer, Inspector Gerald Witherspoon, had solved more homicides than anyone in the history of the Metropolitan Police

Department. Of course, what neither he nor his superiors knew was that he had a great deal of help: namely, his servants. Under the leadership of Mrs. Jeffries, the widow of a Yorkshire policeman, the entire household and their friends used their considerable resources on each and every case. They dug up gossip, followed suspects, and hunted down clues with the tenacity of hounds on the scent. But that wasn't the only reason Mrs. Goodge considered herself blessed, for not only had the Almighty given her a chance to do something useful in the later years of her life, but he'd also given her something she'd not had since she'd gone into service at the tender age of twelve—she'd found a family. Her parents had died when she was a child and she'd not been blessed with siblings. Over the years, she'd devoted herself to learning her craft, to becoming the best cook she could possibly be, and to all intents and purposes she'd achieved that goal. But she'd missed having a family, having people she knew she could count on no matter what happened in life. She had that now. She had people who cared about her, and she no longer worried about the future.

Brought together by Mrs. Jeffries, who'd cleverly pushed and prodded to get them out and about whenever the inspector had a new case, the group was an odd lot. It had been Smythe, the coachman and the father of Mrs. Goodge's own precious godchild, Amanda Belle, who had first figured out what Mrs. Jeffries was up to. But it hadn't taken long for Wiggins, the footman, and Betsy, the former housemaid and now Smythe's wife and the mother of her darling, to suss it out as well. Then Phyllis had come along and joined the household, and at first, she'd been a bit skittish about joining in, but she'd eventually got on board as well and now she was one of them. They weren't related by blood, but they'd become family.

"Justice is important," Mrs. Jeffries agreed. "And we were all lucky to end up here." The clock struck the hour. "Gracious, it's already past noon. I thought Wiggins would be back by now."

"There might have been a long line at the chemist shop," the cook replied. "And Mr. Waldman is very slow in fixing the prescriptions. It was good of the lad to offer to get my medicine for me."

"I wasn't being critical," Mrs. Jeffries said quickly. "But I do tend to worry when one of them is gone longer than I think they ought to be gone. Oh, you know what I mean, Mrs. Goodge. I've seen you glancing at the clock whenever Wiggins or Phyllis is ten minutes late getting back from an errand."

"That's true enough." She sighed. "But considerin' how close we get to the kind of evil that some are capable of doin', it's only natural we'd worry when one of the chicks is out of our sight."

Mrs. Jeffries laughed. "I don't think Wiggins would appreciate being thought of in those terms; he considers himself a fully grown man."

"He'll always be one of my chicks," the cook declared. "Just like Betsy and Phyllis and for that matter, even Smythe, though he's now got almost as much gray in his hair as I do."

"I still can't understand why Chief Superintendent Barrows sent for me. Why should he want me to consult?"

Inspector Gerald Witherspoon asked as he and Constable Barnes got down from the hansom cab. "This isn't our division, and from the message we received, it seems as if the victim isn't someone of great importance—not that any one human being is more worthy than another when it comes to murder. Oh dear, that sounded dreadful and it's not what I meant at all." He stopped, took a deep breath, and pushed his spectacles up his nose.

Gerald Witherspoon was a pale-faced man of late middle age with thinning brown hair under his bowler, a rather bony face, and deep-set hazel eyes. He wore a heavy black overcoat with a bright red and green striped scarf dangling around his neck.

"You're making perfect sense, sir," Constable Barnes said. He paid the hansom driver and nodded his thanks. He was a tall, older copper with a ruddy complexion and a head-ful of wavy, iron gray hair under his policeman's helmet. But despite his years, his back was ramrod straight, and he could still bring down a fleeing criminal or break up a nasty fist-fight if the need arose. "We only get called to another district when it's a case the Home Office wants solved quickly, and that generally means the victim is someone rich or connected to the powers that be. I've no idea why we've been told to come here, sir, but I expect there's a good reason."

"I certainly hope so." Witherspoon tossed his scarf around his neck. "I told Mrs. Jeffries I'd be home early today and I don't like to be late. Mrs. Jeffries never says anything but I can always tell she worries when I'm tardy."

"Considering how many killers you've put away, sir, I'm not surprised she'd be concerned. Even murderers have family and friends that might want a bit of revenge against you, sir. But Mrs. Jeffries won't fret today. When we got the message we were needed here, I sent a street lad over to your house to tell her we'd been called out."

"That was thoughtful of you, Constable. But what about your good wife—won't she be upset if you don't show up in time for supper?"

"No, sir, I told the boy to go on to my house when he'd finished at yours. Mrs. Barnes will pop my plate in the warming oven and work on her knitting until I get home."

Barnes moved onto the broad path leading to the wrought iron gate under the archway of the broad, two-story stone building. "Shall we go in, sir?"

Witherspoon started toward the imposing entrance to Highgate Cemetery. There was a small crowd of people milling about. Some were nicely dressed and holding bouquets while others were obviously workmen and gardeners. All of them stared curiously at the two policemen as they walked toward the gate.

"Let's hope someone has thought to send a constable to meet us," Witherspoon said. "This is a huge place, and if we've got to find the body on our own, it might take quite a long time."

"Someone has thought of it, sir." Barnes pointed to the two constables waiting on the far side of the entrance.

The taller of the two came toward them. "I'm Constable Housman, sir. I'm to take you directly to the body."

"I'm Constable Shearing, sir, and I'm to stay here and keep everyone out," the second, shorter constable offered.

"It's this way, sir." Housman gestured toward the broad path leading out to the cemetery proper.

"Do we know that this is definitely a murder?" Witherspoon asked as he and Barnes fell into step behind the young man.

"Yes, sir, she's been strangled."

"That's a dreadful way to die," the inspector murmured.

"Who is the officer in charge?" Barnes asked. He knew that Witherspoon was sensitive to the fact that some officers thought it was unfair that the two of them were often called in to take over. No one would admit it, but when it came time for promotions to be handed out, the publicity from a quickly solved homicide definitely helped move men up the ladder, and the more ambitious coppers were understandably resentful when they lost their case to outsiders from another district.

"It's Inspector Rogers, sir," Constable Housman replied.

Barnes glanced at Witherspoon and saw the relief on his superior's face. Rogers was known as a down-to-earth, reasonable fellow who followed the rules and was a good policeman. He'd been on the force a long time and Barnes was fairly sure he'd heard the man was going to retire soon. Good. That might make things easier for them. Barnes wasn't naive enough to think they'd been sent to another district so the inspector could merely "consult" on a case.

"He's the one that found the clipping in the lady's hand, sir," Constable Housman continued as he turned off the broad avenue and onto a narrow path bordered by closely spaced headstones. "As soon as he saw it, he sent word to the Yard, and they sent a runner back with the message that you were to be called in straight away."

"Clipping?" Witherspoon asked. "You mean from a newspaper?"

"That's right, sir. But I'll let the inspector tell you about it himself," he replied. "I'd not like to speak out of turn, sir."

Barnes smiled wryly. He knew that the young constable was afraid he'd get into trouble with his guv if he said too much about the case. Which meant that even though Rogers had a reputation as a reasonable fellow, he didn't want his men taking too much initiative. Barnes was grateful that Witherspoon wasn't like that. His inspector didn't set too much importance on the command structure and encouraged everyone who worked on a case with him to not only ask questions, but to feel free to offer opinions. To Barnes' way of thinking, one of the reasons for Witherspoon's success was that he was prepared to listen to his men. Witherspoon had only one rule and that was that no one was to speak to the press unless specifically authorized to do so.

"It's very quiet here," Witherspoon murmured.

Housman led them around a headstone and onto a narrow patch of dead grass. "As we said, sir, Inspector Rogers has put constables on all the gates. He didn't want people tramping about while we investigated."

"What about the ones that were already here?" Barnes glanced at a grave that had fresh flowers on it. "This is a huge place—surely there were already people paying their respects and whatnot when the body was discovered. What happened to them?"

"Inspector Rogers cleared them out, sir."

"That explains the crowd at the gate," Barnes murmured. "I'll bet that made him popular."

"Not really. Several of 'em were real put out. But you can speak to him yourselves. He's just over there with the others." Housman stopped and pointed straight ahead to a chubby, gray-haired man wearing a brown tweed coat and flat cap. He stood with three constables in a semicircle on the path. They were looking down at a body sprawled on the ground. Another man, wearing a black greatcoat and old-fashioned top hat, stood a good ten feet away from them, leaning against the wall of a crypt.

Rogers glanced their way. "Ah, good, you're here." He broke away from the group and came toward them, his right arm outstretched toward Witherspoon. "Inspector Witherspoon, I presume. I'm Inspector Rogers," he said as they shook hands. "It's a relief you're finally here. We'd like to get this sorted out and the victim moved to the morgue as soon as possible."

"We got here as quickly as we could," Witherspoon said, but Rogers ignored him and kept talking. He jerked his chin toward the man leaning against the crypt. "That's Mr. Abbot. He's in charge here and just at the moment, he's a bit put out with us."

"I'm not surprised," Barnes interjected. "He's going to get lots of complaints from the people you made go and from the lot that's hanging about by the gate waiting to get in to pay their respects."

Rogers drew back slightly, his eyes narrowing as he looked first at Barnes and then at Witherspoon. "Couldn't be helped. We can't have people walking about disturbing evidence. But back to Mr. Abbot. He's been nagging me to get a move on so he can reopen the gates. He seems a bit squeamish about corpses. Odd, really, as one would assume a man in his occupation would be used to them. But then again, most of the ones he deals with are already nicely sealed up in boxes."

Witherspoon didn't blame the fellow for staying back; he didn't like corpses, either, especially those that had been strangled. "Is he the one who found the victim?"

"No. Mrs. Rivers discovered the dead woman. She'd come to put flowers on her late husband's grave. She comes every week at the same time. As you can imagine, she's quite upset so I've sent her home. We've got her address so you can interview her when you see fit."

"You don't think she had anything to do with the murder?" Witherspoon deliberately kept his gaze on Rogers' face. Examining the corpse would come soon enough.

Rogers shook his head. "She's eighty years old and far too frail to have done the killing, and Mr. Abbot verified that she's here regularly." He waved at the body. "But you have a look and come to your own conclusions. Everyone on the force knows you have your own methods, Inspector. I'll leave you some men and be off. Our division is at your disposal, sir."

"But the Yard hasn't said that I'm in charge," Witherspoon protested. "I was sent here to consult, sir, not to take over the case."

Rogers lifted an eyebrow. "Let's not be coy. You don't have to mind my feelings—we both know that you're in charge here, Inspector. This is now your case. I'm retiring this summer, but I'm vain enough to admit that solving this murder would have been a feather in my cap and a good way to end my career. But I'm a realist and once I saw that clipping, I knew they'd give it to you."

Witherspoon winced inwardly. He'd once been accused of "hogging the limelight" by another officer, and it had stung. He knew there were people who resented him, but there was nothing he could do about it. It wasn't his fault he kept getting assigned to murders in other districts. The one time he'd broached the subject with Barrows, his superior had been markedly unsympathetic and had told him not to be "so ridiculously sensitive to the opinions of others" and that if the Home Office wanted him on a specific case, so be it.

"We were ordered here, sir," Barnes said quickly. "Inspector Witherspoon didn't ask for this." He wanted to make it perfectly clear that his superior was innocent of any backstabbing or manipulating. They were going to need the cooperation of the lads in this division, and Rogers having a dog-in-the-manger attitude wouldn't benefit anyone, least of all the victim.

"I never said he did," Rogers shot back. "But that's neither here nor there—it's his case now." He reached in his pocket, pulled out an envelope, and handed it to Witherspoon. "You'll understand why I contacted the Yard when you read this."

The inspector opened it carefully and drew out a yellowed newspaper clipping. He held it up to the light and squinted at the small print. Barnes leaned in closer so he could read it as well. The article had been ripped from a paper and only a few of the lines were visible.

Today the Metropolitan Police announced the arrest of Carl Christopher of West London for the murder of the Reverend Jasper Claypool. Inspector Gerald Witherspoon apprehended the man at his West London home. A female accomplice to the crime was said to have escaped from the home, but the police have assured the public that they are confident the accomplice will soon be caught.

Witherspoon took a deep breath but said nothing. Barnes was also uncharacteristically silent.

"Now do you see why we notified the Yard and they sent for you?" Rogers said. "You arrested Christopher so I doubt that the chief superintendent sent you here to 'consult.'"

"Carl Christopher was deservedly hung. He murdered two people," Barnes muttered. "But what I don't understand is why this was in the dead woman's hand."

"Do we know who she is?" Witherspoon asked softly.

"Her name is Alice Robinson. She was identified by Constable Pierpoint." He nodded toward a pale-faced lad with sloping thin shoulders and freckles.

"She's known to the police?" Barnes asked sharply.

"Not at all, Constable," Rogers said smoothly. "It was only happenstance that the constable was able to identify her. A few days ago, there was a break-in at the house across the road and he spoke to Mrs. Robinson as a possible witness. But she'd not seen anything."

Witherspoon nodded. He'd deliberately kept his attention focused on Inspector Rogers. He was in no hurry to examine the corpse. "Where did the victim live?"

"Mrs. Robinson owns a lodging house on Magdala Road. It's about a quarter mile from here."

"Have you sent anyone there, sir?" Barnes glanced at the three constables. They weren't doing anything except standing over the body.

"Not as yet." Rogers crossed his arms over his chest. "When I saw the clipping, I decided to do nothing until Inspector Witherspoon arrived. Now that he has, he can handle the investigation in any way he sees fit."

"I take it that means you've not started a search or looked for witnesses?" Witherspoon asked.

"The immediate area has been gone over"—Rogers swept his hand in an arc—"and the constables asked people in the vicinity if they'd seen anyone, but thus far, we've found out nothing. You'll want to conduct your own inquiries, of course. I'll put some of my men at your disposal."

Barnes struggled to keep his expression neutral but it was blooming hard. He turned away and pretended to examine the crime scene. But inside he was seething. As the first officer on the spot, Rogers should have immediately started a search of the grounds as well as making sure that potential witnesses weren't chucked out onto the street without so much as a by-your-leave. The man was doing his best to cock up this investigation before it was even started. The constable couldn't understand it. Rogers was retiring, and even knowing he might lose the case, he should still have had enough pride to do the job properly.

"I'd appreciate any men that you can spare." Witherspoon glanced at the constables standing over the dead woman. "These lads would be most helpful. They can point out the people who were actually in the cemetery when you arrived here."

"That'll be fine." Rogers smiled agreeably. "But I can't spare anyone else. We're busy. This district has seen an increase in robberies since Christmas and I want to leave it nice and tidy when I retire."

"We can bring some constables in from our station." Barnes turned back and gave Rogers a wide grin. "Our lads are well trained in the inspector's methods."

Rogers' smile disappeared and his eyes narrowed in anger.

"Really, Constable"—Witherspoon laughed self-consciously—"I'm sure my methods aren't very different from Inspector Rogers'."

"You're too modest, sir." Barnes wasn't going to stop now. He was righteously angry with Rogers. "There's a reason *you've* solved more murders than anyone in the history of the force. Now, being as Inspector Rogers is so busy, perhaps he'd like to show us the body so that we can get on with a proper investigation."

Davey Marsh was only ten years old but he was already an old hand at working the neighborhood around the Ladbroke Road Police Station. There was always a clerk, copper, or criminal who would pay a few coins for a message to be sent or an errand to be run. But of all the places he went, his favorite was Upper Edmonton Gardens. Everyone at that household was generous. Inspector Witherspoon always gave him at least a sixpence when he sent him there to say he'd be home late, and the servants were even more generous, especially the cook. Mrs. Goodge never let him leave the kitchen without a sweet bun or a slice of pie.

His mouth watered as he rapped on the back door. A few moments later, Wiggins stuck his head out.

"Cor blimey, it's Davey. Come on in, lad." He held the door open wide. "'Ave ya got a message for us?" The footman, a brown-haired man in his early twenties, had blue eyes and even features.

"Constable Barnes sent me," Davey said as Wiggins closed the door and motioned for the boy to follow him. "He said it was real important."

Wiggins nodded and led him into the kitchen. "Young Davey Marsh is 'ere," he announced, "and 'e says 'e's got an important message from Constable Barnes."

"Hello, Davey." Mrs. Jeffries' spirits soared. There was usually only one reason the constable bothered to send a message. "You look like you've grown a bit since I last saw you."

"Mam says I'm growin' so fast she can't keep me in trousers." He laughed. He was a skinny boy wearing a secondhand blue jacket that was too big for him, scuffed brown shoes, and dark green trousers that were two inches above his ankles.

"Take a chair, lad, and have a nice slice of brown bread," Mrs. Goodge ordered. "It was made fresh this morning and I know that boys your age are always hungry." She also knew that he was generally hungry because his family was poor. He had a younger brother and a mother who struggled to make ends meet by working as a washerwoman.

Davey flew to the table, scrapped back a chair, and flopped down. He pushed a lock of dark blond hair off his forehead as he waited for the treat. "Ta, Mrs. Goodge, your bread is good, not like that stale old stuff Mam buys from the baker."

Wiggins took the spot next to Davey as Mrs. Goodge put a plate down in front of the boy. His eyes widened as he saw the huge slice she'd cut him. "Put some butter and jam on it, boy," she ordered. "And I'll cut another slice for you to take home for your brother."

Mrs. Goodge wrapped the bread in paper while the lad ate and the other two waited for him to finish. When he'd eaten the last crumb, Mrs. Jeffries said, "Now, what was the message?"

"Constable Barnes said that the inspector was goin' to be late home tonight because they'd been called out on a murder." Davey rose from his chair. "And now I've got to get goin' to his house so I can tell Mrs. Barnes the same thing." He glanced at the paper-wrapped parcel Mrs. Goodge had laid on the end of the table. "Can I take it?"

"Of course." The cook nodded. "Are you sure that's all the constable said?"

"I'm sure." He hurried around the table and snatched up the bundle.

Mrs. Jeffries frowned. It wasn't like the constable to be so stingy with information. "He didn't say where they were going?"

Davey edged toward the back hall. "All he said was that I was to tell ya that he and the inspector had been called to a murder site in Highgate so your guv'll be home late tonight."

"He didn't happen to mention where in Highgate this murder site might be?" she persisted.

Davey started to shake his head but then stopped and ran a grubby hand across his cheek as he tried to recall what he'd heard. "He didn't say it was where he was goin', but as he and the inspector got into the hansom cab, I heard him shoutin' up to the driver to take 'em to . . . oh . . . now, where was it? It was, it was . . ."

Mrs. Goodge opened her mouth to shout encouragement at the lad, but Mrs. Jeffries raised her hand for silence as they watched Davey's forehead wrinkle in concentration.

"Now I've got it," he cried. "Highgate Cemetery. He told the driver to take 'em to the cemetery."

"Highgate Cemetery?" Wiggins looked doubtful. "Are ya sure? That's not in the inspector's district."

"I'm sure." Davey looked offended. "It might take me a minute to remember, but I know what I heard. But I've got to go now. Constable Barnes and his missus live across the river, and I want to get there and get home in time to give my brother this bread. There's no food in the house and Mam don't have another load of wash to do until tomorrow."

Mrs. Jeffries was already on her feet and heading for the pine sideboard where she kept a stash of coins. She jerked the drawer open and pulled out a handful of coins "Take this, Davey," she said, handing him the money. "And buy something decent to eat tonight."

Davey's jaw dropped as he looked at the coins in his palm. "Ta, Mrs. Jeffries. This'll buy all three of us a nice supper." Grinning, he shoved the money in his pocket and headed down the back hall.

As soon as they heard the door close, Wiggins got to his feet. "Should I get to the cemetery?" Good-natured and easygoing, he was nonetheless sharp-eyed and clever when they were "on the hunt."

"But what about the others?" Mrs. Goodge interjected before the housekeeper could answer him. She glanced at the clock. "It's only half past one. We've enough time to get them here for a meeting."

"But the only thing we could tell them is that there's

been a murder," Mrs. Jeffries pointed out. "We've no other information. No, I think Wiggins should go to Highgate and see what he can find out. I'll pop round to Betsy and Smythe's flat and tell them to be here in the morning for a meeting. Then I'll stop at Ruth's to tell her."

"On the way home, I can let Luty and Hatchet know so they can be here as well," Wiggins offered.

"That's probably best." The cook looked at Mrs. Jeffries. "By then you'll have had a chance to speak to the inspector. Let's just hope that he doesn't come in so late he's too tired to tell you what's what."

Mr. Abbot dashed toward them as Barnes, Witherspoon, and Rogers turned toward the corpse. "You there"—he pointed at Inspector Witherspoon as he raced up the slight incline—"when can I open the gates again? We've a burial scheduled for this afternoon and it'll be most inconvenient if it's delayed. I've already paid the gravediggers and I don't want to have to pay them again tomorrow."

Witherspoon realized that between Inspector Rogers' attitude and Constable Barnes' charging ahead like a bull in a china shop, he might as well do what was expected and take over. "We're moving as quickly as we can, sir, but this is a murder site," he explained. "I'm not sure when we'll be finished."

"I've got a hearse and two coaches coming through the main gate in an hour. Will you be done by then?" Abbot waved his hands about, pointing in the direction of the road. "I don't see what's taking so long. You've been here for hours."

"And we wouldn't be delayed if proper procedure had been followed," Barnes muttered.

Rogers glared at the constable, but held his peace.

"For goodness' sake, Inspector," Abbot cried. "This is a cemetery and we don't just have burials scheduled. There are dozens of people who want to get in to pay their respects to loved ones."

"The police surgeon should be here any moment," Rogers said. "As soon as Inspector Witherspoon examines the body and the surgeon is finished, we'll be out of your way."

"Examine the body?" Abbot exclaimed. "What on earth for? The woman is dead, dead, dead. Can't you just get a van in here and move her along to the morgue?"

Before Witherspoon could reply, they heard footsteps, and everyone turned to see a man and two constables coming their way. The man wore a blue overcoat and bowler hat and carried a physician's bag. The constables carried an empty stretcher.

"It appears the police surgeon has arrived," Rogers said.

"It's about time." Abbot snorted and glanced down at the body. He shuddered and then backed away.

"We'll be finished in a few moments, sir," Witherspoon called. "But we'll need to search this part of the cemetery and we'll need to question your staff."

"And that includes the gravediggers," Barnes added.

"You can do what you like as long as I can open the main gate." Abbot stopped. "The burial is on the other side of the cemetery."

"You can proceed about your business." Witherspoon

turned to Rogers as he spoke. He didn't wish to be harsh, but honestly, the inspector had been a bit remiss in his duty.

Rogers didn't see the inspector's disapproving expression, though. He'd knelt down by the body and was waving at the newcomers. "Dr. Procash, we'll be done here in a moment and then she's all yours."

"When was the body discovered?" Barnes asked.

"Half past nine this morning."

"What time do the gates open?"

"Nine," Rogers replied. "So she couldn't have been dead more than half an hour before she was discovered. Now, can we get on with this? I've a lot to do today." He glanced at Witherspoon. "Ready?"

The inspector took a deep breath and steeled himself before kneeling next to the dead woman. "Yes, of course." He focused on her attire. She wore a rust-colored cloak that had slipped open, revealing a striped gray and rust blouse neatly tucked into a gray skirt. Her hands lay across her stomach, and he noticed she wore a garnet ring on her right hand. His gaze traveled up her torso. A red cord, its ends neatly arranged over her chest, lay draped around her neck. Keeping his eyes away from her face, he moved closer and examined the darkened line around her neck. "It looks like she was strangled from the front," he muttered.

"Either that or the killer rearranged the cord," Rogers replied.

Witherspoon looked at her face and then gasped. At the same moment, he heard Barnes take a deep, sharply drawn breath.

Rogers, who heard both men, looked at them curiously.

"Surely this isn't the first time you've seen a strangulation," he scoffed. "She's not a pretty sight, but I'd think that with all the murders you've solved and your reputation for not letting anyone touch the body till you've had a good look at it would have prepared you for this."

Her tongue was protruding, her lips were blue, and her mouth was open as if she'd just been surprised. Her eyes stared straight up to the sky.

"Murder is never pretty," Witherspoon said slowly. He closed his eyes as memories flooded into his mind. Images of a beautiful red-haired woman with ivory skin and sapphire blue eyes flashed through his consciousness. But her hair was now a dark brown under the sensible straw hat that was smashed askew on the ground beneath her head. Her cheekbones seemed rounded and less defined but it was most definitely she. The eyes were still the same color of sapphire blue.

"One of your constables identified her?" Barnes fixed Rogers with a stony stare. A day that had started out bad had just gotten worse.

"That's right." Rogers straightened as he realized something was very wrong. "She's Mrs. Robinson, Alice Robinson. I've told you already. She's a respectable widow who owns a lodging house near here. Constable Pierpoint was certain it's her."

"But it isn't her," Witherspoon said as he got to his feet and looked down at the woman. "It's someone else entirely."

"What are you talking about?" Rogers rose as well. "My constables don't make identification mistakes. This is Alice Robinson."

"That may be what she's been calling herself," Barnes

said. "But this woman isn't Alice Robinson. Her name is Edith Durant. We've been looking for her for years."

"Looking for her?" Rogers seemed confused. "Why would you be searching for her? What's she done?"

"She's a murderess," Witherspoon said softly. "The only one who ever got away from us."

CHAPTER 2

—◆—

"'Ow come them gates is shut?" Wiggins pointed to the entrance of Highgate Cemetery. "And what's a constable doin' inside there? Are they plantin' someone important?" Upon arriving, he'd studied the crowd and picked his spot carefully. On one side of the entry there were well-dressed men and women with bouquets of flowers or bundles of greenery. Most of them were peering anxiously toward the gates and checking their watches. So he'd crossed to the other side toward the locals, the sort of folks who'd not mind answering a few questions, especially if the person doing the asking was a bit of a rough lad and a know-it-all. He stopped in the middle of a collection of housemaids, street urchins, matrons with shopping baskets, and a couple of sullen-looking workmen who Wiggins guessed were either gravediggers or groundskeepers. "I 'eard they're buryin' a cousin of the Queen," he continued. "That must be why they've got it all locked up."

"Don't be daft," a dark-haired housemaid said to him. "They're not burying any royals today. There's been a murder and the police have got it locked so they can catch the killer."

A red-haired street boy snorted derisively. "You're the one who's daft. The killer is long gone and the gate's only locked to keep the likes of us out."

"Murder," Wiggins cried. "Cor blimey, who was killed?"

The boy shrugged and the maid turned her attention back to the constable pacing behind the wrought iron fence.

"Mrs. Robinson was murdered," a timid voice said from behind him. He whirled around and came face-to-face with a short, slender, brown-haired girl wearing spectacles. She was dressed in a faded maroon and gold jacket.

Wiggins glanced at her skirt and saw that it was a deep forest green instead of the pale lavender or gray of a housemaid. He gave her his friendliest smile. "You're a clever one, aren't ya?"

The girl blushed. "Not really. I just happened to know that it was Mrs. Robinson who they found."

The red-haired lad spun around on his heel. "How did you find out?" he challenged. "They ain't let anyone in since this morning and no matter how much we ask 'em"— he jabbed a finger at the constable behind the gate—"them coppers won't say a word."

"I know it was her because Mrs. Rivers is the one that found her body, and she overheard one of the constables that come to investigate telling the other policeman that the dead lady was Mrs. Robinson. Mrs. Rivers was so upset over what she'd seen and heard that she sent her maid to the chemist's shop where I work for a sleeping powder, and the maid told us what had happened."

"Wonder why anyone would want to kill 'er," Wiggins interjected quickly. The girl seemed to know a bit and he wanted to keep her talking.

"It was probably that ripper feller," the boy answered.

Wiggins ignored him and kept his attention on the young woman. "Was this Mrs. Robinson the sort to 'ave a lot of enemies?"

"I wouldn't know about that." She smiled shyly. "But I do know she owns the lodging house just over on Magdala Lane."

"Do you think she was killed by a robber?" he asked excitedly.

Before she could reply, the housemaid, who'd now lost interest in staring at the constable guarding the gate, turned to them and said, "I'll bet that's what happened. There have been a lot of robberies round this neighborhood lately. The house next door to us got robbed last week, and the thief took every bit of silver that was on the mantelpiece. Dear Lord, can you credit it, getting robbed and killed in broad daylight?" She crossed her arms over her chest and hugged herself defensively.

"You don't know she was robbed," the boy taunted her. "It could just as easy be old Jack. My mam says they never caught him and I'll bet he's back at it. He always left 'em bloody." He looked at the young woman standing next to Wiggins. "Was Mrs. Robinson all cut up?"

She shook her head. "I don't know. The maid just said that Mrs. Rivers had almost tripped over the dead woman and started screaming."

"I think she must've been all bloodied up and that's why the coppers shut the cemetery," another woman—a bread seller by the look of her half-empty baskets—said, joining the conversation.

"Can you show me where Mrs. Robinson's lodging house is?" Wiggins asked the girl wearing spectacles. He kept his voice low so the others wouldn't interrupt.

"Why?" She cocked her head to one side and studied him. Her expression was openly wary, as though she'd just realized he wasn't asking questions out of sheer curiosity. "She'll not be takin' in any new lodgers now, and what's more, even if she weren't dead, you'd not be able to afford her rates. Even Mr. Bristow, the assistant chemist, couldn't pay what she was charging."

"And how do you know that, miss?"

"Because he tried to get lodging there himself. When she first opened up, he went to inquire, and when he come back, he said her rates were almost double what others in the neighborhood were charging." Behind her spectacles, her gray eyes narrowed suspiciously. "And what happened to that heavy accent you had just a minute ago?"

"Nothing 'appened to it." He was a bit offended. His accent was real, though in truth, his speech had improved from being around the others at Upper Edmonton Gardens. "But I can talk proper-like if there's a lovely girl I'm hoping to impress a bit." This wasn't altogether a fib, though he was quite capable of lying his head off while on the hunt, and to be perfectly honest, she wasn't conventionally pretty, but there was something about her, something attractive in the intelligence in her eyes and the shape of her face.

"You're having me on," she said as a blush crept up her cheeks. "No one thinks a girl in spectacles is attractive."

"Now you're bein' silly. They make you look intelligent." He decided to be honest. "And you've got good bones."

She stared at him doubtfully for a moment and then she smiled. "Thank you, that's nice of you to say. If you'd like, I'll show you her lodging house. I've got to get home and it's on my way."

"If you're sure of her real identity then, I'll send a message to the chief superintendent. That'll put the cat amongst the pigeons." Rogers smirked at Barnes. "It'll be hard to say what he'll dislike most." He turned his attention to Witherspoon. "The fact that we've finally got our hands on the one your lot let get away or the fact that because he's already brought you into the case, you'll be the one investigating her murder."

Witherspoon simply stared at him. But Barnes wasn't going to let him have the last word. "Chief Superintendent Barrows can always take him off the case," he said softly.

Rogers laughed and started up the path. "Oh, I doubt he'll do that. Especially once the newspapers get hold of this tidbit"—he glanced back over his shoulder—"and you can be sure they will."

"That mean-spirited jackanapes." Barnes clenched his fist and started after him. "He's going to leak it himself just to embarrass you."

"Come back, Constable," Witherspoon ordered softly. "You're too close to retirement to risk your pension on an altercation with Inspector Rogers."

One of the constables guarding the body spoke up. "Excuse

me for interrupting, sir, but I doubt he'll tell the papers," he said. Like the other two constables hovering nearby, he'd witnessed the whole incident. "His bark is worse than his bite. He's a good and decent man, sir. His pride was just stung when they took this one away from him."

"What's your name?" Witherspoon asked.

"Constable Jones, sir. I'm sorry, I didn't mean to speak out of turn."

"No apology is needed," the inspector replied. "It speaks well of your superior that his men are willing to defend his actions."

"We are, sir," Constable Jones added eagerly. "By the time Inspector Rogers gets back to the station, he'll be right ashamed of himself, sir. He'll not do anything to bring shame on the force, sir, and he holds you in the highest regard."

Barnes was skeptical but held his tongue. Even the most decent of men were capable of behaving badly when their pride had been hurt, but he agreed with Witherspoon that it was a mark in Rogers' favor that his lads spoke up for him.

"How much longer?" Abbot shouted from his post by the crypt wall.

The police surgeon cleared his throat and looked pointedly at the corpse. Witherspoon nodded and said in a voice loud enough for the cemetery director to hear, "We're almost finished, Dr. Procash. We just need to have a quick search of her pockets and then she's all yours."

Barnes knelt down again and opened her cloak. "Once Rogers found the clipping I expect he left her alone." He ran his hand along the inside of the garment, found nothing, and then flipped the material back over the body and checked the outside pockets. "Nothing, sir."

"Check to see if she's a skirt pocket," Witherspoon said.

Taking care to handle the lady respectfully, Barnes braced himself so he wouldn't lose his balance and slipped his hands back inside the cloak. He ran his fingers along both sides of her frame. His eyes suddenly widened as his fingertips brushed against the outline of a familiar object. He looked at Witherspoon and then slowly, slowly worked his right hand into the pocket, grabbed what he hoped was the handle and not the barrel, and then pulled out a gun. "She obviously came here expecting trouble, sir." He held it up to Witherspoon. "She came armed with a derringer."

"Betsy and Smythe said they'll be here tomorrow morning," Mrs. Jeffries said as she settled into her spot at the kitchen table. "And I was able to catch Ruth. She'll be here as well."

"Good." Mrs. Goodge put a bag of flour on her worktable and untied the top. "Let's just hope that Wiggins has a bit of luck with Luty and Hatchet. You never know when those two will take it into their heads to go out of town, and it makes it so much easier when all of us start out together."

"I wish Wiggins would hurry and get back," Phyllis said as she came down the back stairs. She dumped the bundle of dirty linens she carried into the open wicker laundry basket by the newel post. "I'm ever so excited to hear what he's found out." The maid was a young woman with dark blonde hair she pulled back in a loose bun at the nape of her neck, a rather round-shaped face, and a porcelain complexion.

"We don't know that he'll have found out anything," the cook warned.

"He will." Phyllis closed the lid of the basket and latched it. "He's ever so clever—people tell him everything. I don't know how he does it but I'm determined to learn how to do it myself. The upstairs is done." She looked at the table and then at Mrs. Jeffries. "Is there anything else you want done for tea?"

"It's all ready, but we'll wait a bit. It's only just gone half past four. Wiggins might be back soon."

"Then I'll just nip in and give the floor of the wet larder a quick wash. I want to be at the ready tomorrow morning." Before the housekeeper could reply, she'd hurried off down the hall.

"I remember when she didn't want to have anything to do with our investigatin'," Mrs. Goodge said softly.

"She was so happy to finally be in a household where she was treated decently that she was scared that if the inspector found out what we were up to, she'd be tossed out into the street," Mrs. Jeffries murmured. "Considering how difficult her life has been, it's taken a lot of courage for her to decide to help us."

"Life might have beaten her down at one point, but she's learned to fight back," the cook said, chuckling. "You can even tell it by the way she looks. When she first came here, it was like she didn't want the world to notice her, like she was hidin' what a pretty girl she was behind baby fat and clothes fit for an old lady."

"She has lost some weight," Mrs. Jeffries agreed. "And she is taking more care with her appearance and wardrobe. She's grown in confidence."

"Last week she told me that she's saving all her salary and that one day she's going to open her own detective agency."

"Gracious, good for her." Mrs. Jeffries broke off as they heard the back door open and the sound of footsteps pounding up the corridor.

Wiggins yanked his cap off as he burst into the kitchen. "We've 'ad a bit of luck. I found out the victim's name and best of all, I saw where she lives." Fred, the household's mongrel dog, got up from his warm spot near the cooker.

Phyllis came right behind him, drying her wet hands on her apron as she hurried to the table. "I knew you'd find something," she said as he went to the coat rack.

"Take a moment to catch your breath," Mrs. Goodge ordered. "I'll pour you a cup of tea."

Fred butted his head against Wiggins' leg in a bid for more attention. The footman reached down and stroked his fur. "Come on, then, old fellow, let's move to the table so I can have me tea. Cor blimey, that looks good."

Next to the big brown teapot were plates of freshly baked bread and scones, pots of butter and apricot jam, and an open tin of mince tarts.

"Go ahead and fill your plate," the housekeeper said as Mrs. Goodge handed him his tea. "Your news can wait for a few minutes."

"Ta, Mrs. Jeffries." He helped himself to a slice of bread and then reached for the butter. "Luty and Hatchet were out for the afternoon, but I left a message for them to come tomorrow morning."

"Excellent. The others will be here as well," Mrs. Jeffries said.

The room went quiet save for the clink of china and the

scrapping of cutlery as they tucked into their food. Mrs. Goodge waited until Wiggins had two scones and a slice of bread in front of him before she said, "Go on, then, tell us what's what."

"It was a lady named Alice Robinson that was murdered. She owned a lodging house on Magdala Lane in Highgate." He blew on the surface of his mug and then took a quick sip. "And she was killed at the cemetery there, the West Cemetery. The police had the gates locked so I couldn't get in, but a crowd had gathered and I met up with a young lady named Claudia who knew something about the dead woman."

"Was she pretty?" Phyllis asked with a giggle.

"Yes, she's pretty." He grinned. "But that's not why I chatted with 'er. She knew the victim and she's the one that showed me the lodging 'ouse. I was goin' to have a go at tryin' to talk to one of the servants, but before I could think of a way to get inside, the constables arrived and right on their heels was Constable Barnes and our inspector."

He made it sound as if Witherspoon and Barnes had arrived there immediately after Claudia had shown him the house, which, of course, wasn't true. Being a gentleman, he'd insisted on walking her home after she'd pointed out the Robinson place. Unfortunately, though she worked at the local chemist shop, she lived some distance away in Finsbury Park. He got back to the lodging house just in time to see the inspector and Barnes coming from the other direction.

"We're not being critical, Wiggins," Mrs. Jeffries said. "You've done an excellent job."

"Did this girl know anything else about the victim?" Phyllis asked.

Wiggins shook his head. "Not really. But she did tell me that Mrs. Robinson charged a pretty penny for her rooms. Her rates are much higher than any place else in the neighborhood."

Alice Robinson's lodging house was a five-story town house of pale gray brick with a concrete walkway that led up to a short flight of stairs to the door and a second set of steps that went down to a lower ground floor. The front garden was a narrow strip of earth sprinkled with a few tufts of wintery grass and one rather bedraggled-looking bush.

"I hope the local lads won't be put out by my asking Constable Griffiths to oversee the witness statements." Witherspoon stepped back a pace as Barnes banged the brass knocker against the faded blue paint of the front door.

"They looked relieved to have the help," Barnes said. "With the size of the area in the cemetery to be searched and the number of witnesses, we need more help than the three constables Rogers saw fit to give us." He pressed his ear closer to the wood, listening for footsteps. "Sounds like someone's coming."

The door opened and a middle-aged woman with light brown hair and blue eyes stuck her head out. "Yes, may I help you?" Her gaze darted frantically from Barnes in his policeman's uniform to Witherspoon. "Oh dear, has something happened? You're the police. I'm afraid the mistress isn't here."

"We know that, ma'am," Witherspoon said kindly. "May we come inside?"

In answer, she moved back, opened the door wide, and they stepped inside.

Witherspoon swept off his bowler as he surveyed the foyer. It was long and ended at a staircase with a faded carpet and a dark wooden banister. A tall mirror in a dusty, ornate frame was on the wall and just beneath it were a battered brass umbrella urn and a table holding an ivy plant. On the opposite side was a set of double doors and beyond that a poorly lighted corridor leading to the back of the house.

"May we speak to the housekeeper?" Witherspoon said.

She shook her head, her expression dazed. "There isn't one. Oh dear, I don't know what to do. Mrs. Robinson should have been back hours ago and cook is in a right old state. She's been waiting to send the order to the butcher's and Etta isn't here, either . . . Oh dear, do forgive me, sir, I'm babbling." She stopped and took a deep breath.

"That's quite alright, ma'am," the inspector said. "I take it you're in charge of the household in Mrs. Robinson's absence?"

"Not really. Cook is here, but she's in the kitchen. Shall I go get her?"

Witherspoon glanced at Barnes. "The constable here will go and speak with her."

"The back stairs are this way, sir," she said as she started toward the back, but Barnes held up his hand. "Don't bother, ma'am. I can find my way down, ma'am," he said as he disappeared down the hallway.

"Is there anyone else here? Any of Mrs. Robinson's lodgers?"

"No, sir, it's just me and Mrs. Fremont, the cook. The lodgers are all out and Etta, she's the other maid, today is her afternoon off."

"Is there someplace we can sit down?" the inspector said.

"I suppose we could use the drawing room." She hesitated a moment and then opened the double doors and motioned for him to follow.

The room was painted a pale blue with white crown molding around the ceiling. An unlighted crystal chandelier hung over a matching set of French Empire–style sofas upholstered in cream and blue patterned fabric. The black iron fireplace, also unlighted, was topped with a carved wooden mantelpiece upon which stood a set of ceramic white candlesticks. Another faded Oriental carpet, this one big enough to cover most of the room, lay on the floor.

"Please sit down." The maid pointed to one of the sofas but remained standing herself. She smiled timidly. "I'm ever so sorry, sir, I don't know what to do."

"Please sit down yourself," Witherspoon said gently. "Believe me, Mrs. Robinson won't mind. I'm Inspector Witherspoon and the other policeman is Constable Barnes."

"I'm Carrie, sir, Carrie Durridge." She bit her lip and then sat down opposite him. She stared at him with a frantic, frightened expression.

"I'm afraid we've some bad news, Miss Durridge," Witherspoon began. "Mrs. Robinson is dead."

"Dead? But, sir, that can't be. She was perfectly fine this morning. Was she in an accident? Did she have a heart attack?"

"Mrs. Robinson was murdered," he said quickly, wanting to get the worst of it over. "She was strangled."

Carrie gasped. "Oh my Lord, that's terrible." Her eyes filled with tears. "I can't believe it."

"I understand how shocking this must be for you. Have you worked for Mrs. Robinson a long time?"

She dabbed at her eyes with the corner of her apron and shook her head. "No, sir, I've only been here a few months. But she was decent enough to me, and as you said, sir, this is a terrible shock."

"Did Mrs. Robinson have any enemies?" Witherspoon asked. He'd not been sure about telling the maid that Mrs. Robinson was in reality a wanted woman named Edith Durant so he was feeling his way carefully.

"No, no, not that I know of, but she wasn't one to confide in the servants, sir, but I've not seen anything untoward here."

Downstairs, Barnes wasn't having a lot of luck getting Mrs. Fremont to understand exactly what had happened to her mistress. "No, ma'am, it wasn't an accident."

"Someone did her in?" asked the cook, an elderly woman with a red nose, deep-set watery eyes, and frizzy gray hair. She pursed her lips and stared at him from her spot at the head of the kitchen table. "But that's not right. Are you sure?"

"Absolutely, ma'am, her body was found in Highgate Cemetery this morning."

"Highgate Cemetery? What was she doin' there?"

"That's what we're trying to understand, ma'am." Barnes forced himself to be patient. She wasn't a young woman, and considering that he'd just popped into the kitchen without so much as a by-your-leave, perhaps she was doing as well as could be expected. "What time did you expect Mrs. Robinson home today?"

She snorted and motioned for him to take the chair next to her. "Her nibs never explained herself to the likes of us. She left right after breakfast this morning, and all she said to me was that I wasn't to send off the butcher's order until she had a look at it."

"I understand there's only three servants here—is that correct?" Barnes pulled out his little brown notebook and pencil.

"That's right."

"It's an awfully big house for only three staff." Barnes glanced around the cavernous kitchen. The stone floor was dull from lack of polish, the walls were stained with grease and grime, and the cooker was older than he was.

She shrugged. "I do the cooking, Etta does scullery and the landings and helps me with the serving, and Carrie takes care of the rest. The lodgers do their own rooms."

"How long have you worked here?"

"Two years. She hired me when she bought the place." Mrs. Fremont cackled. "She got me on the cheap, but that's how she gets all of us. Mind you, I'm the only one that's stayed more than a few months. She either sacks them like she did poor Annie Linden or they find a better situation."

"Has Mrs. Robinson had any difficulties with anyone lately?"

"I couldn't say, sir. The reason I've kept my position longer than anyone else around here is that I know how to mind my own business. If her nibs was squabbling with anyone that wished her ill, I don't want to know."

"But this is a murder investigation," Barnes reminded her. "She's dead. She's not going to sack you now."

"True, but I'll not be any help to you. I do my work and I keep to myself."

"Was Mrs. Robinson worried or upset about anything lately?" Barnes pressed. "Surely you can tell me that?"

Upstairs, Witherspoon was having an easier time of it with the housemaid.

"Have you noticed any strangers loitering about the area, anyone who struck you as being particularly interested in this house or Mrs. Robinson?" Witherspoon asked.

"Not that I've noticed, sir. But this is a busy neighborhood and there's always people out and about."

"Has Mrs. Robinson seemed worried or unduly upset lately?"

"No, sir, not that I've noticed." Carrie smiled apologetically. "I'm ever so sorry, sir, but I've not noticed anything odd about her."

Witherspoon decided to start over with a few facts. "What time did Mrs. Robinson leave the house today?"

"I'm not sure, sir. She sent me up to clean the box room as soon as she come downstairs this morning at half past seven."

"Was that her normal time to come down?"

"Yes, sir, it was. She was always at the breakfast table with the tenants and that's served at seven forty-five every day," she said and smiled uncertainly. "But today she didn't want me to help serve. She said she'd do it herself. By the time I finished and came downstairs, it was almost nine o'clock and she was already gone."

"As was just about everyone else in the household," Barnes muttered as he stepped inside. "I've finished interviewing Mrs. Fremont. The other housemaid, Etta Morgan, won't be back until this evening," he said to the inspector. "Apparently,

Mrs. Robinson sent the young lady out on an errand. Mrs. Fremont didn't know where. All she heard was Mrs. Robinson telling the girl she could go for her afternoon out as soon as she was finished."

"Etta always stays out late on her day out," Carrie offered. "She goes to visit her parents in Colchester."

"Do you know where Mrs. Robinson sent Miss Morgan this morning?" Witherspoon asked.

"No, sir, like I said, the mistress was gone when I come down, so I went on in and started on the dining room. Mrs. Robinson likes it set up for the evening meal, sir."

"What time do the tenants usually leave?" Witherspoon shifted slightly on the sofa. It was hard as a rock.

"It varies, sir," Carrie explained. "They come and go as they please."

"Mrs. Fremont says they are all businessmen of one kind or another," Barnes said.

"That's right, sir."

The front door suddenly slammed. Witherspoon rose from his seat as Barnes started for the foyer, but before either of them could reach the hall, the drawing room doors flew open and a middle-aged man burst into the room. His hair was more gray than brown and he was respectably dressed in a gray suit and white shirt.

"What's going on here?" His gaze darted from Barnes to Witherspoon to the housemaid. "Durridge, what on earth are you doing in here?"

Carrie had leapt to her feet. "I'm sorry, sir, but the police came and I wasn't sure where to take them."

"You most certainly shouldn't have taken them to the drawing room," he snapped as he stalked toward them. "I don't know what they're doing here, but take them down to the kitchen."

Barnes fixed his gaze on the interloper. "Are you the owner of this house?" he asked in a voice cold enough to chill bones.

"No, but as one of Mrs. Robinson's tenants, I hardly think she'd approve of the maid answering questions about a stolen trunk while she's out doing the shopping."

"So you're merely a tenant here, Mr. uh . . ." Barnes let his voice trail off as he held the man's gaze.

"Andrew Morecomb," he replied, "but that is hardly relevant."

"It's very relevant, sir," the constable interrupted, "and we're not investigating a missing trunk, but a murder. As you've admitted you live here as well as having taken it upon yourself to act on Mrs. Robinson's behalf in her absence, I can therefore assume you've a personal relationship with the dead woman."

Morecomb's eyes widened. "Dead woman?"

"Yes. Miss Durridge is being interviewed about the murder of Alice Robinson, and if you'll wait in your room, we'd like to have a word with you as well."

Mrs. Jeffries raced to the front-room window as she heard a hansom cab pull up to the house. It was already past eight and she'd begun to think that the inspector was going to stay at the station till the wee hours of the night. She pushed the heavy velvet curtain to one side and saw Inspector Witherspoon stepping onto the pavement.

She was waiting by the front door when he stepped

inside. He gave her a wan smile as he took off his bowler and handed it to her. "I take it you received the message that I'd been called out to a murder."

"Yes, sir, young Davey Marsh came around earlier today." She hung up the hat and held out her hand for his overcoat and scarf. "Your dinner is in the warming oven but I thought you might like a quick sherry before you ate."

"You're an angel, Mrs. Jeffries, that is precisely what I need. It has been a somewhat trying day." He headed off down the hall toward the study.

As the inspector wasn't given to exaggeration, Mrs. Jeffries frowned at his back as she hurried after him. She said nothing as he settled into his favorite chair, and she poured both of them a glass of sherry. "Here you are, sir." She handed him a glass of his favorite drink, Harvey's Bristol Cream sherry.

Witherspoon tossed it down his throat and handed her the glass. "As I said, it has been a very incredible day. Another, please."

"Of course, sir." She smiled as if his knocking back a glass of spirits in one gulp was the most usual thing in the world. She poured him another and brought it back to his chair. "Here you are, sir. Gracious, sir, you look exhausted. Why don't you tell me what happened today."

They had long established this pattern; he always told her about his cases and she, in turn, did her best to bolster his confidence. She took her seat and waited.

He said nothing for a few moments then, finally, he said, "Constable Barnes and I were sent to Highgate Cemetery today. The instructions from Barrows were that we were to go there to consult. When we got there, the inspector in charge of the case wasn't all that happy to see us, but nonetheless, we did our duty."

Mrs. Jeffries watched him with growing concern. There was something wrong. She'd never seen the inspector like this.

"The victim was a woman named Alice Robinson," he continued. "She owned a lodging house nearby and had been identified by a local constable. I couldn't quite understand why they'd called me to the scene, but when I got there, it became obvious." He told her about the newspaper clipping.

Mrs. Jeffries went perfectly still. She had a feeling that there was more to come.

"But that wasn't the biggest surprise." He took another sip. "When I finally looked at the body, I realized that this woman wasn't who everyone thought she was."

"Who was she, sir?"

"Edith Durant." His voice was a mere whisper.

Mrs. Jeffries drew a quick, uneven breath and then struggled to bring herself under control before he could notice that his announcement had knocked the wind out of her sails. But her efforts to appear calm were not needed, as the inspector wasn't looking at her, but was staring into the distance with a faraway look in his eyes.

"Odd, isn't it," he muttered. "How one reacts when faced with a circumstance one never thought to see. I honestly thought I'd never see or hear of her again. Yet she's been right here in London for almost two years, practically under my very nose."

"But as you said, sir, you were called to another district,

"But that doesn't matter, not when you're confronted with the evidence of your incompetence. Oh, I don't mean to wallow in self-pity, but that case has always made me feel that if it hadn't been for my late aunt's influence, I'd never even have made it as far as the Records Room. Even worse, when I saw the Durant woman lying there, when I realized who she really was, I found myself thinking that she'd finally got what she deserved."

"But it is perfectly normal that you'd react that way," she protested. In the back of her mind, she wondered how the others would react when she told them who the victim really was. "She committed a dreadful crime and got away with it for years."

"That shouldn't matter. Justice is for everyone, even the guilty. Edith Durant should have been arrested and punished in a court of law. But we stopped looking for her."

"Only when it became obvious she'd left the country," Mrs. Jeffries argued. "As I recall, sir, you and everyone else on the force did everything possible to find her. You had constables watching the train stations, you put out notices to every police district in the country, and at one point, you and Constable Barnes spent hours checking hotels near all the seaports as well as going through all the passenger manifests for ships leaving the country. There was nothing else you could have done."

"But we still never caught her." He smiled bitterly. "And after today, I'm not sure of myself."

"Don't be ridiculous, sir," she said, feeling her temper rising. "You can't let this one incident dictate your attitude about your career. You've accomplished more for the cause of justice than anyone."

"That's not what I meant," he interrupted. "What I'm most afraid of is myself. I'm scared I won't do a proper job of investigating her murder."

Mrs. Jeffries was already at the table when Mrs. Goodge shuffled down the hallway the next morning. "You're up early," she said as she continued on down the passage with Samson, the mean old orange tabby she adored, trailing behind her. Wiggins, being the softhearted sort, had brought the animal here after his owner had been murdered in one of their earlier cases. It had been love at first sight between the cook and the cat.

"I couldn't sleep. Let the cat out. I've made a fresh pot of tea." She poured a cup and sat it in the cook's place.

Mrs. Goodge grunted in reply, opened the back door, and then trundled back to the kitchen. She frowned as she studied the housekeeper's face. "You look like you haven't slept a wink."

"I haven't."

"What's wrong?"

Mrs. Jeffries smiled wanly. "Quite a bit, I'm afraid."

Inspector Witherspoon had dutifully listened to her protests and her assurances that a man of his character would always, always do his duty, but she'd not been sure he'd believed her. As for the details of the crime itself, she'd not gotten much information out of him as he'd decided he wanted his supper. But when she'd gone to clear the table, she'd noticed he'd eaten very little. "The victim we thought was Alice Robinson, isn't."

"Isn't what?" Mrs. Goodge took a big gulp of the hot tea.

"She's Edith Durant," Mrs. Jeffries blurted.

Mrs. Goodge put her mug down. "Edith Durant? I don't believe it."

"It's true and it's upset the inspector greatly." She stopped, unsure of how much of Witherspoon's confession she ought to share. She didn't want to be disloyal, but on the other hand, Mrs. Goodge was both discreet and devoted to their employer. So she told her everything.

When she'd finished her recital, the cook said nothing; she merely sat there with her hands wrapped around her tea mug.

Mrs. Jeffries waited patiently. Finally she said, "Well, what do you think? What should we do?"

"I don't know." Mrs. Goodge shrugged. "But I understand how the inspector feels. That horrible woman committed terrible crimes and left her accomplice to face the music. They hung him."

"Many would say he deserved to hang," Mrs. Jeffries said. She was afraid this was going to happen—that once the others knew who the victim was, they would not be so keen to find her killer. That, as well as her concerns about the inspector, was what had really kept her awake in the night. "He was no innocent who'd been dragged into the situation against his will. He killed so he could have what he wanted. Carl Christopher murdered Jasper Claypool."

"I'm not disputin' that. But Edith Durant did something far worse, for goodness' sake: She killed her own sister."

Mrs. Jeffries nodded but said nothing. When the others got here, she'd have to go over the details of Edith Durant's previous crimes so that Ruth and Phyllis would understand why this was such a disturbing case and, more important, why there might be those in the household who were less than enthusiastic to track down this particular killer.

They sat in the early-morning quiet of the silent house, both of them lost in thoughts of the past. The back door rattled and the cook got up. "I'll let Samson in. He always does his business quickly when it's cold outside."

Constable Barnes cocked his head to one side and studied the two women. "She was a killer and I'm not going to be losing a lot of sleep over the fact that she was dispatched to meet her Maker by someone of her own ilk. So I can understand how the inspector feels."

"Not just the inspector," Mrs. Goodge muttered. "I'm havin' a hard time with it as well. Maybe that woman did get what she deserved. She might have been murdered, but she's had years of freedom and happiness that her victims didn't have. Maybe this is the Lord's way of doin' justice."

"If this were the Lord's justice," Mrs. Jeffries murmured thoughtfully, "he'd not have dumped the woman's body right under our noses unless, of course, he was testing our own commitment to doing what was right." She wasn't sure she meant the words coming out of her mouth.

"We'll do what's right, Mrs. Jeffries," Barnes protested. "Investigating this murder is our job and we'll do it properly. No one has the right to take the law into his or her own hands. I'm just sayin' I can understand how the inspector feels."

As was his habit, Barnes had stopped in to have a quick word with them before getting out with the inspector. He did it every time there was a murder to be investigated. During the course of his work with Witherspoon, it hadn't taken Barnes long to suss out that the inspector had help with his cases, and being a clever sort, he'd soon figured out precisely how his superior was being assisted. But Barnes was a wily old fox, and he'd also realized that the household of Upper Edmonton Gardens and their friends had access to information that the police might never get.

People who'd die before they spoke to a copper would tell them all manner of useful bits and pieces. Even better, they could worm information out of confidential sources such as bankers and even solicitors. So Barnes had made the decision to help them, and now they had a system in place where they passed facts, rumors, and gossip back and forth.

"There was never any doubt that you'd both do your best," Mrs. Jeffries said. "Speaking of which, the inspector was, well, let's just say not overly concerned with the details of the crime scene when we talked last night. What can you tell us?"

"So far, there's not much to go on. Durant owned a lodging house in Highgate and has been there for about two years." He shook his head and frowned. "I can't believe she was that close and none of us spotted her."

"The inspector said she'd changed her appearance," Mrs. Jeffries said.

"True, her hair was a darker color and she wore spectacles, but you could see that it was still her." He told them what they knew thus far, taking care not to leave out anything, no matter how insignificant it might sound. "So far, the lads haven't found anyone in the cemetery who remembers seeing her or who saw anyone else, so we've no witnesses, but we'll keep trying."

"Death by strangulation isn't pleasant," Mrs. Jeffries murmured. "Putting your hands on someone's throat is a very personal way to kill."

"The killer didn't use his hands. She was strangled by a red cord," he corrected.

"A red cord? What kind?"

"We're not sure. It's about as thick as my thumb. The only other fact we know is that when we searched the body, we found a gun. A derringer, to be precise."

CHAPTER 3

"Mrs. Rivers, we understand how shocked you must have been when you discovered Mrs. Robinson's body," Witherspoon said to the small, frail-looking woman dressed from head to toe in widow's black. He and Barnes were in the front parlor of the lady's Highgate town house. She sat in the center of a medallion-back sofa upholstered in gold and brown stripes. Witherspoon and Barnes sat across from her in matching armchairs.

Signs of mourning were everywhere: Black crocheted antimacassars were draped on the back of all the chairs, and every table, cabinet, and bookcase was covered with ebony runners or black-fringed tablecloths. The curtains on the two windows were a dark shade of gray, and a wide black ribbon had been strung around an elderly gentleman's portrait that was hanging over the mantelpiece.

"It was dreadful, Inspector Witherspoon, absolutely

dreadful." She shuddered and dabbed at her eyes with a white handkerchief edged in black lace.

"Can you tell us what happened?" The inspector gave her an encouraging smile.

"It's not an experience I care to recall," she protested.

"Mrs. Rivers, I understand you were taking flowers to your late husband's grave," Barnes said softly.

"Yes." She nodded eagerly. "That's right. I take flowers to Mr. Rivers' grave every week. Sometimes, if the weather is nice and the florist has flowers that aren't too dear, I go twice a week."

"Your late husband must have been a wonderful person to have so devoted a wife," Barnes said.

"It's good of you to say so, Constable," she responded, beaming with pride. "I try to follow the example set by Her Majesty. She's worn nothing but black since she lost her consort, Prince Albert."

"And I'm sure, like Her Majesty, your husband believed in law and order," the constable continued.

She nodded somberly and glanced at the portrait over the fireplace. "He did. Thank you, Constable, for reminding me of my duty. Mr. Rivers would have insisted that no matter how distressing it might be, I must do what is right. Go ahead, gentlemen, ask your questions."

Witherspoon spoke first. "What time did you arrive at the cemetery yesterday?"

"Half past nine. I always get there at half past nine. The florist on the high street opens at nine and I go there to get fresh flowers. I don't move quickly, Inspector, so it takes me a good half an hour to get to the cemetery."

"Did you see anyone when you went inside the main gate?"

"Not that I recall, Inspector, but then again, when one gets to be my age, one tends to watch where one's walking rather than what is going on around them."

"Using your own words, can you tell us about finding the body," Barnes suggested.

"I walked along the main pathway as I always do until it branched off and then I went to my left, towards the Rivers family plot. That was when I practically tripped over that poor woman. At first I thought she must have fainted but then I saw her face and I knew something was terribly wrong."

"What happened then?" Witherspoon pressed.

"I'm not sure, Inspector, but I think I must have screamed. I turned back and moved as quickly as I dared back towards the main gate. I must have still been shouting or making some sort of ruckus because as I got near the chapel, one of the groundsmen came running. I told him what I'd seen. He helped me to the office and Mr. Abbot sent for the police. When the constables arrived"—she swallowed heavily—"they asked me to show them where the body was, which, of course, I did. They wouldn't let me leave until the other inspector arrived. He had a constable bring me home."

"Did you touch the body?" Barnes asked quietly.

"Certainly not," she exclaimed. "I could tell by looking at the woman's face that she was dead."

"And you don't recall seeing anyone while you were there?" Witherspoon leaned toward her.

"No, I don't think so."

Witherspoon tried putting the question another way. "How about when you entered the cemetery—did you see anyone coming out?"

She thought for a moment and then her face brightened. "There was someone. He was coming out as I was going in. He tipped his hat to me and I remember thinking that there was something odd about him."

"What was that?" Barnes asked quickly.

"The man was carrying a bouquet and I thought it strange that one would take flowers out of a cemetery. Usually, one does just the opposite. One brings flowers in to put on a grave."

Mrs. Jeffries heard the back door open and the twang of Luty Belle Crookshank's American accent. "Get a move on, Hatchet. We're late enough as it is."

"We're right on time, madam," Hatchet replied.

As Mrs. Jeffries waited for the two of them to enter, she crossed her fingers that they might have seen the morning newspapers and, therefore, wouldn't be surprised about Edith Durant having been alive, well, and living in London until yesterday. Unfortunately, none of the others had made mention of it so she was fairly sure they'd not had time to read the papers today. In truth, if they had, it would have made telling them easier.

"Dang it, I knew we'd be the last ones here." Luty stopped beneath the archway separating the hall from the kitchen and surveyed the room. She was a tiny, white-haired American with a kind heart, a sharp tongue, and a love of bright clothes. She'd been a witness in one of Witherspoon's earliest cases, had figured out what the household was up to, and then come to them for help on a problem. Ever since, both she and Hatchet insisted on helping whenever the inspector had a homicide. "You haven't started yet, have ya?"

"Of course they haven't begun, madam." Hatchet swept off his shiny black top hat revealing a head full of snowy white hair. He helped Luty take off her peacock blue cloak, shed his own coat, and hung all their garments on the coat tree.

"We've only just sat down," Mrs. Jeffries assured them as Luty raced around the table and yanked out the empty chair across from Betsy. "Where's my baby?" she demanded.

Betsy smiled apologetically. "I'm sorry, Luty, but we had to leave her home. She's got a bit of a sniffle. Our neighbor is sitting with her."

"We didn't want 'er out in this cold air," Smythe added. He was a tall, muscular man with dark hair going gray at the temples. His features were hard and sharp, softened only by the kindness in his brown eyes and his ready smile. He and Betsy were married and the parents of Amanda, who was Luty Belle's godchild. Betsy had been the inspector's housemaid, and Smythe was still the household coachman despite the fact that Witherspoon rarely used his horses and carriage.

Luty's eyes narrowed in a worried frown. "Have you taken her to the doctor?"

"It's just a sniffle," Betsy assured her. "She'll be right as rain in a day or two."

"You'd best take her to the doctor if she's not." Mrs. Goodge reached for the teapot and began to pour. "We can't take any chances with our little one." She was also a godparent to the child as was the inspector. All three of them doted on her.

"We're keepin' a close watch on her," Smythe promised. "Now, what 'ave we got here?"

Everyone at the table turned their attention to Mrs. Jeffries. She nodded her thanks as the cook handed her a mug of tea. "It's a very unusual case."

"Aren't they all," the blonde, middle-aged woman sitting at the far end of the table muttered. Slender as a girl and still very attractive, Lady Ruth Cannonberry was the widow of a peer. She lived across the communal garden and she and the inspector had become very close "friends." The daughter of a country vicar, she very much believed in Christ's instructions to love our neighbors as ourselves. She fed the hungry, clothed the poor, and visited the sick. She also believed that all people were equal in the sight of God, and to that end, she worked tirelessly for women's rights.

"Indeed they are," Mrs. Jeffries said as she took a quick sip of tea. She didn't want to just blurt it out but was somewhat at a loss as to how to tell them that the dead woman was someone they once hoped they'd see hang. "But this one is especially odd."

"What do you mean, Mrs. Jeffries?" Phyllis asked.

"I'll bet it was because the lady was strangled," Wiggins guessed. "Is that what makes this one so strange? We don't usually get them like that. Most times it's a gun or a knife that does 'em in, but we've had this kind before."

"It's not the nature of the crime itself, it's the identity of the victim." Mrs. Jeffries put her cup down.

"Wiggins said the victim was a lady named Alice Robinson," Hatchet said.

"Alice Robinson is an alias." Mrs. Jeffries took a deep breath. "The victim's real name is Edith Durant."

Smythe, who'd just taken a drink of tea, choked, and Betsy let out a squeak of surprise. Luty's hands balled into fists and Hatchet's jaw dropped open.

"I've heard Gerald mention that name," Ruth murmured. "But when I asked him who she was, he always changed the subject."

Phyllis asked, "Who is Edith Durant?"

"She's the one that got away," Wiggins explained. Unlike the others, he didn't appear to be surprised. "I always knew that she'd turn up one day. Mind you, I didn't expect her to be a corpse."

"It's a pity that Mrs. Rivers couldn't give us a better description of the man she saw leaving the cemetery," Witherspoon commented as he and Barnes got down from a hansom cab in front of Edith Durant's lodging house.

"The only thing she remembered was that the flowers he carried were carnations," Barnes complained. "And that'll not do us any good."

They started up the walkway.

"You there, Constable, come here, please."

Both of them turned and saw a gray-haired, portly woman in spectacles waving at them with one hand while in the other she held a shopping basket. "Come here, please," she repeated. "I must speak with you."

Witherspoon looked at Barnes, shrugged, and then both of them trooped back to the pavement. "Yes, ma'am, how may we be of assistance to you?" the inspector asked, smiling politely.

"Are you the ones investigating Mrs. Robinson's murder?" She made it sound like an accusation.

"We are, madam. Uh, may I ask your name?"

"I'm Lavinia Swanson and I think I might have been the last person to see Mrs. Robinson alive." She glanced toward the lodging house. "But then again, she wasn't Mrs. Robinson, was she? It's all very confusing, and frankly, the newspaper accounts weren't very enlightening about the matter. Just who was this woman? We were acquainted and I thought she was a decent lady. Goodness, I've served her tea in my parlor. Now I find that she wasn't who I thought she was."

"Yes, ma'am, I'm sure it's most disconcerting," Witherspoon said. "But may we get back to your having been the last person to see, uh, the victim? Can you tell me the circumstances of this encounter?"

"Circumstances," she repeated as if she'd never heard the word before. "She was going toward the cemetery. I was on my way to Baxter's on the high street to give them my meat order for the week when we met. Naturally, we stopped and chatted. She's always been a polite, sociable sort of person and, frankly, I was a bit surprised by her behavior. She was in a dreadful hurry and barely gave me the time of day." She sniffed disapprovingly.

"Did she say why she was in a rush?" Barnes asked.

"She was meeting a builder. She said her family had a crypt in the cemetery and there were some cracks in the ceiling tiles."

"What time was this?" Witherspoon glanced at the lodging house and saw the curtain on the first floor twitch as it was hastily dropped back into place. Someone was watching them.

"I don't know the exact time, but it was past nine," she replied. "Then we said our good-byes and went our separate ways."

"Did you see anyone else when you were speaking with Mrs. Robinson?" Barnes asked.

"She isn't Mrs. Robinson," Lavinia Swanson corrected him. "She's someone else entirely, and as I said, the newspaper kept referring to her as someone named Durant. Esther Durant."

"Edith Durant," the constable corrected. "But back to my question: Did you see anyone else hanging about? Anyone who seemed to be loitering or who looked as if they didn't belong?"

She shook her head. "No, but I wasn't really looking, you see. I was brought up to keep my eyes to myself and to ignore strangers. There could easily have been other people going into the cemetery—it's a busy place. There's always funerals or people going in to take flowers to their loved ones. As I said, I wasn't paying attention to who was coming or going. But back to my concern, Constable. Exactly who was this woman?"

Barnes glanced at the inspector, who gave a brief nod. "As I said, ma'am, the woman you knew as Mrs. Robinson was, in fact, Edith Durant. We've been looking for her for years."

"Why?"

"To help with our inquiries regarding the murder of two people," the inspector said. There was no point in trying to evade the woman's question. In the morning papers, one newspaper had already hinted that the murdered woman had an unsavory past, and by the time the evening papers came out, all of them would have part if not all of the details about her.

Lavinia's hand flew to her chest and flattened against her heart. "Dear Lord, that's dreadful, and to think that I had her in my home, I served her tea, I let her pet Kingston. How on earth could such a thing happen? Why hadn't the police arrested her?"

"I'm sure, madam, that many people will be asking that very question," Witherspoon said.

Luty was the first to recover her tongue. "Lordy, lordy, are you sayin' what I think you're sayin'?"

"I'm afraid so. Edith Durant has apparently been living right here in London for the past two years. She owns a lodging house near Islington," Mrs. Jeffries said

"According to what the inspector said, she managed to change her appearance enough so that she wasn't easily recognized. Her hair was a darker color, she wore spectacles, and her clothes while of good quality, were definitely far more conservative than the very stylish Edith Durant."

"And she's been gone a long time," Betsy murmured. "And now she's dead, murdered."

"I can't say that I'll lose any sleep over her leavin' this world," Smythe said. "She did terrible things and to my way of thinkin' she got what she deserved."

"God works in mysterious ways," Hatchet added. "Perhaps this was his way of seeing justice done."

"At least we won't need to worry overmuch on this one," Wiggins said. "If we don't catch her killer, it won't be the end of the world."

Mrs. Jeffries glanced at Phyllis and Ruth. From their

expressions, she could see they were shocked by what was being said. "Edith Durant was part of one of our earlier investigations."

"I gather it was a very ugly case," Ruth murmured.

"Murder is always horrid, but you're right, this one was particularly ugly." Mrs. Jeffries took a deep breath. "There were two victims, you see, and Edith Durant was responsible for both their deaths. The first victim was her own sister, her identical twin, Hilda."

"And she got away with that one for years," Wiggins added.

"Hilda and Edith Durant were physically identical twins, but that was the only thing the two had in common. Hilda was a decent, sensible woman who did precisely what was expected of someone from her background and class. Edith was just the opposite; she had no use for the conventions of society and did as she pleased. As is often the case, Hilda's the one who inherited the family money."

"Not that it did her any good." Luty snorted. "Poor woman was killed for it."

"Edith killed her?" Phyllis asked.

"Yes, unfortunately for Hilda, the man she married, Carl Christopher, fell under Edith's spell," Mrs. Jeffries continued. "But before we go any further, there's another important fact you should know. The two twins were so alike, there was only one person who could tell them apart. That was their uncle, a clergyman named Jasper Claypool." She took a quick sip of tea. "When Claypool retired from his parish here, he went to India to build a church."

"And that's when Edith and Carl struck," Wiggins added. "They killed poor Hilda and . . . and . . . well, I'll not tell ya what they did with the body—it's disgustin'—but Edith took her sister's place."

Ruth looked doubtful. "But how was that possible? A person is more than just their physical appearance. Twins may look alike, but surely they sound and walk and even speak differently."

"Edith Durant was a good actress," Mrs. Goodge said. "And this wasn't the first time she'd masqueraded as her sister. Growing up, they'd often made a game of pretending to be one another. What's more, the Durants hadn't come from London so there weren't all that many that knew them well. They even had cousins, the Rileys, who were fooled by Edith and Carl's charade. They got away with it for years and they'd never have been caught if Reverend Claypool hadn't come back to England."

"He was the second victim." Mrs. Jeffries took up the tale. "Carl Christopher shot him before he could tell anyone that the woman pretending to be Hilda Christopher was really Edith."

"How was Hilda killed?" Ruth asked.

"Edith strangled her with a scarf," Betsy said. "Carl confessed to killing Claypool, but when Edith deserted him and escaped, he decided he wasn't going to cover for her crime."

"So you can see why we're all a bit at a loss about this case," Mrs. Jeffries said. "Of course justice must be served, but Edith Durant was a dreadful excuse for a human being. She was the mastermind behind two murders and then she abandoned her lover and saved herself."

The room was quiet for a long moment, and then Phyllis

stood up. "She was never convicted in a court of law, was she?"

"No, but that don't mean nothin'" Luty said. "We know she did it."

"She may have, but it was never proved properly, was it," Phyllis said. "All of you are saying that because you think she might have been a murderer herself, she doesn't deserve to have her own murder investigated?" Phyllis looked from person to person as she spoke. "Is that what you're all saying?"

"I'd not put it exactly like that," Mrs. Goodge said as she shifted in her chair.

"Then how would you put it?" Phyllis demanded.

"She killed her sister and forced Christopher to kill her uncle," Wiggins said defensively. "Then she run for it and got away."

"For all we know she might have killed a dozen more people," Betsy snapped. "She is evil." Her cheeks colored as she spoke, turning a bright, embarrassing red.

"She'd kill anyone who got in 'er way," Smythe added. "She's not got a conscience."

"You weren't here, so git off your high horse and stop judgin' us," Luty cried.

"I'm not judging anyone," Phyllis said. "I'm just asking questions."

"From the tone of your voice, it appears that you're thinkin' we're in the wrong." Wiggins looked down at the tabletop. "And I don't much like it."

"Maybe she didn't like getting murdered," Phyllis countered as she sat back down. "Look, you're right, I wasn't here, and maybe I'm not as smart or as well read as the rest of you, but I do know one thing: If someone like her can get murdered and no one does anything about it, then someone like me doesn't have much hope."

Everyone started to speak at once.

"That's absurd," Hatchet said tightly. "You've not murdered anyone."

"I don't know what you're on about," Wiggins said. "But you're wrong. Murderers have no right to expect justice."

"She had it comin'," Mrs. Goodge snapped.

"She's wicked," Betsy insisted. "She has no heart or conscience."

Mrs. Jeffries said nothing as everyone except Ruth kept insisting that someone as malicious and evil as the late Edith Durant had got what she deserved. Phyllis, for her part, merely stared at the lot of them with a disappointed, rather stony expression on her round face.

As the argument raged, Mrs. Jeffries wondered whether or not they actually believed what they were saying, or whether part of their fury toward the dead woman was nothing more than vanity. It wasn't a pleasant thought, but once the seed had been planted, it took root and sprouted. Were all of them, and she included herself in this, angry because Edith Durant had escaped justice, or was it that she'd been smarter than any of them had realized? If any of them had been just a bit more thoughtful and clever shouldn't they have anticipated that she'd have an escape route of some sort? After she'd fled, they'd had more than one discussion about how they underestimated her.

But enough was enough and it was time to get on with their current case. Mrs. Jeffries balled her hand into a fist and lifted it a few inches. But before she could bang it against the table, Ruth spoke up.

"I'm deeply ashamed," she said.

People stopped talking, some of them in mid-sentence, and silence descended on the kitchen. Finally, Mrs. Goodge said, "What do you mean? Why should you feel ashamed about anything?"

"Because as you told me what she'd done, for a few moments, I was glad that Edith Durant had been murdered, I was happy that she'd been sent to meet her Maker by the same method she'd used to dispatch other poor souls from this life." Ruth sighed heavily. "But I was wrong." She looked at Phyllis. "It would be easy to think this was God's way of exacting vengeance because she got away from human justice. But human justice is all we have, and if we don't do our best to investigate this murder, then we're nothing more than hypocrites. Justice is justice and the murderer of a murderer must be held as accountable as the murderer of an innocent. Otherwise, justice isn't blind, she picks and chooses who gets her help, and that's just plain wrong."

"But she killed people," Luty protested.

"True, but that doesn't give anyone the right to take her life," Ruth exclaimed. "Murder is murder regardless of who the victim might be. If we start deciding who is deserving of justice and who isn't, then where does it end? Perhaps someone will decide that because they don't like my politics or my religion, I'm not entitled to legal protection—and that's not right."

"It most certainly isn't," Mrs. Jeffries declared. "No one has the right to take the law into their hands, not even

to kill a killer. I shall do my very best to help catch whoever murdered Edith Durant." She surveyed the faces at
the table, seeing in each of their expressions their internal
struggles as their consciences did battle with the desire to
see the murder as a kind of divine retribution.

It was Betsy who broke first. "I'll help, too. She was a
horrible person but she shouldn't have been murdered."

"I 'ate to say it"—Smythe grinned at Phyllis and
Ruth—"but you two are right. Once we start pickin' and
choosin', it's not justice, it's vengeance. So count me in as
well."

One by one, the others followed suit, though Wiggins
did leave himself a bit of wiggle room by declaring that
"I'll do me best, but if her killer gets away, it'll not be our
fault, it'll be because God wanted it that way."

"I did as you asked, sir," Carrie Durridge said as she ushered Witherspoon and Barnes into the foyer. "I told the
tenants they should be available today and Mr. Redley and
Mr. Erskine are both upstairs. But Mr. Morecomb complained that you'd already spoken to him, and said he'd be
here after lunch if you needed to talk to him again. Mr.
Teasdale said he had an engagement he couldn't cancel
and that he'd be back late this afternoon. Neither of them
said what time they'd be here. I did my best, sir. I told them
it was important but that didn't seem to make any difference."

Witherspoon gave her a reassuring smile. "Don't look
so worried. I'm sure you handled it properly and we'll
speak with both Mr. Morecomb and Mr. Teasdale in due
course. Are the other gentlemen in their rooms?"

"That's right, sir," she answered, pointing up the staircase. "Mr. Erskine has the room just on the first-floor landing. He's expecting you."

They nodded and went up the staircase. Barnes had raised his hand to knock, when the door opened, revealing a brown-haired man with a handlebar mustache, a portly belly, and a double chin. He was dressed for the business day in gray suit trousers, a white shirt with a blue tie, and a dark blue waistcoat. He stared at them for a moment, his gaze flicking from the inspector to Barnes. "You're the police. The housemaid said you'd be here today." He held his door open and waved them inside. "I'm John Erskine. Come in and let's get this over with. I don't have much time. I've a business engagement."

"We'll be as quick as possible," Witherspoon said as he and Barnes stepped inside. The door opened onto a small sitting room furnished with a horsehair love seat, a matching wing chair, a secretary, and one lone window with a gray and green patterned curtain hanging at the window. An open door led to a bedroom with an iron bedstead covered with a cream-colored chenille bedspread.

"Sit down, please." Erskine pointed to the love seat as he eased his frame into the chair. "I'm very sorry to hear about the poor woman's murder, but nonetheless, I doubt I'll be of any use in your inquiries. I know nothing about this matter."

They took their seats and the constable whipped out his little brown notebook and pencil.

"How long have you lived here?" Witherspoon asked.

"I've been here since November," Erskine replied.

"What is your occupation, sir?" Barnes asked.

"I'm a sales agent for Canadian Furs. We supply skins

for the coat and hat trade both here and on the Continent. We've an office in High Holborn."

"How did you come to rent lodgings here?" Barnes asked. "Were you acquainted with the deceased?"

"No, no, never met the woman until she became my landlady. This establishment was recommended to me," he said. "It's clean and the food is good. I travel quite frequently and this is convenient to the railroad stations. I must say, I was surprised to find out that Mrs. Robinson wasn't who I thought she was. This morning's newspaper reported that she used an alias of some sort."

"That's correct, sir. Her real name was Edith Durant," Witherspoon said.

Erskine stared at them, his expression openly curious. "The paper was a bit vague about why she used a name different from her own, but there was a hint that she'd been involved in some sort of unsavory activities."

"She was a suspect in an unsolved murder and we've been looking for her for a long time," the inspector said.

"Murder." Erskine's eyes widened as he spoke. "My Lord, who on earth would have thought her capable of such a thing? She ran a respectable house, minded her own business, and seemed a perfectly decent sort of person."

"When was the last time you saw her, sir?" Barnes looked up from his notebook.

"Yesterday morning at breakfast. Mrs. Robinson always presided over the breakfast table, though actually, she did more serving than presiding. Or rather, I suppose I ought to refer to her as Miss Durant." He frowned in confusion. "I'm afraid I don't quite know what to make of this. It's difficult to think one has been living under the roof of a person implicated in a terrible crime."

"Do you know if Miss Durant had any enemies?" Witherspoon asked.

"If she did, she certainly didn't mention it to me." Erskine's eyebrows drew together. "As I said, Inspector, I was merely her tenant. We were cordial to one another but that was the extent of our relationship."

"Has anything happened recently that you felt was strange or unusual?" Witherspoon pressed. "Anything out of the ordinary."

"No, nothing . . ." His voice trailed off. "Wait a moment, there was something odd that happened. It was two days ago. I came home late in the evening because I'd had a business dinner, and when I stopped to pick up my post, I heard Mrs. Robinson." He broke off and smiled. "Sorry, I can't help but think of her as Mrs. Robinson."

"That's understandable, sir," Witherspoon assured him. "Go on, please."

"She always put the post on the table in the foyer so I was standing there when I heard her shouting."

"Shouting," Barnes prompted. "At who?"

"I don't know." Erskine shrugged. "You see, I didn't see her. I only heard her. Her rooms are upstairs on the first floor, just across the hall from mine. Her door was closed but I could quite clearly hear her shouting at someone."

"What was she saying?" Witherspoon was annoyed with himself. He ought to have searched Alice Robinson's rooms before he began interviewing the tenants.

"I couldn't hear everything, of course. Only a few words

here and there, but I heard her yell that she'd not put up with such nonsense."

"And you're sure this was the evening before she was murdered?"

"Positive, Inspector." His mouth gaped open as he realized the significance of what he'd just said. "My word, I'd not thought of that. She might have been arguing with her killer."

"Do you know who was in the room with her?" Witherspoon asked.

Erskine shook his head. "The door slammed and the shouting suddenly stopped. But I have no idea who she was arguing with. I went into the kitchen and got a drink of water and then I went up to my rooms. I was tired and just wanted to get some rest."

"What was her manner at breakfast yesterday?"

Erskine stroked his mustache. "The same as always, Inspector."

"She didn't seem upset or preoccupied?"

"Not that I could see. But you might want to ask one of the others. We were all there, but I wasn't paying attention to anything but my food and my morning paper."

Witherspoon glanced at Barnes and they both stood up. "Thank you for your time, sir," the inspector said as they moved to the door.

"Sorry I couldn't be more helpful." Erskine heaved himself out of the chair. "But as I said, I really didn't know the woman at all."

When they came out onto the landing, Carrie was standing at the bottom of the staircase. "Mr. Redley's room is on the second floor." She pointed up.

"Thank you, miss." Witherspoon smiled at the maid.

"But we're going to have a look at Mrs. Robinson's rooms before we continue with the interviews."

"Shall I tell Mr. Redley you'll see him later? He did mention that he needed to get to work today." She started up the stairs. "He's got a bit of a temper when he's in a state, sir, and I'd not like him to be inconvenienced."

"Then we'll see him this afternoon. Perhaps by then Mr. Morecomb and Mr. Teasdale will also be available," Witherspoon said as Carrie reached the landing.

"Yes, sir, I'll go up and let him know."

They crossed the hallway to the opposite door and Barnes grabbed the knob and gave it a twist. "It's locked, sir. Which isn't surprising considering what we know of Edith Durant's character."

Witherspoon moved to the banister and looked up to where Carrie's footsteps could be heard clomping across the next landing. "Do you have the key to Mrs. Robinson's room?" he called.

"No, sir." Her face appeared above him. "I've no idea where she kept it, sir. If you'll give me a minute, I'll go down and ask Mrs. Fremont."

"I don't want any of you thinkin' I'm deliberately not going to do my part in this one." Mrs. Goodge crossed her arms over her chest. "Ruth and Phyllis have both given my conscience a good prod. I can see that I was wrong to think the victim deserved to be murdered. But make no mistake, this is going to be a tough case. The woman was living under an assumed name and she's only been in London for two years. None of my sources will be of much help with this kind of a situation."

"You don't know that, Mrs. Goodge," Phyllis said. "You're right about the tradespeople that come into the kitchen—Highgate is a long ways off so most of the locals here won't know anything. But you're bound to know someone from the old days that works or lives up that way."

The cook had a network of delivery boys, van drivers, tinkers, rag and bone sellers, gasmen, and even builders who regularly trooped through her kitchen. Freshly baked buns, biscuits, and cakes kept her visitors in their chairs while she poured cups of tea and got them talking about the suspects in the inspector's cases. As so many of those investigations had involved the rich and powerful, it was easy to get information. The upper crust were notoriously indiscreet in front of those they considered their inferiors and didn't bother to hold their tongues. But tradespeople, hansom drivers, and servants all had ears with which to hear and mouths with which to repeat what they'd heard, so lots of lovely bits of gossip and news came her way.

Additionally, Mrs. Goodge had spent most of her life working for some of the finest households in England, and she had a host of old colleagues who she called upon when needed.

"I suppose I can always contact Ida Leacock," the cook mused. "There isn't much that goes on in this town that she doesn't know about."

"I'll have a go at the local shopkeepers," Phyllis offered. "Even if she's only lived in the neighborhood two years, someone may know something."

"If the baby is better tomorrow, I'll take her out in her pram to the local parks." Betsy glanced at Smythe to see his reaction. He tended to be a bit overprotective of Amanda. But he nodded in agreement.

"I've got some local sources up that way I can tap," Smythe added. "And I'll check the local cab stands to see if anyone dropped a fare at the main gate of the cemetery close to the time of the murder." He looked at Mrs. Jeffries. "Do we know the time?"

"She was probably killed between nine and half past." Mrs. Jeffries told them what she'd learned from the inspector and from Constable Barnes. She took her time, taking care to make sure she left nothing out. When she'd finished, she reached for the teapot and poured a fresh cup.

"So she was murdered with a red cord?" Hatchet mused. "I wonder if that is significant."

"Significant how?" Mrs. Jeffries added sugar and cream to her tea. She'd wondered the same herself.

"I'm no expert, but in many cultures colors have meaning." He frowned as he cast his mind back to his younger days when he was footloose, fancy-free, and wandering in the Far East. "For instance, in China, white is the color of mourning and red is usually associated with prosperity and good fortune."

"Gettin' strangled with a red cord don't sound prosperous to me." Luty snorted. "Seems to me that when people are doin' a killin', they just grab what's handy."

"True, Luty, but in that case, why not use a knife or some sort of heavy object?" Ruth asked. "Every house in London has both of those items."

"Why didn't Edith Durant use her gun?" Wiggins leaned forward, plopping his arms onto the table. "She 'ad a derringer in her pocket. Why didn't she use it when she was attacked?"

"Perhaps she panicked," Mrs. Jeffries replied.

"She did," Phyllis stated. She pushed back from the table and got up. "Didn't the constable tell you that the ends of the red cords were lying across her chest?" She glanced at the cook and the housekeeper as she spoke.

"That's right." Mrs. Goodge nodded. "But I don't see how that means she got so flustered she couldn't grab her gun."

"But it does." Phyllis tapped Wiggins on the shoulder. "Can you get up, please? I want to show everyone."

Wiggins looked a bit confused but did as she asked. Phyllis darted over to the coat tree and fumbled through the cloaks, coats, hats, and mufflers until she found what she needed: a long black wool scarf that belonged to Mrs. Goodge. She looked at the cook. "May I use this?"

"Of course," she replied.

Phyllis rushed back to Wiggins. Keeping her hands on the ends of the garment, she stood on tiptoe and draped it around his neck. "Now, let's pretend you're Edith Durant."

"That won't work." Betsy got up. "Wiggins is six foot tall and as I remember, Edith Durant was about my height." She went around the table until she was beside Wiggins. "Do it with me."

"You're right—it'll work better with someone her size," Phyllis agreed as she pulled the scarf off Wiggins' neck and moved in front of Betsy.

Phyllis draped the scarf around Betsy's neck. "When I pull these ends together, I want you to try and stop me while at the same time reaching into your pocket for a gun."

She started to draw the ends across Betsy's chest.

"Just a minute. Let's do this right." Betsy glanced at the table. "Wrap a serviette around a spoon and give it to me," she instructed Wiggins.

By this time everyone knew what Phyllis was doing and they watched her closely, especially Mrs. Jeffries.

"Wind it tight," Luty ordered as Wiggins grabbed the crumpled white cotton square and wound it around a spoon.

"Try to make it the same size as a derringer," Ruth suggested.

He snatched another serviette, twisted it onto the spoon, and handed it to Betsy.

Betsy tucked it in the pocket of her skirt. "Good. Now I'm ready. Go ahead."

"Be careful." Smythe half rose from his chair. "I'm fond of that neck, so don't squeeze too much."

"I'll not hurt her," Phyllis promised. She pulled at the two ends. "Now."

Betsy began clawing at the material as it tightened around her neck. "Harder," she ordered. "Pull it tighter."

Phyllis winced but did as instructed, yanking harder on the scarf while still not wanting to go too far. Betsy grabbed, snatched, and tried her best to get the noose off her neck, but Phyllis held it tight enough that she couldn't.

"That's enough," Mrs. Jeffries said. "We can all see what must have happened."

Phyllis dropped the ends and Betsy flipped the material away from her neck. "Are you alright? I didn't hurt you?" the maid asked worriedly.

"Of course not," Betsy assured her. "What's more, now

we know why Edith didn't use her gun. When you've got something around your neck, you instinctively try to get it off. Once Phyllis started to tighten the scarf, I didn't even think of reaching into my pocket, so it's a good bet that Edith didn't, either."

"Especially as her killer meant business and wanted the woman dead," Mrs. Goodge said.

"But we've learned something else important as well." Mrs. Jeffries watched Phyllis as she spoke.

"What?" Wiggins asked.

"The killer could just as easily have been a woman as a man."

Phyllis' demonstration signaled the end of the meeting. As soon as everyone had gone, Phyllis started to help clear up the table but Mrs. Jeffries sent her on her way.

Mrs. Goodge pulled a battered tray off the shelf from under her worktable. "Phyllis is quite clever, isn't she," she commented as she began to gather dirty cups and spoons.

"Indeed she is, but I don't think that's the reason she knew about what happens to a person when they're being strangled." Mrs. Jeffries sat down heavily in her chair. She hated the thoughts that were crowding into her head, but she'd been watching the maid's face and hadn't liked what she'd seen.

"What do you mean by that?" Mrs. Goodge shoved the tray onto the table and sat down.

"Did you notice that during the demonstration, even with the excitement of being right and making her point, Phyllis went very pale, and that when it was over and she looked away for a moment, her lips were trembling?"

"I can't say that I did. I don't like where this conversation is heading, Hepzibah. Are you trying to say what I think you're saying?"

"I hope to God I'm wrong and that perhaps Phyllis simply figured out the obvious, namely, that people panic when they're being strangled."

"But you don't really believe it do you?" Mrs. Goodge sighed. "You think she knew because it happened to her."

"Yes, I do."

"But Phyllis isn't dead—she's alive and well."

"True, and I'm not implying that someone actually tried to murder her, but it's certainly within the bounds of possibility that a parent or one of her former masters put their hands around her throat to scare her."

"People can be terrible, can't they," Mrs. Goodge muttered. "Especially to those who are dependent on them."

"Unfortunately, yes. One master with a nasty temper or one mistress who's just had her best dress ruined by an inexperienced maid is quite capable of all manner of dreadful behavior."

"When I was just starting in service, working as a scullery maid, the master's son burned his tongue on the soup so he threw it at the serving maid. The bowl shattered and the girl was scalded with hot liquid as well as glass. When she got her quarterly wages, they'd taken the cost of the broken dish out of what little they paid her. They were horrible people." Mrs. Goodge shook her head in disgust.

"I didn't mean to stir up unpleasant memories," Mrs. Jeffries apologized. "Please don't let me upset you."

The cook waved her hand dismissively. "I'm not upset.

Those things happened and we accepted them as a matter of course. I think you're right about Phyllis, though. She rarely speaks of her past and to my knowledge, never mentions her family except to say they're all dead. She might have been miserable in the past but at least now she's with the inspector and he'll not let anyone mistreat her ever again."

CHAPTER 4

In the end, they had to break into the room. None of the servants knew where another key might be, and there wasn't one on the landing, hidden under either of the two potted cactus plants, or on top of the doorjamb nor had there been a key found on Edith's person when she'd been killed.

"Either the killer took the key or she had a hiding place somewhere else here in the house." Barnes grunted as he worked the thin edge of a crowbar between the lock and the door.

"It'd take days to search the whole house for an item as small as a key." The inspector winced as wood splintered and the lock gave.

Barnes put the tool down against the doorframe and stepped inside.

Witherspoon followed him, stopping next to the constable

as they both stared at the late Edith Durant's private quarters. There was nothing of genteel poverty here, no frayed rugs, limp curtains, faded upholstery, or mismatched furniture.

An Empire-style three-seater couch in cream-colored satin and two matching chairs sat on an opulent maroon and cream patterned rug. Velvet burgundy curtains topped with elaborate valences draped the two windows, and a small but elegant crystal chandelier hung from the ceiling. The walls were painted a pale pink and decorated with paintings of landscapes, seascapes, and pastoral scenes. A white marble fireplace was on the far wall and above that hung a long mirror in a carved gold gilt frame. A walnut secretary was in the corner. A curio cabinet filled with ceramic shepherds, brass bells, and two brightly painted wooden boxes decorated with inlaid mother-of-pearl was next to the door.

"She kept the good stuff for herself, didn't she." Barnes moved farther into the room. "Nothing tatty here, sir, is there. She made sure her quarters were luxurious."

"Indeed she did," Witherspoon agreed. "But that's very much in keeping with what we knew of the woman's character." He picked up a silver calling card case from the table next to the sofa. It was enameled with brilliantly colored bees, dragonflies, and flowers. "This would fetch a pretty price, I expect. I wonder who cleaned her rooms. I can't see her on her hands and knees doing the cleaning."

Barnes snorted, selected a small, brass box from the knickknacks on a corner table, and flipped it open. "I've got a feeling she kept everyone out of here, sir. She'd not want to risk one of her staff stealing from her."

"Yes, you're probably right." He nodded at the box. "Is there anything inside?"

"Empty." Barnes put it down and pointed to an open door at the opposite end of the room. "Do you want me to take the bedroom, sir?"

"You might as well." He nodded as he started for the secretary. "I'll start in here."

Barnes went into the bedroom and paused just inside the door. Like the sitting room, it was luxuriously furnished. A gauzy white canopy crowned a huge four-poster that was covered with a shiny satin spread in ruby red. A carved box the size of a trunk stood at the foot of the bed and directly across from that was a dressing table. A double wardrobe stood on one side of the window and a matching chest of drawers stood on the other.

He searched the dressing table first, opening the lone drawer but finding nothing but two vials of almond oil, a tin of zinc oxide, a jar of Madame Celeste's face cream, and a broken hat pin. He ran his fingers around the inside of the drawer but found nothing. Closing it up, he went through the chest of drawers, starting with the bottom one and working his way up. But again, he found nothing untoward, only extra woolens, ancient corsets, old-fashioned petticoats, night-dresses, stockings, and two cloth coin purses, both of which were empty. Frustrated, he closed the top drawer and stalked to the wardrobe. He knew there was something here. Every copper's sense he had told him that Edith Durant had been up to her old tricks before she died, and he was sure she would have kept her secrets close by. He opened the left door. Four starched white blouses and a row of conservative gray, brown, and blue skirts in sensible cottons and wools hung on this side. Two pair of shoes, one brown and one black, rested on the wardrobe floor. Both of them had low heels.

He pulled open the right-hand door and grinned. "Now this is more like it. This is the Edith Durant I remember." Emerald green silks, coral satins, and gowns in every known shade of blue hung in a neat row. The constable was no expert, but even he could tell these dresses didn't come cheap. A black satin evening bag hung on the hook and on the floor were five pair of shoes, all with high heels and in a variety of colors, none of which were black or brown.

He pushed the gowns aside and ran his fingers over the back of the wardrobe, looking for a secret compartment. But he felt nothing except bare wood. He did the same on the other side and had just started to close the doors when he happened to glance down.

It took a moment before he realized that the shoes on each side of the wardrobe were at different levels. The fancy shoes were a good six inches higher than the plain ones. He knelt down, swept the shoes onto the carpet, and studied the floor of the wardrobe, noting that the wood jutted out over the base of the piece by half an inch on both sides of the structure but that it was only noticeable when the doors were open. He grabbed the jutting lip between his finger and thumb and tugged up. The wood lifted easily, revealing a space big enough to hold a small ledger. "Inspector, I've found something," he yelled as he pulled it out.

Phyllis was so depressed she could scream. Her shoulders slumped as she trudged toward the last shop on the high street. She'd already been to the baker's, where she'd been told in no uncertain terms that they didn't ever discuss their patrons; the greengrocer's, where the stall had been manned by a young woman who apparently was such a half-wit she couldn't understand simple inquiries; the butcher's and the grocer's shop, both of which had such a constant stream of customers that Phyllis had given up trying to learn anything; and even the draper's emporium, where they'd looked at her blankly when she'd inquired about Alice Robinson. Add to that, once the excitement of this morning's demonstration had worn off, she'd found herself thinking about things best left in the past.

She stopped and shifted her shopping basket to her other arm. Inside was a tin of Adams Furniture Polish, a bun, and a pound of carrots. Mrs. Jeffries had given her a list of actual items the household needed before she'd set out today, not that it had done any good at all. Thus far, she'd learned absolutely nothing and the only place left to inquire was the ironmonger's. Fat lot of good that would do, but still, she had to try. It was true that the others had been at this far longer than she had, but as someone who'd once seen a person she loved denied justice, she'd have died before she'd ever claim anyone, even someone as wicked as Wiggins claimed Edith Durant was, should be denied their day in a proper court of law.

She glanced at the soot-colored clouds blanketing the sky. She'd better hurry; it looked like rain and she'd not brought her brolly. Reaching the door, she peeked in the window and saw that the clerk was a young man.

Closing her eyes, she took a deep breath and thought back to Betsy's encouraging words. "You're a lovely girl, Phyllis. You've got to believe in yourself. Just put a big smile on your face and you'll dazzle them into telling you everything." Phyllis knew she wasn't as pretty as Betsy, but she wasn't a troll, either. Besides, what did she have to lose? Smiling brightly, she went into the shop.

Wiggins turned, keeping his back toward the late Edith Durant's home in case the inspector or a constable who knew him by sight might happen to step outside. He blew on his hands to keep them warm and wished he'd worn his gloves. It might be the middle of March but the gray, over-cast day was downright cold, especially if you'd been out-side for over an hour now.

He'd gone up and down the street several times, keeping his gaze on the servant's entrances of the neighboring homes, hoping for a chance to chat with someone. He'd been about to give up when a young lad had appeared in the side walkway of the town house directly across the street from the lodging house. The boy had glanced over his shoulder and then scur-ried off like the hounds of hell were nipping at his heels. Taking care to stay back a decent distance, Wiggins took off after him. He waited till both he and the boy had rounded the corner before he tried making contact.

"Excuse me," he called. "But you've dropped this." He held up a sixpence.

The boy turned and stared at him sullenly. "What did ya say?" He looked to be about ten years old and had a thin face, blue eyes, and curly blond hair sticking out from be-neath the red and gray wool cap on his head. "Was ya talkin' to me?"

Wiggins moved close enough for him to see the coin properly. "I said, I think ya dropped this."

He hesitated, moved to where Wiggins stood, and then

held out a grubby, dirt-encrusted hand. "Yeah, I did. Thanks for findin' it."

Wiggins put the money in his hand and grinned. "There's more where this came from if you can 'elp me."

The boy stumbled backward a step before he caught himself. "Help ya? How?" His eyes narrowed suspiciously.

"Don't get all stroppy on me." Wiggins laughed to put the lad at ease. "I'm just wantin' to buy you a cup of tea and some buns. I want to ask a few questions."

"Questions about what?"

"About the woman that lived across the road from the house you just came out of." He jerked his thumb in the direction of the lodging house.

"You mean Mrs. Robinson, the lady that got murdered over at Highgate?"

"That's right. I work for a newspaper and my guv wants me to find out a few bits and pieces about the dead lady."

"Why?"

"To sell papers, of course." He shrugged and turned away. "But if you're not interested . . ."

"I'll talk to ya." The lad tugged on his sleeve. "Come on, you can buy me that cup of tea and I'll tell ya what I know."

Wiggins knew he had him. "But do you know anything?"

"'Course I do." The lad grinned. "My mistress hated Mrs. Robinson—she called her a toffee-nosed cow who thought herself above the rest of us. Come on, then, let's go. I've plenty of time. The mistress is out shopping, the housekeeper is havin' a lie-down, and today's the cook's afternoon out, so no one will notice 'ow long I'm gone."

Five minutes later they were settled at a workingman's café, with two cups of tea and a plate of buns on their table.

It was too late for the breakfast trade and the lunch crowd wouldn't be in for another hour, so they had the place to themselves except for two men—wearing the flat caps and heavy work boots of day laborers—who sat at the counter. Outside, the overcast sky had finally made up its mind and a light rain began to fall.

"Go on, then." Wiggins pointed to the pastry. "'Elp yourself." He could tell by the way the boy stared at the plate of food that he was hungry. The child obviously came from one of those miserable households that scrimped on food for their servants. Wiggins started to get angry and then forced himself to calm down. If he let his feelings show, it might scare the lad and he didn't want that.

"Ta, mister, this is right decent of ya. My name is Freddie Ricks. What's yours?" He grabbed a bun and stuffed it into his mouth.

"Me, my name is Albert Jones." It was a fake name, one that he often used when he was on the hunt. He'd picked it because it was easy to remember and he hoped it was the sort of name a real newsman might have. He sipped his tea while Freddie ate one, then two of the four buns from the plate.

"That was good," Freddie said, licking the crumbs off his thumbs.

"Glad you enjoyed it, Freddie," Wiggins said. "You can have the rest to take 'ome if you like, but before that, why don't you tell me why your mistress called Mrs. Robinson a toffee-nosed cow."

"I can't make heads nor tails of this." Witherspoon frowned at the ledger. They'd opened it on Edith's dressing table. "But I've a feeling it's important."

"She'd not have hidden it if it wasn't," Barnes said. "But it looks like she was using some sort of code. At least her handwriting is legible."

They stared at the most recent entry in the half-filled ledger.

Georgie Porgie   D/Neck 500   March 3rd, Paris   100

"'Georgie Porgie.' That's the name of a nursery rhyme. I know because I heard Mrs. Goodge saying it as she played with Amanda." Witherspoon looked at Barnes.

"It is, sir," Barnes replied. "'Georgie Porgie, Puddin' and Pie, / kissed the girls and made them cry, / When the boys came out to play, / Georgie Porgie ran away.'"

"But what can it mean?" Witherspoon looked down at the book, his gaze going to the previous entry. It was just as odd.

Mutton Chops   SilCan(2) 25   March 1, Colchester   5

And the one above it was equally strange.

Bobby Shafto   Seascp 100   Feb 27, London   10

"It could be anything," Witherspoon muttered. He flicked to the previous page and ran his finger down the first column. "Mutton Chops, Bobby Shafto. Oh, here's a new one: Jack Sprat."

"'Jack Sprat could eat no fat,'" Barnes muttered. "This must be a code, sir. It's the only explanation. Obviously Edith was more than just a landlady and she was using this ledger to keep track of something she was involved in."

Witherspoon flicked back through the book. "The same names are repeated but there're also several other ones, equally nonsensical. The entries are much the same, too: initials or a word that doesn't make sense followed by a number, then a date and a city."

"Perhaps they meant something to her, sir." He spoke slowly as the idea took shape in his mind. "The names, I mean. Perhaps she used them as a way of identifying a person without using his or her real name."

"That's possible, I suppose." Witherspoon looked doubtful. "But if it was her ledger, why not just use real names?"

Barnes shrugged. "She was a strange woman, but I know one thing about her—she had a reason for everything she did. If you'll recall, sir, she was able to get away the last time not only because she was bold and daring, but because she'd planned ahead."

"We don't know that for a fact. She might have just been lucky."

"No one is that lucky, sir," Barnes argued. "Once she got out of the Christopher house, she must have had cash stashed in secret places around the city. That's the only way she could have gotten away so fast and gone so far. We were watching all the ports and train stations, so she must have had money in order to buy her way out of the country."

"So you're saying that this ledger is her thinking ahead again?"

"I am, sir," Barnes said. "It'll take us a while to figure out what the entries mean, but when we do, we'll find that she kept this thing as some sort of protection."

"In that case, it was woefully ineffective," Witherspoon said. "She's dead, so it obviously didn't do her any good."

"That's true, sir, but maybe her killer didn't realize she had it."

"Or perhaps they didn't care." The inspector closed the ledger. "I think we're going to find that no matter what name Edith Durant used, she was still the sort of person who made a lot of enemies and one of those enemies murdered her."

"Agreed, sir. I just wish we knew what the entries meant."

"We'll figure it out eventually, and once we do, I'm sure it'll show she was doing something criminal."

"There might be a faster way, sir," Barnes said. "If she was up to something illegal, someone in London will know about it. Why don't I send word to a few of my informants and see what we can find?"

Phyllis concentrated on doing precisely as Betsy had instructed when she opened the door and stepped inside. Her head was high, her shoulders back, and there was the tiniest sway to her hips as she walked. The clerk's mouth gaped open as he stared at her.

His Adam's apple bobbed up and down as he swallowed convulsively. "May I be of assistance, miss?" he asked in a high-pitched squeak.

Phyllis was stunned. No one, least of all a man, had ever reacted to her in such a manner. She'd always considered her features too plain and her figure too plump to ever catch a man's eye. But perhaps Betsy was right? Perhaps it was just a matter of confidence and carriage that caused the male of the species to take notice.

She didn't speak till she reached the counter, then she put her basket down and looked him directly in the eye. "I certainly hope so," she murmured. She was making it up as she went along, her mind frantically going over all the advice Betsy had given her. *Don't be afraid to use honeyed words,* Betsy had said. *No matter how silly it might sound, flattery works wonders, especially with a man.*

"What can I do for you?" he asked again.

"Sorry, I didn't mean to stare," she apologized. "But it's not often that I find myself having to ask for help from such an attractive stranger. I'm in a bit of a desperate situation here and I was told that you were someone who might be able to help me. I was told you have a remarkable memory."

She couldn't believe she'd actually said those words and she half expected him to laugh in her face, but he didn't. He simply gaped at her as a blush crept up his cheeks. "Oh dear, I've been too forward. Please forgive me."

"No, no, there's nothing to forgive." He straightened his shoulders. "I wouldn't say my memory was remarkable, miss"—he glanced at her ringless finger—"but I am known to be someone who can recollect even the smallest detail. Now, tell me, how I can help you?"

Unfortunately for Phyllis, her mind chose that very moment to go completely blank. For a few moments, there was nothing but an awkward silence.

"Miss," he prompted. "You were asking for my help."

"Oh yes." She nodded as if it all flooded back to her. "My mistress sent me to this neighborhood to pick up a parcel for her. But I've lost the address. The only thing I can recall her saying is that it was just across the road from the lodging house owned by that lady who was murdered. The girl at the greengrocer's told me that the poor murdered lady used to shop here and that you were so clever, you would know where she lived." She watched him carefully as she spoke but saw nothing in his expression that made her think he didn't believe her.

"You mean Mrs. Robinson?"

"Was that her name, then? The murdered lady. I couldn't remember."

"That's her," he said. "She was in here just last week. She lives on Magdala Lane. It's not far from here. She bought two yards of oilcloth. The heavy kind used to keep out the wet."

Barnes went downstairs with the ledger while the inspector went up to the next landing to interview Gordon Redley. There were two sets of rooms here as well. He went to the door on his right and knocked softly.

It opened immediately, revealing a thin, balding man wearing a blue suit and a white shirt open at the collar. "I've been waiting for you." He waved him inside. "I'm Gordon Redley. The maid said you'd be coming to speak to me this afternoon. I expected you earlier."

"I'm sorry to have inconvenienced you, Mr. Redley," Witherspoon apologized as he stepped over the threshold, "but it couldn't be helped. We had an urgent matter to deal with."

The rooms were the same floor plan as Edith Durant's but that's where the similarity ended. Here the furniture consisted of a faded gray-green lumpy-looking couch and two overstuffed armchairs with misshapen antimacassars draped along the top. Two bookcases, a scratched secretary, and a side table made up the rest of the furnishings, and through the open door a bed with an iron bedstead was visible.

"I hardly think searching my landlady's rooms consti-
tutes an urgent matter. But you're here now and I'd like to
get this matter put to rest as quickly as possible." Redley
frowned at the rain splattering the window and then
pointed to the sofa. "Please sit down. I'm in a bit of hurry.
I've an appointment in the city, and now that it's wet outside, it's going to take even longer to get there."

"I'm Inspector Gerald Witherspoon"—he introduced
himself as he took his seat—"and I'll be as quick about this
as possible. I take it you're aware that Mrs. Robinson was
murdered yesterday."

"Mrs. Robinson." He smiled cynically as he eased into
a chair. "Don't you mean Miss Durant, Miss Edith Durant?
But yes, I'm aware that she was murdered. Everyone in the
household knows she's dead. But I've no idea how I can be
of any help to you. I know nothing about it."

"When was the last time you saw her?"

"At breakfast yesterday," he replied.

"And did you notice anything unusual about her manner?" Witherspoon knew he had to go through the same
litany of questions he'd asked the others in the house. He
was already fairly sure he knew the answers.

"The only thing that was odd was that she was serving
breakfast herself rather than the maid," Redley replied.

"She didn't normally serve the meal?"

"Not usually, no, but it wasn't the first time she'd done it."
He waved a hand around the room. "As you can see, Inspector, this is quite a large house but Mrs. Robinson didn't have
a lot of staff. She was cheap that way and she often had the
serving girl off doing something else. I heard someone

thumping about in the box room only the night before, so she probably had the girl upstairs again doing heavy cleaning."

Witherspoon nodded. "How long have you lived here, sir?"

Redley's hazel eyes narrowed in thought. "I think it's been three and a half months. Yes, yes, that's correct. I took up residence here at the end of November."

"What do you do, sir?" Witherspoon realized that as the man's expression had changed, he suddenly looked familiar.

"I'm an acquisitions representative for the New World Art Company. They're based in New York. We buy the rights to reproduce and manufacture objects of art and ceramics and sculptures."

"Have we met before, Mr. Redley?"

Redley drew back in surprise. "I don't know what you mean, Inspector. I've never seen you before in my life nor have I ever frequented the sort of places you'd have been likely to meet me."

"I wasn't implying that I'd met you in my professional capacity as a policeman," he said quickly. "Actually, now that I look a bit more closely, I think I must have been mistaken."

"I should certainly hope so." He sniffed in disapproval. "Can we get on with this? The traffic getting into the city is dreadful so I need to leave soon."

"Have you seen anyone suspicious hanging around the neighborhood?"

"No."

"Do you know of anyone that had a reason to want to harm the victim?" He shifted his weight, trying to get comfortable. The sofa cushion was hard as a rock.

Redley stroked his chin. "Well, one doesn't like to speak

out of turn, but Mrs. Robinson had a dispute quite recently. She's had some harsh words with a neighbor."

"Which neighbor?"

"The lady next door, a Mrs. Travers."

"What kind of problem was it?"

"I don't know the exact nature of the dispute," Redley replied, "and Mrs. Robinson wasn't one to discuss her business with anyone."

"Then how do you know she was having difficulties with anyone?" he pressed.

"Because I accidentally overheard a rather heated exchange between the two women." He closed the top button on his shirt.

"When was this?"

"It was this past Sunday." He stood up, crossed the room, and grabbed a blue tie that had been hanging on the bedroom side of the open door.

"What exactly did you overhear?"

He flipped up his collar, draped the tie around his neck, and tucked it inside. "I've already told you what I heard: They were arguing. There's a nice garden out the back and I'd gone out to get some air. That's when I heard them quarreling."

"What were they arguing about?" Yee gods, he thought, getting information out of this fellow was as slow as pouring treacle in a cold kitchen.

"I didn't hear everything, I only heard Mrs. Travers yelling that if Mrs. Robinson didn't cease her accusations, she'd see her in court."

"What did Mrs. Robinson say?"

He frowned. "I don't know. She moved close to Mrs.

Travers and whispered something. Then she turned on her heel and stalked off."

"You *heard* this from your spot in the garden?" Witherspoon knew that if he was telling the truth, he wasn't just listening to the quarrel, he must have been watching as well.

Redley glowered in annoyance. "Alright, I'll admit it. When I heard them going at it, I peeked through the slats in the fence. That's when I saw Mrs. Robinson walk to the woman and whisper in her ear. Then she stalked away. But that wasn't the end of it. As she was going down the path, Mrs. Travers suddenly shouted at her. She yelled that she could make it most uncomfortable if Mrs. Robinson didn't stay away from her, that Mrs. Robinson might not like being dragged through the London courts."

"She didn't like her much." Freddie Ricks bobbed his chin up and down for emphasis. "Mrs. Gray, she's the mistress, was always tellin' people that it wasn't right the way that woman come into the neighborhood and started renting out rooms. Said it made the area common."

"Are you sayin' that Mrs. Gray didn't like Mrs. Robinson or that she didn't like the fact there were lodgers across the road from her?" Wiggins was beginning to suspect young Freddie had been hungry enough to gild the lily and had exaggerated about knowing "something."

Freddie stared at him, his expression puzzled.

"I mean, had Mrs. Robinson said or done something rude or nasty to your mistress, or was she just annoyed that there was a lodging house on your street?"

"I guess ya could say it was somethin' rude, and Mrs. Gray thought it was mean, but the rest of us thought it was funny." He giggled. "Even Mrs. Riddle, she's the cook, laughed when she heard about it." He pointed to the last bun on the plate. "If it's all the same to you, I'd rather eat that now than take it back with me."

"Go ahead and have it," Wiggins said. "But before you do, tell me what you're on about. What did Mrs. Gray think was mean?"

"Mrs. Robinson wouldn't rent rooms to Mrs. Gray's cousin." He reached for the bun.

Wiggins yanked the plate to his side of the table. "I need more details than that. Bein' refused a room shouldn't have made the ladies enemies. Maybe Mrs. Robinson was full up?"

"She wasn't," Freddie protested. "Mrs. Gray had checked with Mrs. Robinson's housemaid and Annie told her there were two empty rooms." His gaze went to the plate and he licked his lips.

Wiggins shoved it across to him. "Go on, then, take a bite and then tell me the rest."

Freddie snatched the bun, stuffed a bite in his mouth, and chewed frantically. "Not much more to tell." He swallowed. "Mrs. Gray didn't want to be stuck with her cousin. He was in London for six months on a job of some sort and with him bein' a relation and all, she couldn't charge him rent. But she's right cheap and she didn't want the cost of feedin' him. So she marched over there and demanded to know why her cousin couldn't have a room. Mrs. Robinson told Mrs. Gray that his references weren't good enough."

"Mrs. Gray told you this, did she?"

"'Course not. I heard the story from Mrs. Riddle who

got it directly from Mrs. Fremont when they was both down at the pub." He took another bite.

"Who is Mrs. Fremont?"

"Mrs. Robinson's cook. She and Mrs. Riddle are friends. They drink together at the pub sometimes."

"Your mistress doesn't mind if her female servants go to the pub?"

Freddie shrugged. "She does, but there's naught she can do about it." He stuffed the last bite into his mouth.

"She could give her the sack."

"Nah, she'd not do that. She pays miserable wages and Mrs. Riddle is a right good cook. She can even make them cheap cuts of meat taste decent, so Mrs. Gray leaves her alone."

The two laborers shoved away from the counter and left, letting in a cold blast of air as they opened the door and stepped out. Wiggins glanced out the window and saw that the rain had eased off. He wasn't sure what to make of this information; it sounded like the sort of neighborhood squabble that happens all the time. But then again, maybe he should dig a bit deeper and keep the lad chatting a little more. "How about you, then, Freddie. What do you do there?"

"Mrs. Gray tells the neighbors that I'm a footman"—he snorted in derision—"but I'm not really. I do whatever I'm told to. My sister got me the position when our mum passed away last September. I help with the heavy cleaning, polish the master's and mistress's shoes and their son's, too, when he's home from school. I run a lot of errands, clean grates, beat rugs, whatever needs doin'. The wages aren't much, but it's a roof over my head and I get to live with Meg."

"Is that your sister?" Wiggins asked softly.

"Yeah, she's the maid." He grinned. "Meg thinks Mrs. Robinson told our mistress she wouldn't rent her cousin a room because she wanted to get a bit of her own back. She'd found out that Mrs. Gray had told all the neighbors havin' a lodgin' house on the street made us common as muck."

"What do ya mean 'e ain't 'ere?" Smythe was incredulous. "Where is 'e? What's got into the fella? 'E's got a business to run."

He had a glare that could make grown men cringe, but Lily, the tall, black-haired barmaid, wasn't in the least intimidated. "That don't mean he's got to be here every minute," she said.

"But this is the second time lately that 'e's not been where 'e ought to be." Smythe was in the Dirty Duck Pub, and unfortunately for him, Blimpey Groggins, the owner of said establishment, was not in attendance.

Whenever they had a new case, the Dirty Duck was always Smythe's first stop. Groggins was a buyer and seller of information and Smythe figured he was probably his best customer. He never haggled over the high fees, didn't pester Blimpey about the details of how he obtained information, and paid promptly in cold, hard cash.

"It's not his fault." Lily dried a shot glass and put it on the tray in front of her. "He's got shingles."

"Shingles!"

"He's had them for a week now and his Nell only got him to go to the doctor today. Mind you, there's naught the sawbones can do about it. I know, my mam had 'em real bad last winter and they liked to kill her."

Smythe didn't want to be hard, but this was going to put him back a bit. It wasn't as if he couldn't do a bit of sleuthing on his own—he most certainly could—but considering the resources Blimpey had at his fingertips, it seemed stupid not to use him. He charged an arm and a leg, but Smythe could well afford his fees. Smythe might appear to be a coachman, but the truth was, he was rich and Blimpey was one of the few people who knew it. He'd come back from Australia years ago with a fortune.

"Where are they?" he asked.

Lily slapped the tea towel over her shoulder and picked up the tray of shot glasses. "Where are what?"

"The shingles. Are they on his face or his legs . . ."

"They're on his side and he's been a right old bear since they popped out." She shoved the tray onto the back counter and crossed her arms over her ample bosom. "Truth to tell, all of us 'ere are hoping he stays away till he's fixed, good and proper."

"How long does that take?"

She shrugged. "Don't remember 'ow long it took me mam, but it wasn't just a day or two. Mind you, I don't think Blimpey's got 'em as bad as she did. She had them on her face and around her eyes."

"So Blimpey doesn't 'ave a nasty case of them?" Smythe knew where Blimpey lived, and if need be, he'd drop in and see him. He had a feeling that with this particular case, he'd most definitely need the man's help.

"Oh, for God's sake, Smythe, he's got the ruddy shingles. Bad case or not, he'll be mean as a bear with a burr up its arse, so like I said, those of us that work here are hopin' he bloomin' well stays home. The last thing we need is for the likes of you wavin' lolly under his nose and gettin' him back here before he's healed."

By this time, Jane, the other barmaid, and Eldon, Blimpey's man-of-all-work, had slipped in and stood just behind Lily. They nodded in agreement as she spoke and Smythe knew he was beaten. If he ever wanted a beer that hadn't been spit in or worse, he'd better back off. "Alright, you've made your point. I understand. I'll leave 'im alone. But you 'ave him send me a message the minute 'e's back and able to work."

Luty's day wasn't going any better than Smythe's. She stood in the huge inner office of Prentiss, Prentiss, Harrison and McKay and glared at her lawyers. "What do ya mean? Of course ya can find out who inherits the woman's money. Isn't that what you lawyers are always doin', stickin' your nose into other people's business?"

"That's true, madam," Edgar Prentiss, the elderly head of the firm, replied. "However, as we generally only stick our respective noses into affairs directly concerned with protecting your business interests, we're at a bit of a loss here as to what you expect us to do."

"I've just told ya what I need." She surveyed the four solicitors who were entrusted with a large part of her legal business. Prentiss, bald, hawk-nosed, and wearing an old-fashioned wing tip collar and black tie, sat behind a massive rosewood desk. Michael Harrison, blond haired, blue-eyed, and thin as a railroad tie, stood to his right, and next to him was James McKay, a burly black-haired Irishman without an ounce of humor in his makeup. To the left of Prentiss, stood the youngest and by far the best-looking of the bunch,

Dennis Avery. Brown haired, tall, and well built, he struggled to keep a grin off his face.

"But, madam, we've no authority to go snooping about in this . . . er, Mrs. Robinson's estate," Prentiss said slowly, as though explaining something to a dim-witted child.

Luty's eyes narrowed. She knew his tone was deliberate. They'd argued many a time over a woman's proper place in the world. He was a hidebound old conservative who thought a female couldn't understand a balance sheet, shouldn't vote, and ought to let the menfolk make all the important decisions. But he was also one of the best legal minds in England. "Oh, git off yer high horse, Edgar," she retorted, using his Christian name because she knew it would annoy him. "You've pulled plenty of stunts in your time so don't give me that 'we've no authority' nonsense."

"Really, madam, I hardly think what we may or may not have done in the past is relevant here," Harrison sputtered.

Luty ignored him. "Her name was Edith Durant, and now that she's dead, if she has a will, it'll soon be a matter of public record. For goodness' sake, they publish 'em in the newspapers."

"Edith Durant. Isn't she the woman who was found murdered in Highgate Cemetery?" Harrison charged.

"What of it?" She wished she'd not come here; there were already too many people in London who'd figured out Inspector Witherspoon had help on his cases, and she didn't want her lawyers adding to that number. Her gaze shifted to Dennis Avery. He'd lost the battle and was grinning from ear to ear. Then he winked at her. She blinked. She wasn't mistaken—the fellow had actually given her wink.

"The manner of her death isn't relevant." Prentiss gave

Harrison a quick frown before turning his attention to Luty. "Precisely what were you hoping to learn from the contents of her will?"

Luty was ready for this one. "She owned a lodging house. I've heard there's a lot of freehold property in that neighborhood, and if that's the case, I was thinkin' about buyin' it. But if she's gone and left it to a relative . . ." She broke off and shrugged.

"In that case, madam, we can most certainly obtain the information you need. You should have told us this to begin with," Prentiss lectured. "If we'd known this was about business, our attitudes would have been completely different."

Avery snickered and quickly masked the sound with a cough.

"What did you think this was about?" she demanded.

Prentiss cleared his throat. "Well, we . . . uh . . . er . . ."

"Uh, er, what?" she snapped. "What did you think I was doin'?"

"We thought you were simply curious about the dead woman," McKay said quickly. "It wouldn't be the first time you've been inquisitive about murder victims . . ." His voice trailed off as she fixed him with a steely glare.

"What Mr. McKay meant was . . ." Prentiss began.

Luty cut him off. "I know what he meant. You all thought I was just bein' a busybody and stickin' my nose into a dead woman's business. You think I'm some kind of ghoul."

She was incredibly relieved. These men were excellent at protecting her interests, but they were short on imagination and thought she was just being a typical nosy female. From the stricken expressions on their faces, she'd bet her next hot dinner that none of them realized that she made inquiries because she was helping Inspector Witherspoon. She flicked another glance at Avery. He winked again. Dang, she thought, he knows what I'm up to.

She yanked a handkerchief out of her sleeve and dabbed at her eyes. "That's right mean of ya. Just because a woman is a little curious every once in a while."

"Oh dear, madam, please don't be upset. We meant nothing of the sort." Prentiss leapt up, pushed past Harrison and McKay, and flew around the desk. He grabbed Luty's hand. "We meant no offense whatsoever." He tossed Harrison a quick glare. "My colleague used an unfortunate choice of words."

"That's right, Mrs. Crookshank, I used an unfortunate turn of phrase. I meant no offense whatsoever. I'm sure a woman of your character would never let a ghoulish thought enter her mind."

"Let me get you some water, or tea." Prentiss pleaded.

Once more, she cut him off. "No, no, that's alright." She sniffed and dabbed at her eyes again. "Sometimes I'm overly sensitive. If young Mr. Avery would just help me out to my carriage, I'll be on my way."

"But, madam, I don't want you thinking . . ."

"I'm fine, Mr. Prentiss. You've apologized and that's the end of the matter. Come on"—she peeked at Avery over her handkerchief—"I need to go now."

"Of course, ma'am." Avery charged forward, took her arm, and led her out into the hall. "Well, madam, you've certainly put the fear of God into them," he whispered as he closed the door.

"Good, but when you go back, be sure and tell 'em their positions are safe. I'll not have anyone sittin' around frettin' about their jobs."

"Thank you, ma'am, you're very kind," he said. He led her through a narrow corridor and out into the main hall.

She snorted. "Kindness is only part of it. People worryin' about where their next meal is comin' from can't concentrate on their work."

But they both knew she was just sputtering for the sake of it and that she had a reputation among those who worked for her as being sympathetic, caring, and a bit of a soft touch.

Nevertheless, he nodded as though he were agreeing with her. "Of course, madam. I'll tell them you were laughing over the incident by the time I put you in your carriage. Will that do?"

"That'll do nicely."

"Good." He grinned again. "Now, ma'am, why don't you tell me specifically what it is you'd like me to find out?"

"You're smart as well as handsome." She laughed. "First of all, find out if Edith Durant had a will, second, who gits the goods, and third, anything else that you think is interestin'."

CHAPTER 5

Constable Barnes was in the foyer leafing through his little brown notebook but flipped it closed when Witherspoon came down the staircase. "As you instructed, sir, I've sent the ledger to Y Division with a note asking Inspector Rogers to take a look at it."

"Thank you, Constable. I think it's the least we could do. I don't want to exclude him completely from this investigation. Perhaps Inspector Rogers will have some idea of what it might mean. After all, this is his district."

Barnes doubted it but kept his opinion to himself. "Etta Morgan, the other housemaid, is downstairs, sir. I'll go down and interview her then I'd like to have another word with Mrs. Fremont."

"Excellent idea, Constable. The poor woman was in a bit of a state yesterday. Perhaps today she'll be able to give us some useful information."

"Yes, sir." Barnes started for the back stairs.

"Just a moment," Witherspoon called. "If I'm not mistaken, Mrs. Fremont has been here longer than the other servants."

"That's right, sir. Is there something specific you want me to ask her?"

"Two things, Constable. One, find out if she knows who did Edith Durant's legal work. If the deceased truly owned this house, she must have had a solicitor to handle the matter. Yet we've searched every desk and drawer in the place and found nothing: no deeds, no conveyance reports, not even any bills for household repairs or fixtures."

"I'll ask her, sir," Barnes said. "But I don't have much hope she'll know anything. The one fact I was able to get out of Mrs. Fremont was that her mistress wasn't in the habit of telling them anything about her business."

"That's the impression I've had as well."

"Maybe we should take another look, sir," Barnes suggested. "This is a big house, but Constable Pierpoint should be back soon from Y Division, and he and Constable Griffiths can have another hunt. Maybe a fresh pair of eyes will spot something we overlooked."

"Alright. If Mrs. Fremont and the other servants can't even give us a name, we'll call in every available constable and search the place again. The second thing I want you to ask is if Mrs. Fremont had ever seen a red cord lying about. You know, from a set of old curtains or a bed canopy. Ask the other servants as well."

"You think the killer took the murder weapon from here?"

"I've no idea. I'm merely trying to eliminate that as a possibility." He perked up as he spoke, realizing that once again his "inner voice" was guiding him. "If we get lucky and find out where the cord might have come from, it will most certainly narrow the number of suspects."

The front door opened and Morecomb, struggling with his umbrella against the wind, yanked it shut and stepped inside. "Miserable weather," he groused as he slammed the door and dumped the umbrella into the battered brass stand.

"I'll be in the kitchen, sir." Barnes nodded politely to Morecomb before disappearing down the hall.

"Good. You're back," the inspector said cheerfully.

Morecomb put his hat and coat on the coat rack. "My meeting took less time than expected. Durridge said you needed to speak with me again, and frankly, Inspector, I'd like to get it done with so I can go about my business. I'm a busy man."

"I shall be as quick as possible." Witherspoon opened the double doors leading to the drawing room. "Let's go in here."

Morecomb followed him. The room was so dim he could barely make out the furniture. Someone, possibly out of respect for the fact that there had been a death in the house, had pulled both sets of curtains shut. Witherspoon hesitated briefly and then decided he didn't want to sit in the dark, so he crossed to the nearest window and flung open the drapes. Daylight, not particularly bright because it was raining outside, filtered enough light into the room so that he could see properly. He'd learned that it was always a good idea to watch a person's face when one was asking questions. When he turned, he saw that Morecomb had taken a seat on one of the sofas.

The inspector sat down across from him. "When was the last time you spoke with Mrs. Robinson?"

"I've already told you that." Morecomb gave an exasperated sigh. "It was at breakfast yesterday morning."

"Yes, sir, I know that's what you said, but I wanted to make certain your recollection was correct." Witherspoon smiled faintly to take the sting out of his words, but really, sometimes he got a bit annoyed with people who acted as if a murder investigation was a dreadful inconvenience to them. "You didn't see her after breakfast?"

"I did not." He crossed his arms over his chest. "As soon as I'd eaten, I went upstairs for my briefcase and left for my appointments."

"When you left the house, did you notice anyone hanging about the area?"

"This is a busy street and there were any number of people out," he began.

Witherspoon cut him off. "I understand that. What I meant was, did you see anyone who looked out of place or who appeared to have an undue interest in this house?"

"You mean anyone suspicious?" Morecomb shook his head. "No, I didn't see anyone like that. Why? Do you think the murderer followed her from here?"

"We've formed no opinion as yet; we're merely ascertaining any and all possibilities. Were the other tenants still here when you left?" Witherspoon found timelines very useful and it certainly wouldn't hurt to know the household's whereabouts prior to the murder.

Morecomb ran a hand through his damp hair as he considered the question. "I believe that Mr. Erskine had gone. Yes, I remember he was in the foyer putting on his coat when I went upstairs, but as for Mr. Teasdale and Mr. Redley, I've no idea if they were still here when I left or not.

Why? What does it matter where we might have been before Mrs. Robinson was killed?"

The inspector ignored his comment. "So there were still people in the house after you'd gone. What time did you leave?"

"I told you yesterday, I left at my usual time, eight fifteen. My first appointment was at nine."

"Where was that, sir?"

"What do you mean? Are you asking me where I was when she was killed?"

"Yes, sir, I am," Witherspoon replied.

For a moment, Morecomb simply gaped at him. "I'm a respectable businessman," he finally sputtered. "And I'll not have the police pestering my clients and casting aspersions on my good name."

"Exactly what is it you do?"

"I sell safes. You know, metal boxes and vaults for people to store their valuables. For God's sake, Inspector, do you want to ruin me just because I happen to live here? It wasn't my fault the woman got herself murdered."

"It's a routine inquiry, Mr. Morecomb," Witherspoon explained patiently.

"Routine or not, my customers expect me to maintain the very highest standards of ethics. The very hint of a scandal could send my sales plummeting. I work on commission, sir, and my competitors would love nothing more than to see me embroiled in a nasty murder inquiry."

Witherspoon tried again. "We're not trying to embroil you in anything."

"That won't matter. Once people find out you've been nosing about asking questions, my reputation is shot," he snapped. "The companies I represent won't take kindly to it, either. Everyone thinks those Americans are easygoing and friendly, but when it comes to business, they're as ruthless as a Barbary pirate."

"You represent an American company?" The inspector interrupted in hopes of stopping the fellow's tirade.

He nodded vigorously. "They manufacture fireproof office safes, and I'm also an agent for an English company, McCarty's of Wolverhampton. They build walk-in specialty vaults for both commercial and domestic use. So you see, Inspector, this isn't the sort of situation which is going to enhance my reputation or my pocketbook."

Constable Barnes put his teacup down on the table. "You're sure you've never seen a red cord about the house?" he asked.

Mrs. Fremont shook her head. "Not that I can remember. Do you want another cuppa?"

"No, thank you, Mrs. Fremont. Is there anything else you can tell me about the household? Anything that might help us find who killed Mrs. Robinson?" He'd given up asking questions and was now trying to find out what he could by just chatting. That method seemed to be working far better than formally interviewing her.

The cook was putting dishes into the top of the sideboard. "Well, like I told you before, she wasn't one to discuss her business with the likes of us, but we do have eyes and ears and sometimes we see things that were best left in the dark, if you know what I mean."

"What kind of things?"

She put a serving platter onto the shelf and closed the

door. "The kind the mistress didn't want people to know about." She cocked her head to one side and met his gaze. "I know you want to find out who killed her and that's fine, you're doin' your job. But what's goin' to happen to us? I gave you the name of the solicitor she used and I know that'll help you."

"It should be very helpful." He wasn't sure what she wanted, but he didn't want her to stop talking.

"Good. Now I need you to do something for us."

"Us?" he repeated.

"Me and Carrie and Etta. I want you to ask that solicitor what's goin' to happen to us. We've got no place to go and I'm not thinkin' that her nibs was the type to remember her servants in her will, if she even had a will."

Barnes stared at her for a long moment. Her face was the ruddy color of a heavy drinker, and he was certain that she had a bottle of cheap gin hidden somewhere here in the kitchen. He could see the fear in her eyes and he didn't doubt that the other servants, Carrie Durridge, the middle-aged housemaid, and Etta Morgan, were scared as well. Life was hard when you were at the bottom of the heap and he, for one, wasn't going to make it any harder for these poor women. "We'll ask him if there has been any provision made for the servants," he promised.

She snorted. "I'm not goin' to hold my breath, Constable, but if we could at least keep a roof over our head while we're lookin' for other positions, it'd be a help. I'm a fair cook and both the maids are hardworking. What we're most scared of is being chucked out without any warning. Those things happen, you know. Plus, we're due our quarterly wages at the end of the month. We need to be paid."

Barnes nodded. "You can depend on the inspector. He'll be sure to bring this up with the solicitor."

"Fair enough," she replied. "Her nibs weren't a saint, but then again, who is? You know that I sleep upstairs because Carrie has the room down here so she can let the tenants in late at night. There's a bell that rings directly in her room, so that her nibs didn't have to get up and let them in herself."

He wasn't sure he did know this fact, but he nodded anyway.

"Two weeks ago, I had to come down to the kitchen late in the night to take a headache powder. It was about midnight, I think. I used the front stairs because two of the tenants were still out, so there was light enough to see by. I got my powder and started back up to my room. Just as I reached the landing, I saw Mrs. Robinson comin' out of Mr. Teasdale's room. Luckily for me, it was a cold night and she was in a rush so she just hurried on to her own quarters, otherwise, I'd have been done for. She'd not have liked me knowin' that she was spending nights with Mr. Teasdale. Mind you, he is a good-looking devil."

"That's it?" Barnes could think of several instances when he and his wife were first married and they'd lived in lodgings and had to summon the landlady. He gritted his teeth against a shudder as an image of a pair of large rats skittering across their sitting room floor sprang into his mind. "That's what makes you think she was romantically involved with him? She might have been in his room because he'd taken ill or he'd seen a rodent or something like that."

Mrs. Fremont snickered. "Don't be daft, Constable. You're not catching rats wearing a fancy nightgown and that's what she was wearing when I saw her. What's more, that wasn't the only time. The very next night, I saw her going into Mr. Teasdale's room again."

"Lady Cannonberry, how wonderful to see you." The Reverend Reginald Pontefract rose from behind his massive desk as the maid ushered Ruth into the study of St. John's rectory. He was a tall, slender man dressed in a black suit and clerical collar, as befitted his position in the church. She hadn't seen him in years, and she noted that his short-cropped rather coarse brown hair was now threaded with gray, there were deep lines around his hazel eyes, and his nose, always prominent, seemed even more so as his chin had receded as he'd aged. She supposed he was surprised by her appearance as well; she was certainly not the young matron she'd been the last time they'd met.

"I'm so sorry to barge in on you," she apologized as he came toward her. "But I was in the neighborhood and saw the notice that you were collecting contributions for the widows and orphans fund. I wanted to make a contribution and, of course, see you. I do hope I haven't interrupted your schedule too much."

This was, of course, not true, though in all fairness she did intend to make a generous donation. She'd come here because thus far, her efforts to learn anything useful had been futile. Last night, she'd mentioned the murder at a dinner party but none of the other guests knew anything, and this morning, she'd brought it up while chairing a meeting of the financial committee for her women's suffrage group. But none of the other women knew anything about Edith Durant/ Alice Robinson or the neighborhood where she'd lived.

But Ruth wasn't one to give up. When her meeting had ended, she'd sat down at her elegant French secretary and gone through both her and the late Lord Cannonberry's various correspondence papers. She'd found Reginald Pontefract's name and address on a note he'd written informing her of his new church appointment. She barely remembered the good reverend—he'd actually been a childhood neighbor of the Cannonberry country estate—and she'd almost stuffed the paper back into the bottom drawer, but then the address caught her eye. Pontefract was now the vicar of St. Peter's Highgate Hill. She hadn't been sure how close his church might be to the lodging house, but she'd decided it was worth the risk. Luckily, when she'd reached the neighborhood, she'd discovered both the church and rectory were only a few streets away from the victim's home on Magdala Lane.

"You are a most welcome interruption, Lady Cannonberry. It's been ages since I've seen you. It's generous of you to take the trouble to come personally to make a contribution." He took her arm and led her to a leather chair next to the fireplace.

As she sank into the seat, she glanced around the cavernous room and noted it was far more luxurious than her father's simple study had been. Gold-plated candlesticks stood at each end of the marble mantelpiece and a multicolored Persian rug covered the polished oak floor. Small, elegant sculptures, museum-quality ceramics, and a collection of Japanese-style tea sets were displayed on the floor-to-ceiling bookshelves opposite the ornate desk. Her hackles started to rise but she got ahold of herself. It wasn't her place to judge. Perhaps this room and its outrageously expensive furnishings weren't his doing—this was, after all, the rectory. But still, a pittance of the value of the room's furnishings could feed an orphanage for a year.

"Mary." He caught the maid before the door had closed. "Bring us tea, please."

"Right away, sir," the girl said as she slipped out.

"I don't want to put you to any trouble," Ruth protested.

"It's no trouble at all." He sat down on the chair opposite and studied her. A slight smile played around her thin lips. "We've not seen one another for quite a long while."

"It's actually been a number of years." She clasped her hands together in her lap.

"It was at Lord Cannonberry's funeral," he continued. "I have thought of you often since then." He leaned toward her. "You've been widowed for a long time. I'm sure it must be very lonely for you."

"Not really. I do keep very busy and I've many friends." Ruth smiled uneasily.

"Oh yes, I've heard you've joined one of those organizations that agitate for women voting and owning property and doing all manner of things the Bible most assuredly says they oughtn't." He reached over and patted her hand. "But that's understandable. Without the guidance of a strong man in your life, it's easy to get confused and make inappropriate choices."

She finally remembered why she'd avoided him for all these years. She didn't like him. But she needed information. "That, of course, is a matter of opinion."

"Oh no, I don't think so. The Good Book is quite clear that a woman should obey."

"My father, who, if you'll recall, was quite a renowned

biblical scholar, most certainly didn't share that view," she interrupted.

"Your father believed strongly that our Lord came to spread only a message of love and acceptance. He wasn't comfortable with many other aspects of the Christian tradition."

"You mean like blind obedience to the dictates of society, slavery, and the oppression of women and native peoples in those countries we've decided we've a right to colonize?" She gave him a tight smile. "You're right, he had no patience for such things and, frankly, neither do I." She clamped her mouth shut to keep from saying anything further. She was on the hunt here and this most certainly wasn't the way to loosen his tongue.

But he didn't seem to take offense. Instead, he laughed. "I look forward to many interesting debates with you on the subject. I do so like a challenge."

"You've never married yourself?" she asked innocently. She knew he was unwed. She was beginning to understand why.

"I've never been blessed with the happiness of matrimony." He moved even closer, so close she feared he was going to slip off the edge of the chair. "But perhaps that will change for me one day. The Lord does provide and I take it as a good sign that he sent you here to me today."

Etta Morgan was a thin young woman with a pale, pinched face, slightly buck teeth, and dark brown hair pulled into a bun on the nape of her neck "But I wasn't even here when Mrs. Robinson left the house." She put the basket of vegetables the greengrocer had just delivered on the counter next to the sink. "So I can't really tell you much."

"I understand that," Constable Barnes reassured her. "I just need to ask you a few questions. Why don't you have a seat." He nodded toward the empty chair across the table from where he sat.

"I've got to get the veg scrubbed for supper. Mrs. Fremont is making a casserole with the last of the boiled beef from yesterday."

"Mrs. Fremont has gone upstairs for a nap," he replied. "And I overheard her tell Miss Durridge that she'd be down later this afternoon, so you've plenty of time. Please, Miss Morgan, sit down."

"None of us know what's going to happen now that Mrs. Robinson is gone, but Mrs. Fremont says we've got to take care of the tenants. They have paid for their lodgings and meals up to the end of the month." She pulled out a chair and sat down. "That means they can't chuck us out till then, right?"

He wasn't sure what to say. Now that he had the solicitor's name and address, he'd no idea what was going to happen once they contacted him. On the other hand, the lass had a point; the lodgers did have rights. "I expect you'll be fine until then."

She brightened a bit. "I hope so."

"So do I," he said honestly. "Now, when was the last time you saw Mrs. Robinson?"

"Yesterday," Etta said. "As soon as breakfast was over, she sent me to the East End with a package."

"What time was that?"

"I don't know the exact time. I'd just come up from the kitchen and the clock in there has been broken since I've been here. But I think it was about twenty past eight," she replied. "I'd started to do the clearing up when she told me to leave it. She said that Mrs. Fremont would do it and I was to deliver a package for her."

"What kind of a package?"

"A small one. It was wrapped in brown paper."

"Where did you take it?"

"To the Black Swan—that's a pub on the Commercial Road. I gave it to Mr. McConnell." Her eyes widened. "I didn't do anything wrong, Constable. I took it right to where she told me."

"I'm sure you did, Miss Morgan. By any chance did Mrs. Robinson tell you what was in the package?"

She pursed her lips and shook her head. "No, she just give me the omnibus fare and told me where to take it. It took ages to get there as well. I got lost twice and I was ever so worried I'd not be able to find my way back in time to meet Nancy—she's my friend. We're from the same town and she's got the same afternoon out as I do. We take the train together so we can go home. It makes it nice, sir. We get to visit that bit longer before we have to come back. With there being two of us we don't mind coming back a bit after dark."

He asked her the same questions he'd asked the other staff, and like them, she hadn't seen anyone suspicious hanging about the neighborhood, nor had she seen a red cord or noticed Mrs. Robinson behaving any differently than she usually did. Barnes flipped the notebook shut. "Thank you,

Miss Morgan." He started to get up and then eased back into his seat. "How long have you worked here?"

"Almost a year." She grinned. "I've lasted longer than most. Generally they either get the sack or move on to someplace better."

"Mrs. Robinson was a difficult mistress?"

"Only about some things. As long as we didn't cross her and did our work, she didn't mind what we did. The place I used to work, they'd never have let a housemaid stay out after dark, and they'd have sacked you right away if you went to a pub. I don't care for the taste of gin or ale, so I don't go to pubs, but Mrs. Fremont and the other girl that used to work here, Annie, they popped into the pub around the corner every day after lunch and sometimes in the evenings as well." She jerked her thumb up toward the ceiling. "Cook still does."

"That's very interesting." Barnes opened his notebook to a clean page. "What kind of things was Mrs. Robinson strict about?"

Teasdale hadn't returned to the lodging house by the time the inspector and Barnes were finished with their respective interviews so they went to a café on the high street to eat. Over a late lunch of fried chops and boiled cabbage, they talked about the case. Barnes in particular made certain he told the inspector everything he'd heard from Etta Morgan and Mrs. Fremont.

"At least now we know she had a solicitor." Witherspoon buttoned his overcoat as they left the café. The rain had stopped but the temperature had dropped sharply and a cold wind had come in from the west. "We'll go and see him tomorrow morning. Perhaps he'll be able to reassure the household about their circumstances."

"But they'll be able to stay until the end of the month," Barnes said. "The cook pointed out that the tenants are paid through the end of the month."

"I don't suppose there's much hope that Edith Durant made any provisions whatsoever in her will for her servants. Which is unfortunate. From what you said, both the cook and Miss Morgan are dreadfully worried about what's to become of them. Still, they're fully trained so they ought to be able to find new positions."

"Do you want me to send a Y Division constable or one of our lads to the Black Swan?" Barnes asked as they turned the corner to Magdala Lane.

"I don't wish to offend Inspector Rogers any further, but frankly, I'd feel better if we sent Constable Griffiths."

"Are we going to stop by Y Division tomorrow and see if anyone there has made heads or tails of the ledger?"

Witherspoon thought for a moment. "Perhaps we ought to stop by the station when we're finished today. We could get Inspector Rogers' thoughts on the ledger and I could give him a quick report. I don't want him to feel as if we've taken over completely."

"He already thinks that," Barnes said bluntly. "What's more, from the bits and pieces I've heard from the Y Division lads, Rogers wasn't exaggerating when he told us he was busy."

They stopped as they were now directly across the road from the Durant house. "You mean there really are more burglaries than usual?" Witherspoon stepped off the curb and waited for a cooper's van and a lad pulling a flatbed handcart loaded with butcher's boxes to go past. "I thought Inspector Rogers might be exaggerating when he told us that, you know, as a way to salvage his pride because he was losing the case."

Barnes waited till the cart was a good ways down the road before he answered. "Sounds like he was telling the truth, sir. Thieves have targeted wealthy houses and made off with a fortune in stolen jewelry, silver, and even some coin collections. Superintendent Huntley is putting a lot of pressure on his inspectors to find the culprits."

Witherspoon nodded. "Right, then, we'll not add to his burden at the moment. But we'll need to know about the ledger."

"I'll stop by tomorrow morning and pick it up," Barnes said. "They'll let us know if they've cracked the code, sir." They had reached the lodging house. The constable glanced at the house next door and then at Witherspoon. "Should I check to see if Mr. Teasdale is back or do you want me with you during the interview with Mrs. Travers?"

"With me, please. You're much better at reading facial expressions than I am." He started up the stairs of the Travers house. When they reached the door, the constable banged the brass knocker against the wood. A few moments later, a red-headed housemaid stuck her head out and stared at them curiously. "Can I help you?"

"We'd like to speak to Mrs. Travers," Witherspoon said.

The girl nodded. "I'll see if she's receiving." She started to close the door, but stopped when Barnes flattened his hand against the wood.

"This isn't a social call, miss," he said softly. "Please

tell Mrs. Travers she can either speak to us here or she's welcome to come down to the station."

"Yes, sir." Surprised, she opened the door wide and ushered them inside. "Please wait here," she muttered before bobbing a quick curtsey and disappearing down the corridor.

"I don't like bullying young women, sir, but I didn't think we had time to play by-your-leave with the girl."

"You did right, Constable. You got us inside and she's gone to fetch her mistress. Like you, I get tired of the gentry thinking we're no more than hired lackeys who can be put off whenever it suits them." He surveyed the foyer as he spoke. "This looks to be the same floor plan as the Durant place. I'd guess that all the houses along this road were built at the same time and, from the looks of things, by the same builder."

"It's done up a bit better. The wallpaper is lovely," he said, pointing to the pale green and white striped walls, "and the chandelier's been polished properly."

"That's very observant of you, Constable." A woman stepped into the hall. "I'm Mrs. Travers. My maid says you wish to speak to me."

They turned and saw a tall, thin woman with blue eyes, brown hair, a pale complexion, and a long, narrow nose. Witherspoon introduced himself and the constable. "Thank you for seeing us, Mrs. Travers. We'll try not to take too much of your time, but as I'm sure you know, your next-door neighbor was murdered and we do have a few questions for you."

"I'd heard, of course, and I must say, I wasn't surprised."

She turned and waved them toward the double doors of the drawing room. "Come along, then. We might as well sit down."

The wallpaper in the drawing room was the same as in the foyer, the only difference being the bottom half of the room was paneled in a white-painted wainscot. The sofa and chairs were upholstered in a colorful emerald green and white print pattern and the cabinets and tables were covered with fringed shawls and table runners in various shades of green, blue, white, and yellow. The contrast between here and the Durant house was painfully evident.

"Please make yourselves comfortable." She sat down on the sofa and waited while they took the two chairs opposite her. "So, you're here to speak to me about Mrs. Robinson's murder."

"That's correct, ma'am," Witherspoon said.

"I don't know that I can be very helpful, Inspector, but I'll do my best."

"When was the last time you saw your neighbor?" He glanced at Barnes and noted that he had his notebook and pencil at the ready.

"Yesterday morning. I saw her from my window."

"What time?" Barnes asked.

"I didn't note the time, but I think it was before nine."

"Have you seen anyone hanging about here that struck you as being odd or out of place?" Witherspoon asked.

"I've noticed nothing." She smiled faintly.

"Mrs. Travers, is there anyone else in your household?" The inspector unbuttoned his coat.

"My staff, of course. I've a live-in maid, a cook, and a

daily woman that comes in to do the heavy cleaning. I'm a widow. My son lives in Liverpool and my daughter is in Leeds."

"Mrs. Travers, we've been told that you and the deceased had an argument prior to her being murdered."

"An argument?" Her eyebrows shot up. "That's hardly what I would call it. That insufferable woman threatened me."

"Threatened you in what way?"

"In the most frightening way possible." She met his gaze. "She said she was going to kill me."

Mrs. Jeffries took her place at the head of the table. From the expressions on the faces around the table, she had the feeling this meeting might be brief. None of them looked particularly pleased with themselves. "Who would like to go first?"

For a moment, no one spoke, then Phyllis raised her hand. "I will. My report won't take long because I trooped all over the high street near the lodging house but I didn't find out much."

"You ain't the only one." Luty snorted. "I wasted my day trying to light a fire under my lawyers. I finally got one of 'em to get off his backside and promise he'd try to find out if Edith Durant had a will or who might inherit her property, but that's all I got done."

"Go ahead," Mrs. Jeffries said to Phyllis.

"Like I said, I trotted along to every shop on the street and couldn't get anything really useful out of anyone," she began.

"Did people not know anything about the victim or was

it that you couldn't get anyone to talk to you about her?" Mrs. Jeffries took a sip of tea.

"A little of both," she admitted. "But I did find out one thing when I went to the ironmonger's shop." She told them about Edith Durant's last purchase of oilcloth. "I know it's not much, but at least it is a bit of information," she concluded.

"We don't know that it isn't important," Mrs. Jeffries assured her. Though in truth, oilcloth had so many uses in a household, the purchase probably meant nothing. Just last week she'd sent Wiggins to get some so she could keep the damp out of the top shelf in the dry larder. "Now, who would like to go next?"

"I've not got much to tell," Smythe said. "But I did find out that none of the hansoms at the cab stand on Highgate Hill remembered droppin' off any fares at the cemetery entrance."

"Edith Durant walked to the cemetery," Wiggins said quickly. "Leastways that's what my source told me."

"But maybe her killer didn't," the coachman pointed out. He was still aggravated that he'd not been able to talk to Blimpey Groggins, and his irritation had mounted as he'd spent half the day talking to hansom drivers, most of whom hadn't even heard about the murder.

"And that is very useful information," Mrs. Jeffries interjected. She sensed that everyone was trying hard to do their part because they were fighting their own feelings about the Durant murder, but nonetheless, perhaps it was time to remind them that Rome wasn't built in a day and that on many of their previous cases it had taken time before they got any results from their efforts. "Very useful indeed but I'd like all of you to remember that sometimes it takes more than a day or two before we feel we're genuinely 'on the hunt.' I don't think any of you ought to feel you're doing anything wrong."

"We didn't until you brought it up," Mrs. Goodge muttered in a loud enough voice for everyone to hear. "It's not my fault that Edith Durant—or Alice Robinson as she was callin' herself—wasn't a person any of my former colleagues would know about, and what's more, Highgate Hill is too far for my local sources to service so it's no good me askin' any of them if they know anything."

"And I can't take the baby all that way when it's so wet outside," Betsy protested. "She's got the sniffles already."

"I think we're doin' our part." Luty jabbed her finger in the air. "It's not like we're standin' back waitin' for information to fall into our laps. I've got one of my lawyers havin' a look at who if anyone might be inheritin' from Durant."

"Really, Mrs. Jeffries, I do think your comments are somewhat off the mark. I'm working several sources to learn what I can about the late, unlamented Edith Durant," Hatchet snapped.

All of them, except for Ruth who was staring off in the distance, began talking at once.

Mrs. Jeffries stood up. "Wait a moment, please." She raised her voice to make them hear her. "I expressed myself badly and you've misunderstood. I think you're doing a splendid job with what is possibly our most difficult case. All I was trying to say is that we mustn't expect too much of ourselves and that as we move along, our inquiries will bear fruit."

"Oh, I thought you were hintin' we weren't doin' what we should be doin'. My mistake," Mrs. Goodge said.

"Sorry, Mrs. J." Smythe grinned. "Today wasn't one of me best and I heard what I thought you was sayin' instead of what you was really sayin'."

"I'm sorry, too." Betsy laughed. "Goodness, we are a sorry bunch, aren't we? We can't decide whether we're doing our very best or whether our own feelings about the dead woman are keeping us from asking the right questions."

"I think we're doing fine." Ruth gave herself a little shake. Her encounter with the Reverend Reginald Pontefract had distracted her so she'd missed the undercurrents of tension at the table. Since fleeing the rectory, she'd been filled with a vague sense of guilt and that had upset her greatly. She wasn't a vain or silly woman, but she wasn't a fool, either.

She wasn't the only one on the hunt—the good reverend was as well, only he was looking for a rich wife and she fit his requirements perfectly. Widowed, wealthy, and childless. No wonder he'd been so delighted when she'd willingly stepped into his lair. She caught herself as she realized what she was thinking. Gracious, what was wrong with her? She'd taken a few strands of yarn and knitted an entire sweater. Just because he'd watched her like a cat eyeing a wounded canary didn't mean he had anything in mind except . . . except . . . Oh, nonsense, she told herself sternly, you think entirely too much of yourself.

Yet, still, she remembered the way he'd looked at her and how excited he'd been when she'd made her donation. Five pounds wasn't a pittance, but he'd carried on as if she'd agreed to fund half a dozen missionaries for a year in Africa. He'd wanted to thank her by having her to dinner tomorrow night, and the thought of being alone with him at the rectory had alarmed her so badly, she'd heard herself insisting he come to dinner at her home instead. She had no intention of being alone with him in the rectory. But why did she feel so guilty? He was an old acquaintance of her father's and she'd gone there with the best of intentions. Gracious, she'd never liked the fellow and, from what she saw today, she still didn't. Nonetheless, she felt as if she'd betrayed Gerald Witherspoon. Still, it couldn't be helped. When serving the cause of justice, one did what one had to do.

"Ruth." Mrs. Jeffries' voice interrupted her reverie. "Would you care to say something?"

She smiled self-consciously. "I don't have much to share. To be completely truthful, I learned very little today."

"It sounds as if you had a bit of luck, then?" Hatchet said brightly.

"Not really. I went to a source that lives on Highgate Hill, an old acquaintance of my late husband. A vicar," she admitted. "But no one from the Robinson household attends his church."

"And bein' a vicar, I don't suppose he'd stoop to listen to gossip," Mrs. Goodge sighed. "Pity, really, he'd be in a position to get an earful."

Ruth's spirits lifted and she laughed. "True, he would." Surely, if she was clever enough, she could get something useful out of Reginald Pontefract. She had to try.

"I think we've got to do somethin' a bit different," Phyllis said.

"Like what?" Mrs. Goodge demanded.

"I've been thinkin' about it. So I asked myself, if Edith Durant was running a lodging house and more or less still hiding from the police, who would be part of her world? Who would have reason to want her dead?"

"Knowin' her character, I expect lots of people wouldn't mind if she was six feet under." Luty took a sip of tea.

"But, like us, most of the people she harmed in the past—those that she hurt when she was playactin' at being her sister—they probably didn't know she was back in London," Phyllis countered. "Look, I'm not explaining it right, but it seems to me that whoever killed her might be someone from now."

"My source says she doesn't have any social connections," Wiggins said. "The lad I spoke to says there was never visitors or parties or that sort of thing at the lodging house. What's more, none of the tenants seem to stay more than a few months, so it'd not be likely they'd want to kill her, and she can't keep help—they come and go almost as quickly as the tenants." He told them everything he'd learned from Freddie Ricks.

"But that's what I mean," Phyllis said as soon as he'd finished. "Your lad said she had two empty rooms to let and she wouldn't rent them because her nose was out of joint over something her neighbor said. That doesn't make sense. From what you've all told me about her, she was greedy. So why did she let empty rooms sit there when she could have been making a bit of money off them?"

No one said anything for a moment.

"She's right." Mrs. Jeffries tapped her finger against the rim of her mug. "We've got to take a closer look at the household, and I think we've got to start with her tenants."

"Why would your next-door neighbor threaten to murder you?" Witherspoon asked.

"Because she's mad," Mrs. Travers said shortly. "She's

insane. I've never liked having a lodging house next door. Before she came here, it was an ordinary house. But when she bought it, she started taking in all manner of strange men."

"Taking in lodgers hardly makes her a madwoman," Witherspoon said gently.

"Of course it doesn't," she snapped. "It was her behavior that convinced me she was insane. We'd never really had much to do with one another except to nod politely when we passed on the street. But then she came to my house and accused me of spying on her and even coming onto her property. She said she'd seen me peeking over the fence when she was in the back garden and that it was her private place. That she didn't even allow her tenants to go back there."

"When was this?" Barnes asked.

"When was what? The argument or the alleged time I was spying on her?" She folded her arms over her chest.

"Both."

"The argument, if one could call it that, was this past Sunday. She came storming over here, pushed her way past my maid, and accosted me outside as I was pruning my rosebushes. She screamed like a madwoman, saying all sorts of nonsensical things. She said she'd seen me watching her and that she'd found evidence I'd been in her sanctuary. That's what she called it, her sanctuary." She pointed toward the back of the house. "Both houses have long, narrow gardens, Inspector, and she's got the back section of hers walled off with bamboo. She claimed I trespassed, that I somehow miraculously found a key to her side gate or leapt over the fence to have a good look around her garden. But that's absurd. I've no interest in her or her property. As to when this incident is supposed to have occurred, it was the previous Friday evening. I tried to tell her she was mistaken, that no one could possibly have been trying to spy on her nor would anyone want to do such a thing. My house was completely empty that particular night. Even the cook and the maid were gone. But she refused to believe me. She kept shouting at me, demanding I tell her who I was working for, who'd paid me to keep an eye on her, and that sort of nonsense. I must tell you, Inspector, I was quite alarmed. Luckily my maid and the man from the gasworks who'd come to have a look at the cooker came out, and that seemed to frighten her enough to leave."

"Exactly when did she threaten you?" Witherspoon asked.

"Just as she was leaving. She was almost at the side gate when suddenly she turned. She came back and looked me straight in the eye, and then she whispered that she'd kill me if I came on her property again."

CHAPTER 6

"Gracious, sir, you look very tired," Mrs. Jeffries said as she hung up the inspector's coat and hat. "It's very late. Do you want your dinner straightaway or would you like a glass of sherry?"

"A sherry would be lovely." He headed down the hall and she hurried after him, delighted that despite his fatigue and the late hour, he wanted to chat.

A few minutes later, she handed him a glass, took her own seat, and waited while he took a long sip of his drink.

"That is precisely what I needed." He put the glass on the table next to him. "It's been the most confusing day, Mrs. Jeffries. We've found out a huge amount of information, but I don't know what to make of any of it."

"Now, sir, you always say that when you're at this point in an investigation." She took a quick sip from her own glass to buy a bit of time. The inspector was having his usual crisis of confidence and she needed to bolster his faith in himself. But she must get the words right. "You know good and well that once your 'inner voice' begins working, it muddles up your thinking process for a day or two. Honestly, sir, if you didn't look so exhausted, I'd say you were teasing me. Tell me what happened, sir. That always helps you to sort the wheat from the chaff."

He gave her a wan smile. "How well you know me, Mrs. Jeffries." He began by telling her about their search of Edith Durant's room and the discovery of the ledger.

"You've no idea what it could mean?" she asked when he paused to take a breath.

"None," he admitted. "But both Constable Barnes and I are sure it's important. We've passed it along to Y Division in the hopes that Inspector Rogers or one of his chaps might be able to make heads or tails of it. Who knows, it might be some sort of code the local lads have seen before, but I doubt they'll be able to give it much attention. Apparently, there's been an alarming number of burglaries in the area and Y Division is under a lot of pressure to make some arrests."

Mrs. Jeffries wanted to see that ledger. "Will you be taking it to the Yard, then?"

"Constable Barnes is picking it up tomorrow morning."

"You could take it to Ladbroke Road," she interrupted. "You've some very clever constables there. Perhaps one of them will be able to help." She held her breath, silently praying that he'd agree.

He scratched his chin. "That's a very good idea. If none of our men have any good ideas, we can always send it along to the Yard." He grinned suddenly. "I can take it over personally in a day or two. By then, Chief Superintendent Barrows will be demanding I stop what I'm doing and give him a full report on the investigation. I'd rather like to see him take a look at the ledger."

She chuckled. "I've full faith in you, sir. I'm sure by the time the chief wants his report, you'll know what the entries in the book mean."

He smiled, pleased by the compliment. "Let's hope you're right. After that, we continued with our interviews." Witherspoon told her about their second interview with Morecomb as well as what he'd learned from Gordon Redley and John Erskine.

"Erskine overheard Edith Durant arguing with someone the night before the murder," she clarified. "Was he absolutely positive, sir?"

"He was. Unfortunately, instead of going upstairs and seeing who this unknown person might have been, he trotted into the kitchen for a drink of water. But I actually think that Gordon Redley's account of Edith Durant's quarrel with her neighbor was more suspicious."

"In what way, sir?" She took a sip of sherry.

"Because the two accounts differed in one very important respect, and neither Constable Barnes nor I have any idea which of the two of them might be lying," he explained. "Gordon Redley stated that he heard and saw Mrs. Travers tell the victim that if she didn't cease her accusations, she'd see her in court, and it was at that point that Edith Durant told Mrs. Travers that if she came on her property again, she'd kill her. She then turned and marched off, but as she was walking away, Mrs. Travers allegedly shouted at her again. It was something like, she could make it most uncomfortable if Mrs. Robinson didn't stay away from her, that Mrs. Robinson might not like being dragged through the London courts."

"Gracious, sir, that's most extraordinary." Mrs. Jeffries hoped she could remember all this. "What do you think she meant?"

"That's just it. When we asked her about the difference between her recollection of the incident and what Gordon Redley claimed he'd heard and saw, Mrs. Travers insisted he was wrong, that she'd made no such statements. Fortunately, we've witnesses to her account. Her maid and the man from the gasworks came out of the house when they heard the shouting start. I can ask one of them to verify what happened." He frowned as a thought struck him. "But what if they went back to the kitchen before the incident happened?"

The absurdity of the idea almost made her laugh. "This was high drama, sir, so I very much doubt either of them moved an inch. But even if they did go inside, I'm sure that the maid would have peeked through a door or window."

"Yes, if threats were being bandied back and forth, I suppose they'd have wanted to insure that Mrs. Travers was safe." He drained his glass and handed it to her. "Let's have another, shall we."

She allowed herself a smile as she crossed the room and refilled their glasses. He actually believed what he'd just said. Despite everything he'd seen as a policeman, the inspector still believed in the inherent goodness in people and ascribed only the best motives for their behavior. For her part, Mrs. Jeffries would bet her next hot dinner that Mrs. Travers' safety was the last thing either the maid or the man from the gasworks was concerned about. It was far more likely that they were both hoping the argument would accelerate into fisticuffs. But she kept her opinion to herself as she came back to her seat and handed him his glass. "Here you are, sir." She took her seat. "You've learned a huge amount today, sir."

"Indeed we have, Mrs. Jeffries, and not just from the tenants, either." He took a quick sip. "Constable Barnes spoke to the cook again and he took a statement from the housemaid who was out all day yesterday. I must say, according to the maid, Edith Durant was a very odd employer."

"In what way, sir?"

"She was an unusual combination of both strictness and leniency. Apparently, her servants, including the young female ones, could stay out as late as they liked and go to pubs. But they weren't allowed to go into her room and the only time they were allowed in the tenants' quarters was when they changed the linens once a fortnight. But, and this is the interesting part, Edith Durant herself supervised them when the beds were changed. According to Etta Morgan, she'd use her passkey to enter the room and then she'd allow either Miss Morgan or Carrie Durridge to change the linens. But she stayed and watched them the whole time."

"It's a strange way to behave, sir, but perhaps she did it to avoid either herself or her staff from being accused of stealing from the tenants," she suggested. Considering what she knew of Edith Durant's character, she didn't believe for a moment the woman was trying to protect her servants or herself from a bogus charge of thieving, but she wanted to insure that the inspector thought about any and all possibilities to explain Durant's behavior.

"That's possible, I suppose," he mused. "But it doesn't seem to fit her character, now, does it. Nonetheless, I'll keep it in mind when I speak to Carrie Durridge again. She was the one person we didn't have time to re-interview today and I've a number of questions I didn't think to ask before. I'd like to know what happened to the keys."

"You mean the one to Edith's room?"

"And the passkey," he said. "That's not turned up, either."

From down the hall, the clock struck the hour. Witherspoon drained his glass and stood up. "I'll have my dinner now, Mrs. Jeffries, and if you'd be so kind as to keep me company, I'll tell you what else we learned today."

Mrs. Jeffries shifted her weight on the hard straight-backed chair and rocked her shoulders from side to side, trying to work the strain out of her tense muscles. It was past midnight and she'd been at her desk since bidding the inspector a cheerful "good night" just after nine o'clock. Holding her arms out toward the lantern, she stretched her cramped fingers as hard as she could. For the past three hours, she'd written down every little detail about this case that she could remember, and she sincerely hoped she had remembered them all.

She glanced toward her window, noting the pale light from the gas lamp across the road. Even though it was well past her usual bedtime, she was far too excited to sleep. Everyone had done their best, but they'd learned very few facts. Thank goodness the inspector had done a bit better. She sighed heavily and wondered if despite their assertions that they believed everyone, even a murderess, deserved justice, they weren't fooling themselves. Perhaps their own inner demons were keeping them from doing their best.

She frowned as the idea took root in her mind and started to bloom. No. She shook her head. She refused to believe such a thing. She rubbed her hands together, massaging her aching fingers and digging hard into her palms to relieve the ache. But once the thought was in her mind, it refused to go away. What if all of them, including her, had deluded themselves into thinking they were actually working on this case, when their "inner minds," which she honestly believed they all possessed, were actually forcing them to work in accordance with their own preconceived notions of right and wrong? "You're being ridiculous," she muttered. But was she? All of them knew that Edith Durant was a killer, and even though they'd been shamed by both Phyllis and Ruth into doing their duty, she wondered if they were victims of their own prejudices. Today the inspector had discovered more information than all of them combined.

No, she refused to believe they'd given in to their prejudices and not done the best they could. Today was merely a lackluster day; it happened sometimes. She picked up the paper and began to study the notes she'd made. Things would be different tomorrow. Better. She'd send Wiggins to the Black Swan to see if he could learn anything useful. She'd ask Ruth or Luty to have a good look at Mrs. Travers and see if there was more to the altercation between the two women than met the eye. Tomorrow, she'd ask Hatchet and Smythe to make inquiries about the tenants at the lodging house, and she'd see if Betsy might be able to find out the names of any of Durant's former servants. She'd also ask Phyllis and Mrs. Goodge to continue finding out every morsel of gossip there was to be had about the late, unlamented Edith Durant.

Barnes knocked on the door of the duty office at Y Division headquarters, waited till he heard a voice tell him to enter, and then stepped inside. It was an overcast gray day and despite the early hour, the lamp on the desk was lighted.

Inspector Rogers looked up from the file he'd been studying and then frowned when he saw his visitor. "I didn't set the press on Inspector Witherspoon," he announced. "I'll not have you nor anyone else thinking I'd do such a thing to a fellow officer."

"But they got the story very quickly," Barnes pointed out as he advanced into the small office. "Her real name was in the evening papers that very day."

"That's true, but they didn't get it from me," he retorted. "We got off on the wrong foot at our first meeting and that was my fault. I'll admit to that, but I most certainly did not tell the press anything about this case, not then, not now, not ever."

"I know, sir."

"You know?" Rogers drew back in surprise.

Barnes smiled. "May I sit down? These are new boots and they're hurting my feet."

Rogers pointed to the empty chair in front of the desk. "Right, then, tell me how you know it wasn't me."

"Your reputation sir." Barnes sighed in pleasure as he took his seat. "Several of your lads made it a point to tell me and Inspector Witherspoon that you were a decent, honorable officer who was dedicated to doin' a proper job."

Rogers stared at the constable for a long moment, then his mouth quirked up in a grin. "So you're takin' the word of men who work for me?"

"Them and a few of my sources at the Yard. You're held in pretty high esteem, sir. Oh Lord, why do they make these boots with such a tight fit?"

After the altercation at the cemetery, Barnes had quietly checked with several of his old colleagues at Scotland Yard and learned that Rogers was highly regarded by the rank and file as well as the top brass. He'd not done it out of spite or anger, but only because he'd wanted to be prepared in case Rogers attempted to sabotage the investigation. It wouldn't be the first time someone had tried to hobble one of Inspector Witherspoon's cases.

"It's decent of you to say so, Constable," Rogers replied softly. "And I very much appreciate the sentiment. Would you like a cup of tea? I can send down to the canteen."

Barnes shook his head. He'd had a cup both at home and with Mrs. Jeffries and Mrs. Goodge at Upper Edmonton Gardens. "No thanks, sir, I'm fine."

"Right, then, down to business." He opened the top drawer and pulled out the ledger. "No one here can figure it out. The entries obviously mean something, but as to what that might be, we simply don't know." He shoved it across his desk. "I've taken a good long look at it and had a couple of my brighter lads and the other two duty inspectors see if they could understand it, but it was no good. I'm sorry, Constable Barnes, we tried our best."

"I'm sure you did, sir." Barnes picked it up.

"What will you do now?"

"Take it to the Yard, I expect." He got to his feet. "I'll have to see what Inspector Witherspoon wants to do with it."

"Perhaps her solicitor might be able to shed some light on it," Rogers suggested. "I'm assuming, of course, that as a property owner she had someone to handle her legal affairs."

"She did," he agreed. "That's actually not a bad idea. The victim had no close friends or relatives."

"She has relatives," Rogers interrupted. "She's a niece in Edinburgh that she visits every month. You didn't know that?"

"No, we didn't. How did you find out?"

"From the officer who originally identified her as Alice Robinson," Rogers replied. "Remember, I told you she was questioned as a witness in a burglary. A trunk was stolen from one of the houses across the road. When Constable Pierpoint asked if she'd seen anything during the time period the trunk was taken, she told him she wasn't home. That she'd left for the train station. She goes to Edinburgh once a month to visit her niece."

Barnes wondered why none of the tenants nor the servants had mentioned this fact. "But she doesn't have a niece in Edinburgh. When Edith Durant went on the run, we contacted every member of her family. The Durants were all dead, the Rileys, Edith's cousins, loathed her, and the Claypools hadn't seen nor heard from her in years."

"But blood is thicker than water," Rogers mused. "And maybe this niece is a relative of Carl Christopher."

"The only relative Christopher had was a sister and she moved to Italy years before Carl Christopher married into the Durant family. She came back when he was arrested and bankrupted herself paying for his defense when he went to trial. She'd not have anything to do with Edith Durant."

"Well, she obviously had some reason for going to Scotland, unless, of course, she was lying to Constable Pierpoint." Rogers clamped his hand over his mouth as he yawned. "Sorry, I'm a bit tired."

"Have you been on duty all night?" Barnes asked. He looked more closely at Inspector Rogers and realized the poor fellow looked awful; his eyes were red rimmed, his face pale, and there was enough stubble on his cheeks to indicate he needed a shave.

Rogers smiled wanly. "Unfortunately, yes, but I'm not the only one. Everyone's working extra hours. I've had to double the constables out on patrol and every inspector in the division is doing additional shifts. It makes us tired and irritable." He cleared his throat. "Please tell Inspector Witherspoon I'm sorry for my behavior at the cemetery. He's a good officer and from what I've heard, an exemplary human being. My only excuse is that I was exhausted."

"I'll tell him, sir." Barnes sat back down in the chair he'd just vacated. "Is it the burglaries?"

Rogers nodded, his expression glum. "It's like an epidemic. It's like nothing I've ever seen before, and we're all completely baffled."

"How so?"

"The thieves are targeting small but valuable items: jewelry, silver, small paintings, ceramics, things like that, the sort of stuff that should be easy to trace." Rogers leaned forward. "But none of it has shown up in the usual places. We're keeping an eye on a couple of dodgy art dealers, but so far, nothing from that quarter. Nor has any of the jewelry or silver turned up at any of the street markets or pawn-shops. We've put a lot of pressure on our snitches, but none of them have heard of anything being moved. We've got all the known thieves under constant surveillance and the burglaries are still happening, so it's none of them. It's as if the thieves pinched the stuff and then did nothing with it. They're certainly not moving it along the usual routes for stolen goods."

"What about the local fences? Wouldn't they have some idea?"

"Everyone claims to know nothing." He sighed. "And we've leaned on some of the boys pretty hard. The Home Office has stuck their oar in now and there's pressure being put on the superintendent for us to make an arrest. But we don't even have any suspects."

Wiggins hadn't thought that a simple trip to the East End would end up with him running for his life. He was fairly sure Mrs. Jeffries hadn't known it, either, when she asked him at their morning meeting to go along to the Black Swan and snoop about a bit. But he was in serious trouble now. The four toughs had fanned out and were blocking the far end of the mews. He looked the other way, wincing when he saw it was a dead end. There was nothing to do but go back into the pub. He either had to face the angry barkeep or risk his neck with the toughs, and considering it would be four against one, he thought he'd take his chances with the barkeep.

The Black Swan was on the Commercial Road, so if he could make it to the street, he might have a chance of getting away with his body parts intact. Blast, who'd a thought a few harmless questions could get him in this kind of a mess.

Taking a deep breath, he whirled around, yanked the door open, and raced inside. He ran down the narrow hallway to the public bar and into the small, crowded room. He charged toward the street door, grazing the shoulder of an old man at the end of the counter, leapt over a stool, and dodged to his left to avoid the hulking brute who'd suddenly popped up to block his way.

"Get back 'ere," the barkeep yelled. But Wiggins knew he daren't stop. He lunged for the door handle just as he felt a hand grabbing at the back of his coat. Clawing at the knob, he got the door open and flew through it onto the street. The four toughs were now coming at him from around the corner and the hulking brute was right on his heels. Just ahead of him was the street, crowded with omnibuses, carts, vans, hansoms, and four-wheelers, all of which were moving fast.

"Don't let 'im git away. Surround 'im," one of the toughs shouted.

Wiggins dashed into the street, leaping in front of a cooper's van, getting safely past it only to have to swerve to his left to avoid being run down by a hansom cab. This was his only chance, and he took it. He dodged around a handcart loaded with cockles and eels and directly into the path of a carriage. Ignoring the swearing and the shouting as drivers pulled on hand brakes and horses reared, Wiggins jumped, leapt, and weaved in and out of the traffic. Reaching the other side, he didn't stop, but continued running. He intended to get as far away from the Black Swan as possible, so he didn't look back, he simply ran down the pavement doing his best to avoid smashing into anyone unlucky enough to be in his path. He skidded to a halt as he rounded the corner and saw a fixed-point constable.

He gasped for breath and glanced over his shoulder but didn't see either the brute from the pub or the four toughs. Swallowing hard, he leaned against a lamppost to give his shaking legs a rest. His heart was pounding and he thought his lungs would burst, but it took only a few minutes before he straightened up and continued on, moving nonchalantly past the constable. His pursuers were gone, too. Apparently they didn't want to explain to the copper why they were chasing him. But nonetheless, Wiggins didn't feel really safe until he reached Whitechapel Station and boarded a train for the West End of London and home.

"Mr. Teasdale, we'd hoped to have a word with you yesterday," Witherspoon said as he took a seat.

"I was unavoidably detained," Teasdale said smoothly. "Business, Inspector. Frankly, sir, I've no idea why you thought it so important to speak to me. I know nothing of this matter."

Tall, well-built, and impeccably dressed, Norman Teasdale leaned against the mantel of the drawing room and stared at the inspector. He was a handsome man—dark brown hair with just a bit of gray at the temples, brown eyes, and perfect features save for the beginnings of a double chin.

The inspector nodded as if in agreement, then said, "That's as may be, but we do need to question you. How long have you been a tenant here?"

"Six months. My company transferred me here from the Continent. Previously I was in Rome."

"Who is your employer?"

Teasdale raised an eyebrow. "Is that relevant, Inspector?"

"It's a standard question, sir," Witherspoon replied.

"Well, I suppose you could say I don't work for any one individual company; I act as an agent for a consortium of wine growers and food importers."

"But I thought you said your company sent you here," Witherspoon pressed.

"What I meant to say was that the companies I represent offered me some substantial incentives to relocate here." He pushed away from the mantel. "My principals feel there's no reason that fine wines, preserved meats, and delicious Italian cheeses can't be appreciated by the sophisticated citizens of London."

"When was the last time you saw Mrs. Robinson?"

"At breakfast on the day she was killed."

"What was your relationship with Mrs. Robinson?"

"I was her tenant, Inspector."

"Was that all?" Witherspoon pressed.

"I don't know what you're trying to imply, Inspector," he said coldly. "She was my landlady and, other than that, I had no relationship with her."

"That's not what we've been told, Mr. Teasdale. We have it on good authority that you and the deceased were more than landlady and tenant. Two witnesses have stated that you had an . . . uh, very personal relationship with her." He was exaggerating just to see if it would have any effect. Mrs. Fremont, the cook, was the only witness who'd seen the victim going into Teasdale's rooms, but then again, she'd seen it two nights in a row.

Teasdale's mouth opened and then snapped shut. "They were lying."

"Mr. Teasdale, really, you'll save us both a great deal of time and trouble if you'll just tell me the truth. What was the true nature of your relationship with Mrs. Robinson?"

He said nothing for a long moment and then he flopped into a chair. "Alright, I'll admit it, we did have a personal relationship. We were lovers."

"Were you aware of her true identity?"

"I'm not sure how to answer that, Inspector."

"Just tell me the truth, sir. Were you aware that she was Edith Durant and not Alice Robinson?"

"I knew that Alice Robinson wasn't her real name, but I had no idea she was wanted for murder. I didn't find that out until after she was dead. You've got to understand, Inspector, we both knew our relationship was temporary and that's the way we wanted it. I didn't ask a lot of questions. She had her life and I had mine."

"But surely you must have had some curiosity about her?" Witherspoon didn't understand people like Norman Teasdale. He'd been shy around women all his life and had thought he was destined to be alone forever, but then he'd found happiness with Ruth, and he wanted to know everything about her. "Are you saying you didn't care for her at all?"

"Of course I cared, Inspector, but she made it quite clear she didn't want to answer questions. The one time I asked her why she went to Edinburgh once a month she almost threw me out."

"Edinburgh?" Witherspoon interrupted. "She went to Edinburgh?"

"That's what I just said, Inspector. She told the servants she was going there to see her niece, but I knew that wasn't true. One of the few things she did tell me was that she had no close relatives." He smiled skeptically. "But when I asked her about it, she told me that if I wanted to continue living here, I'd mind my own business and not ask so many questions."

"You've no idea why she made these trips?" Witherspoon wondered why neither the servants nor the other tenants had mentioned this particular fact.

"No, Inspector, and as I said, the one time I mentioned it, she made it perfectly clear it was none of my business."

"Where did you go after breakfast on the day Mrs. Robinson was killed?"

Surprised by the change of subject, he blinked. "I went to work. I had appointments set up with three different clients that day."

"What time did you leave the house?"

"Right after breakfast. I went up to get my order book and was at Upper Holloway Station by half past eight. Really, Inspector, surely you don't think I had anything to do with her murder."

"I'm merely asking for an accounting of your movements, sir," Witherspoon explained. "It's standard procedure, sir. Where did you go from the station?"

"To see my first customer." He got up and began to pace the room.

But the inspector wasn't going to give up because the fellow was getting a tad annoyed. He wanted facts, verifiable facts. "Who was that, sir?"

He stopped in his tracks, his expression outraged. "You're not going to bother my customers, Inspector. I'll not have it. You'll ruin my business. I don't sell my wines or foodstuffs to the local corner shop, Inspector, I sell to expensive hotels and restaurants, not the sort of people that will appreciate the police barging in and asking a lot of foolish questions about me."

"I'm afraid I must insist," Witherspoon pressed. "You do understand, until we can verify your whereabouts at the time of the murder, we must consider you a suspect."

"But I had no reason to kill her," he cried.

"You've admitted you had an intimate relationship with the deceased."

"For God's sake, what's that got to do with it? I've already told you. It was temporary and it was an arrangement that suited us both."

"But we only have your word for that, sir. For all we know, Edith Durant or Alice Robinson, as you knew her, may have wanted far more from you than just a 'temporary' romance." Witherspoon was no expert on the motives of the fair sex, but his relationship with Ruth had helped him understand women a bit better. She had very recently hinted that she hoped their association was going to be both long lasting and exclusive. "Perhaps you wished to end the relationship and she refused," he continued. "Edith Durant was no shy young maiden. Had she wanted to, there are any number of ways she could have embarrassed you and caused you difficulties. Now, sir, I promise you we'll be discreet, but I must know which customer you were with at nine o'clock on the day of the murder."

* * *

"Are you sure they'll serve us?" The thin, pale young woman with bright red hair and deep-set blue eyes glanced nervously at the freshly painted exterior of the Highgate Hill Tea Shop and then back at her companion.

"Of course they will." Phyllis lifted her chin, smiled confidently, and led the two of them inside. It was past the hour for morning tea and not close enough to lunch for the place to be busy, so only two of the tables had customers. A black-jacketed waiter hurried across the polished wood floor in their direction.

"A table for two, please. We'd like tea." She kept a pleasant smile on her face as she spoke, but despite her earlier bravado, she'd admit to being just a bit apprehensive. This was the first time in her life she'd entered a posh establishment as a customer and not a servant carrying packages for a mistress. But she refused to give in to her insecurities. At the morning meeting, Mrs. Jeffries had made it clear that she valued and respected Phyllis' abilities when they were on the hunt. She'd apologized for giving Phyllis the difficult task of tracking down gossip about a woman who had very few connections in her own neighborhood. Phyllis had left Upper Edmonton Gardens full of confidence and determined not to let the housekeeper down.

"Will the table by the window do for you, miss?" the waiter asked.

"That will be fine."

As soon as they were settled and she'd ordered, she smiled at the young woman sitting across from her.

Annie Linden, former housemaid to Edith Durant, was

gazing at her surroundings with her mouth slightly open. When she caught Phyllis' eye, she smiled self-consciously. "Sorry, I didn't mean to be gawking. But I'm not used to places like this."

"I wasn't, either, until very recently," Phyllis admitted. "But people like us have as much right to enjoy the finer things in life as anyone else. Just because we weren't born rich and we've got to work to earn our living, doesn't mean we aren't as deserving as anyone else."

"Still, this is awfully nice of you," Annie said. "Tea will cost a lot more here than it would at the road stand. It's only sixpence there."

"Don't worry about how much it costs. I'm grateful you're going to help me out." Phyllis couldn't believe how lucky she'd gotten. In the first shop she had gone into this morning, the one where the clerk yesterday wouldn't say a ruddy word, fortune had smiled on her and a talkative young miss was behind the counter. When she'd mentioned the murder and the lodging house, the girl had shrugged, said she didn't know anything about Alice Robinson, and then pointed at a young woman trudging past the window. "But she'll be able to help you. If your paper wants the goods on Alice Robinson, you'd best speak to that one. She worked for the woman until recently and now she's doing agency work until she finds something permanent. She's been all over the neighborhood looking for a position."

Phyllis hadn't wasted any time; she'd raced across the road and accosted Annie Linden, boldly declaring she worked for a newspaper and would pay her for her time and information. If the girl was doing temporary work, she must be desperate for money. Phyllis had done it herself before she got the job at Upper Edmonton Gardens and she knew how awful it was.

"Here you are, miss." The waiter put down the tea things as well as a plate with four small, delicate frosted cakes. She waited till the waiter had gone before she poured. "Help yourself to a cake," she offered as she handed Annie a cup of tea.

"Ta." Annie smiled broadly, picked up one of the pastries, and took a bite. "Hmm . . . this is good."

"I'm glad you're enjoying it." Phyllis gave her a few minutes to eat before she started asking questions. "I understand you used to work for Alice Robinson?"

Annie nodded and licked a speck of white frosting off her finger. "I did, but she give me the sack and it weren't my fault. But she was so angry, she wouldn't listen to me."

"What do you mean?" Phyllis took a sip of her tea. "What happened?"

"I didn't hear the bell ringing—that's what." She frowned heavily. "The first time it happened was with Mr. Redley. He came home late and claims he rung the bell for five minutes but I never heard a thing."

"I don't understand. You were the one who let the gentlemen in at night?" Phyllis already knew this, as Mrs. Jeffries had passed along all the details about the household that she'd gotten out of both the inspector and Constable Barnes. But experience had taught her that acting as if you didn't know anything often got you quite a bit more.

Annie picked up the second cake, took a bite, and swallowed. "I was. It was part of my duties. Mrs. Robinson's tenants were business gentlemen and sometimes they had to be out late. She didn't like getting up in the night, so I

had the room downstairs and I was to let them in so she'd
not be disturbed. I didn't mind. I got my own room and I'd
never had that before. But like I was saying, that first time
it happened I must have slept like the dead, so Mr. Redley
went to the front and got Mrs. Robinson up. She wasn't
happy about it, but she didn't sack me then."

"When did she sack you?"

"The next night. I slept hard then, too, and Mr. Morecomb ended up waking her out of her sleep. The next
morning, she told me to pack my things and get out." Her
eyes filled with tears. "And it weren't fair. I worked hard
there and did more than my fair share."

Phyllis knew exactly how the girl must have felt; she
knew what it was like to be tossed into the street through
no real fault of your own. Suddenly, she wasn't as concerned about the case as she was about Annie. "That's so
unfair. Maybe you were taking ill. Maybe that's why you
slept so heavily."

"But I wasn't. There weren't nothing wrong the next
morning but a bad headache."

"But anyone can have a bad night." Phyllis smiled sym-
pathetically.

"I'm a light sleeper," she insisted. "And it hadn't ever
happened before."

Phyllis thought of something else Mrs. Jeffries had
shared with them at their morning meeting. "Had you been
out that night? Gone to the pub or something like that?"

Annie bit her lip and looked away. "So what if I was? I
wasn't drunk. Besides, we was allowed out once supper
was over and the washing up done. The tenants didn't need
us and Mrs. Robinson either went out somewhere or went

up to her quarters. It wasn't like we wasn't doin' our work, so sometimes Mrs. Fremont and I would nip out to the pub for a drink, and as long as we were back by nine, when the doors was locked, then Mrs. Robinson didn't mind."

Phyllis nodded as though this was the most ordinary situation in the world, but in truth, there were very few households that allowed their female servants out at night. That frequently didn't stop a lot of them from going out, but usually it was done without the master's or mistress's knowledge. "Had you and Mrs. Fremont been to the pub the night you slept so soundly?"

"Just me." She shoved the last of the cake in her mouth. "Mrs. Fremont's knees were acting up so she stayed home. But I didn't have much to drink. The pub was real crowded that night and the woman standing next to me jostled my elbow and my second drink went all over my skirt and it was my best one, too. Mind you, though, she was decent about it. She give me a bottle she'd bought for herself to make up for it."

"She gave you a whole bottle because she'd spilled one drink?" Phyllis wasn't that familiar with the cost of alcohol, but even with her limited knowledge, that didn't sound right.

Annie shook her head. "She was makin' up for ruining my skirt, not spilling my drink. Besides, she was the sort of woman who could afford to be a bit generous. She was dressed fancy and acted like the ruddy Queen."

With the ledger and the other reports from Y Division tucked under his arm, Barnes climbed the front stairs of the lodging house. He knocked lightly on the door, opened it, and stepped inside.

The inspector was coming down the stairs, Carrie Durridge trailing behind him. "I'm only asking because Etta and Mrs. Fremont are in a state," she said. "They're concerned with what's going to happen."

"I understand that, Miss Durridge," he said as they reached the foyer. He nodded to the constable.

"So what should I do, sir?" Carrie tugged at the inspector's sleeve to get his attention.

"For the time being, stay here and continue working. We'll be seeing Mrs. Robinson's solicitor this afternoon."

"But will we be paid, sir? That's what we want to know. The quarter is over at the end of the month and we want to make sure we get our wages," she persisted.

Witherspoon had no idea about the legality of the situation, but he didn't want the tenants or the servants scattering to the four winds just yet.

"There's money for the quarterly wages." Barnes waved one of the reports he'd carried in under his arm. "Mrs. Robinson had an account for the household expenses at the London and County Bank in Islington."

Carrie heaved a sigh of relief. "Oh, thank goodness. I'll go tell the others."

As soon as she disappeared, Witherspoon turned to the constable with a grateful smile. "Thank goodness you came when you did. The maid's been dogging my footsteps since I got here. Of course, I don't blame the poor woman. I'm sure all of them are concerned about their future. But how did you find out about the bank account?"

"Inspector Rogers had some of his men check the local banks when he got wind of the fact that we didn't find any of Edith Durant's papers here. His men did a good job in that respect. They also got witness statements from the locals near the cemetery entrance, and his lads have found a tinker who saw two men and a woman going into the cemetery before Durant was killed."

"Together?"

Barnes shook his head. "No, all three were separate."

"Can the tinker identify either of them?" Witherspoon asked hopefully.

"The woman wore a cloak over her head but he might be able to identify one of the men. He's a local person, so he'd be available if we need him. Trouble is, just because he only saw three people doesn't mean they were the only ones that went inside. There might have been others goin' in and out."

"What about the man Mrs. Rivers saw coming out of the cemetery when she was going in, the one carrying the bouquet?"

Barnes grinned. "He's not a killer, Inspector, he's a flower thief. The lads at Y Division know all about him. Apparently, the groundsmen and the gardeners at Highgate have complained about him for months. Two or three times a week he steals a freshly laid bouquet off one of the graves and makes off with it. They've caught him a couple of times and he's been fined, but he always goes back and does it again."

"He steals flowers off a grave?" the inspector muttered, his expression incredulous. "Good gracious, is nothing sacred?"

"Not to some people, sir." He handed over the reports and the ledger. "Inspector Rogers passed the ledger around to his best and brightest, sir, but none of them can make heads nor tails of it."

"That's not surprising," Witherspoon murmured. "Let's hold on to it for a day or two, Constable. Perhaps after we speak to the Durant solicitor, he'll have some idea that would be helpful. Failing that, we'll see if any of our lads at the Ladbroke Road Station can decipher what it might mean."

There was a knock at the front door just as Carrie reappeared from the kitchen. "Cook and Etta are very relieved, sir." She flashed him a quick smile as she hurried toward the front door and yanked it open. "It's another policeman, sir," she called as Constable Jones stepped into the foyer.

He was breathing hard and his face was flushed as if he'd been running. "Inspector Rogers sent me, sir," he said to Witherspoon. "We received a message right after the constable left. I was trying to catch up with him and that's why I'm out of breath." He handed the inspector a folded piece of paper. "This is for you, sir."

Witherspoon opened it, and as his eyes flicked across the page, his expression became increasingly morose.

"That doesn't seem like good news, sir," Barnes murmured.

He handed the paper to Barnes. "It isn't. Chief Superintendent Barrows wants us to come to the Yard right away."

CHAPTER 7

———

Smythe lengthened his stride as Erskine disappeared around the corner. He didn't know where his quarry was going but he wasn't going to lose him now. When Erskine came out of the lodging house dressed in his tidy business suit this morning, Smythe had been sure he'd make for his office in High Holborn, but instead, he'd gone to one of the oldest sections of the East End, Whitechapel. It was a maze of narrow cobblestone streets enclosed by brick buildings caked with dirt and grime and shops selling second- and thirdhand goods. Ragged children peered out the dirty windows of overcrowded flats and worn-out women trudged from one food stall to another looking for something they could afford for their families. Lean and hungry-looking men stood around on the streets hoping for a bit of work as day laborers. The air smelled of rot and vinegar with an occasional whiff of cabbage tossed in for good measure. It was a miserable place and Smythe had once known it well.

Ahead of him, Erskine cut into a passageway and Smythe hurried to keep up with him. Blast a Spaniard, the fellow was supposed to be a businessman, so what was he doing in this part of London? There weren't many around this neighborhood looking to buy Canadian furs for their missus.

Erskine reached the end of the passageway and turned to his right. Smythe slowed his steps, waiting a few seconds before moving ahead. He came out on a narrow road enclosed on the far side by the back end of a derelict warehouse and on this side, there was a paved courtyard leading to a pub called the Hanged Man. Erskine was just disappearing through the front door.

Smythe hesitated for a brief moment. He'd heard of this place and what he'd heard hadn't been good. Even the local constables, a tough lot from the Leman Street Station, avoided the place unless they had no other choice, and he'd heard gossip that there'd been gang leaders that had gone inside and never been seen again. Still, common sense told him that people liked to tell tales and most of the talk about the Hanged Man was probably exaggerated.

He shrugged, crossed the courtyard, and went inside. The lighting was so dim he stood by the entrance, waiting for his eyes to adjust. When he could see properly, he saw it was just a pub. Shelves filled with bottles, barrels, and jugs stood behind the bar; long, shallow benches were along the walls; and there were half a dozen tables, all but one of which was occupied. Rough-looking men drinking pints crowded the bar and several women dressed in tatty-looking finery that showed off their bosoms sat on the benches and at some of the tables drinking gin.

He spotted Erskine at the table near the edge of the counter. He was in earnest conversation with two men. Smythe strode to the bar and wedged himself into a spot at the end. He nodded apologetically as he jostled his neighbor's arm, a cockles and eel vendor, judging by the smell of him. The man shot him a dirty look but Smythe didn't care, he was as close to Erskine as possible.

The barman, a balding fellow with a handlebar mustache, eyed him suspiciously. "I've never seen you in here before."

"Never been 'ere before." Smythe met his gaze and held it. He heard the shuffle of feet and the scraping of stools as the others at the bar moved away from him. Showing any weakness or fear would be deadly, so Smythe straightened up to his full height and held his ground.

"You from around here?" Baldy swiped at the counter with a dirty, greasy rag as he spoke.

"I'm from lots of places and this is the first time I've 'ad to answer a bunch of bleedin' questions to get a pint. Is this a pub or not?" he demanded.

By this time, everyone in the pub was listening to their exchange.

"This is my pub"—the publican glared at him—"and I serve who I want."

"Are you sayin' you'll not serve me a drink?" Smythe hardened his voice and threw back his shoulders in an attempt to look mean. From his left, he heard the stools at Erskine's table scraping against the wood floor and knew that lot had gotten to their feet.

He glanced at the entrance to make sure the coast was clear in case he had to make a run for it but now two huge bruisers were flanking the doorway. The room had gone quiet and he could feel everyone's eyes on him. He turned and saw Erskine pointing at him. Blast a Spaniard, this was quickly going to hell in a handbasket.

Instead of answering, Baldy reached under the bar and pulled out a ruddy huge club. Two of the men from Erskine's table started toward him, and it was then that Smythe shoved his hand in his trouser pocket and found what he hoped would get him out of the pub in one piece. He pushed away from the bar, swerved to his left, and raced to the center of the room. He moved so fast no one had time to react, and that was what he counted on. Yanking his hand out of his pocket, he raised his arm and opened his fingers. Sixpences, shillings, florins, and even some half crowns cascaded to the floor.

For a split second, no one moved, then almost as one, they rushed toward the money. "Good God, look, it's a half crown," one of the women shouted as she shoved her companion out of the way and dived for the coin. Within seconds the room was in bedlam as they pushed and shoved one another out of the way to get to the money. The two thugs by the door leapt in as well giving Smythe a chance to skirt the edge of the crowd and break for the door. He headed for the crowded streets of the Commercial Road. He didn't look behind him, but he knew someone was after him because he could hear them pounding against the pavement. He raced around the corner and skidded to a halt, turning to face his pursuer. It was one of the brutes that'd been guarding the door. He was big, ugly, stupid-looking, and charging toward him like a mad bull. As he estimated the man's speed, Smythe balled his hands into fists before swiveling to his side and sticking his foot out just in time to send the brute crashing to his knees.

"Oyyy," the man screamed in a surprisingly high-pitched, girlish voice as he tumbled forward. Smythe leapt onto his back, pushing him to the ground and planting his knee in the fellow's spine. "Why were you followin' me?" he demanded. "All I wanted was a ruddy drink."

"I'm just doin' what I was told." His assailant gasped out the words. "They told me to mess you about a bit. I wasn't really goin' to 'urt ya." He bucked hard, trying to dislodge Smythe.

Smythe flattened his arm across the back of the man's neck and pressed. He'd picked up this move from an opal miner in the outback of Australia; it was vicious enough to stop an attacker without actually hurting him too badly. "Who sent you after me?"

"Who do ya bleedin' well think? It was the bloke you was followin'. He offered me two quid to do it." His voice was raspy, his breathing harsh. "Come on, leave off, you've got me down. Bloody 'ell, I shoulda told Erskine to do it 'imself."

Smythe knew he didn't have a lot of time to ask questions. By now, the money he'd tossed to the floor would be scooped up and the other brute would probably come looking for his mate. He pulled his arm off the ruffian's neck. "Why did Erksine want me messed up?"

"'Ow the bleedin' 'ell should I know? We didn't chat about it when he offered me the lolly. All I 'eard was that he spotted you followin' 'im and didn't like it."

He heard footsteps coming. Time to go. "Tell Erskine 'e made a mistake." Smythe leapt up. "I was just thirsty."

"Yeah, and I'm the Queen's ruddy cousin," the man answered, sneering as he struggled onto his knees.

But the sarcasm was lost as Smythe was already gone.

"Should I wait out here, sir?" Barnes sucked in a lungful of air as he and Witherspoon stopped outside the office of Chief Superintendent Barrows. They'd taken a hansom to the modern redbrick building that was known as New Scotland Yard and raced up the three flights of stairs.

Witherspoon was well aware of the hierarchy that governed the Metropolitan Police Department, and by rights, he should merely nod assent and then go see Barrows alone. But that didn't seem fair to him, since he didn't consider the constable to be a subordinate but a full partner. "No, I should like you to come in, Constable. Chief Superintendent Barrows may have information for us about this matter, and if that is the case, you might have questions or other insights about this crime that will be very useful." He turned and rapped sharply on the door.

Barnes was inordinately pleased, but kept a somber, no-nonsense expression on his face as he followed his inspector. Chief Superintendent Barrows, recently promoted and moved to one of the "turret" offices with a nice view of the Thames, looked up from the open file on his desk. His horn-rimmed spectacles slipped down his long nose and his mouth flattened in disapproval as his gaze flicked from Witherspoon to Barnes and back.

"I insisted Constable Barnes come in with me," Witherspoon said quickly. "I wanted him to hear firsthand any new information the Yard might have obtained about this case." The inspector wanted to make it clear that Barnes was innocent of violating the unwritten protocols governing the police.

"I didn't ask you here because we've any new information," Barrows snapped. "I was hoping you would have some for me." He poked his finger on the open file. "All I've had so far is the first report. She was murdered two days ago, Inspector, and I've had one report."

"We've been very busy, sir," Witherspoon protested. "And we have learned a bit more since that first report."

"Have you learned the identity of the killer?"

"No, sir, not as yet, but we're moving forward on the case."

Barrows sighed, took his glasses off, dropped them next to the file, and stood up. He walked to the window and gazed out at the traffic on the Thames. "Look, Witherspoon, I know you have your methods, and in the past, they've worked well. But we do have procedures that are equally useful."

"I follow all established procedures, sir. I wasn't aware that I'd done anything wrong on this case," the inspector said.

"It's not a matter of doing anything wrong." Barrows swung back to them. "It's more that you don't seem to understand the damage that's been done to the force because of this case."

Barnes knew what was coming next. Disgusted, he looked down at the floor because he didn't want the inspector to see the look of contempt he was afraid he couldn't hide. Barrows had always been a copper first and a bureaucrat second, but this latest promotion seemed to have changed him. He'd heard rumors that the chief was now more interested in showing off the view from his office and getting good press cuttings than he was in pursuing justice. Barnes hadn't believed it, but he did now. He'd seen the articles in both the *Times* and the other dailies and they'd not been kind to the police. Most of the newspapers had started out writing about the Durant murder and then gone on to the other scandals and mishaps that had dogged the force for the past few years.

"I'm sorry we didn't catch Edith Durant years ago," Witherspoon said. "But she most certainly wasn't the first criminal to get away from the Metropolitan Police Force. With all due respect, sir, there have been a number of miscreants who escaped us and were never brought to justice."

Barnes' chin jerked sharply as he looked up. Witherspoon stared calmly at Barrows. The constable hadn't expected this; he'd thought the inspector would quietly apologize and try to smooth Barrows' ruffled feathers. The chief obviously hadn't expected it, either, because he was gaping at the inspector in openmouthed surprise.

"I'm not being insubordinate, sir," Witherspoon continued. "I'm merely stating facts."

Barrows finally got himself under control. "And the fact is that the department is being smeared in the press just when we've begun to regain the confidence of the public." He tried for a conciliatory smile. "I'm not being critical of your methods, Inspector. Believe me, no one is more aware of your service record than I am. You've caught more murderers than anyone in the history of the department and that is part of the problem."

Barnes couldn't stay silent. "How can that be a problem, sir? Aren't we supposed to catch killers?"

Barrows came back to his chair, flopped down, and motioned for them to take the two straight-backed chairs in front of his desk. "Of course we are and I fully expect you'll find the culprit in this crime." He looked at Witherspoon. "But every time you're on a case, the press expects a miracle, and frankly, since there has been such negative press the past few years, your successes have helped us to regain the confidence of the public and we'd like to keep it that way."

The inspector unbuttoned his overcoat as he sat down. "I'm not sure I understand, sir."

"Between the Trafalgar Square riots, the Whitechapel murders, and the Cleveland Street scandal, the department has had to overcome the public perception that we're either incompetent or corrupt."

"But we're neither, sir." The inspector took off his bowler.

"Yes, yes, I know that, but our friends on Fleet Street like to sell newspapers, and dredging up our old failures helps them in that endeavor. We've worked diligently to improve our standing and regain the public's confidence, and to some extent, we've succeeded. But when the press got wind of the Durant murder and, more important, that she was a suspect we let get away, they've been merciless." He sighed. "That's why we've been hoping you'd make an arrest quickly and this whole matter would go away."

"We're making progress sir," Witherspoon assured him.

"But you've no real suspects, right?"

"I wouldn't put it quite like that, sir," Witherspoon said. "There are several people who had recent disputes with the victim. We're looking at them more closely."

"Do you have any idea why Durant was at the cemetery?"

"According to a witness who saw her only moments

before the murder, she was going in to speak to a builder. She told the witness her family had a crypt there."

"They don't," Barrows said. "I sent a constable to the business office to check when I got your first report, and no one by the name of Durant, Riley, or Claypool has a crypt or tomb or even so much as a headstone in the place. So unless Durant has family under another name—and believe me, with that woman it's certainly possible—she didn't go to the cemetery to meet anyone but her killer."

The porter, an older man wearing a misshapen blue suit that hung limply on his skinny frame, pointed to the first door down the corridor. "Yes, sir, that's Mr. Teasdale's office."

Hatchet had been delighted when Mrs. Jeffries had asked him to take a closer look at two of Edith Durant's lodgers. Thus far, despite his bluffs that he had his sources checking on any number of things, he'd found out nothing. He was loathe to let Luty know that particular fact. The woman was ridiculously competitive. What's more, his usual sources were sadly lacking at the moment so he was more than happy to take on this task.

Hatchet smiled gratefully. "Excellent. Then I'm at the right place."

Norman Teasdale's place of business was on the ground floor of a three-story older brown brick building on Baker Street. At their meeting this morning, Mrs. Jeffries had pointed out that they really knew very little about the individuals who lived in Edith Durant's house. He'd been given the task of finding out what he could about Norman Teasdale and Andrew Morecomb. She'd supplied him with the addresses of the two men's offices, and he'd gone to More-comb's place of business first only to find that even though the building existed, no one there had ever heard of him nor were any of the offices let to someone selling safes and vaults. That information had cost him a bit of coin, but it was well worth the money. Besides, he could easily afford it.

"He's not here now," the porter continued helpfully. "He usually only comes in later in the afternoon." He broke off, nodding at a businessman in a black overcoat and bowler hat who hurried past them.

"Surely he has a clerk I can speak with." Hatchet watched the businessman disappear up the stairs, noticing that the fellow carried a briefcase.

"He doesn't." The porter shook his head as he spoke. "Mr. Teasdale spends most of his time out and about, sir. His business is sellin' fancy wines and cheeses . . ."

"Yes, I know, that's why I wanted to meet with him," Hatchet lied.

"He usually comes back to his office around three o'clock, sir. He has to record his orders, sir, and then he gives me the tally sheet for the lad to take to the telegraph office."

"That won't do me any good. I need to see him now." This was looking more and more like Teasdale was a legitimate businessman. After finding out about Morecomb, Hatchet wanted to make sure about Teasdale before the afternoon meeting at Upper Edmonton Gardens. He wasn't certain what was going on with Edith Durant's tenants, but his instincts told him he was onto something. "I'll be on a train to Birmingham."

The porter scratched his stubbly chin. "This time of day

Mr. Teasdale is either at the customs house clearing his shipments or at the train station making sure they're shipped out properly to his customers. He's got customers everywhere—Manchester, Newcastle, Leeds. He works hard, does Mr. Teasdale, and takes his responsibilities seriously. He always wants to be certain his clients get their wines and cheeses right on time. Like he says, when you're bringing bits in from other countries, you've got to make sure the paperwork is in order and make sure the shipments go out on the proper train. He's a good gent, is Mr. Teasdale."

"You sound as if you like him."

"I do, sir." He shot a malevolent glance toward the staircase. "He's not like some that work here. There's them that won't give you the time of day let alone a 'good morning, Jim.'" He snorted. "But the rules here says I've got to greet everyone properly when they walk through the front door whether they're decent to me or not. Mr. Teasdale isn't like that. He always has a nice 'hello' and asks if my arthritis is bothering me. He's very generous, too. Last year one of his shipments was returned so he give me a nice bottle of wine, a salami, and two different cheeses. Mind you, I didn't much care for the cheese, and if truth be told, the salami upset my stomach, but the wine was lovely, real posh stuff it was. The missus and I enjoyed it."

"I'm sorry I'm going to miss seeing him," Hatchet said truthfully. "He sounds a perfect fellow to do business with."

"You might meet him at the customs house." The porter jerked his head toward the right. "It's not far from here. I can give you directions."

"But you're not absolutely sure he'll be there, are you?" Hatchet said.

"No, sir, I'm not. Would you like to leave your card, sir? I'll make sure he gets it."

"That won't be necessary." Hatchet reached into his pocket, pulled out a shilling, and handed it to the porter. "Thank you for your assistance. When Mr. Teasdale returns, please tell him I'll be in town next week and I'll try to stop by and see him then. My name is Mr. Hawkins and I represent several hotels in the midlands that are interested in procuring his goods."

"Thank you, sir," the porter said, grinning broadly as he took the money.

"By the way, I need to send a telegram. Which lad does that for you?" Hatchet asked casually.

"Young Willie Bates is reliable. He's a blond lad who hangs about on the corner, sir. Tell him that Jonesy sent you and he'll not rob you blind."

Mrs. Jeffries tiptoed down the back hall and stepped outside. She closed the door quietly, not wanting to disturb Mrs. Goodge, who was hosting one of her old colleagues with tea and treats. The wind was raw and high so she fastened her cloak and strode briskly toward the path on the other side of the small, brick terrace.

The walkway was a large oval separating the houses from the foliage, trees, flower beds, bushes, and shrubbery of the garden proper. Her feet crunched against the gravel as she started walking. She'd come out to have a good think and she sincerely hoped the cold, windy day would keep the neighbors safely inside their warm houses. There was so much she had to consider about this case, and frankly, she wasn't sure what to do next. She wanted to see the ledger but knew that might be difficult. Constable Barnes had said he'd try to make sure the inspector brought it home with him this evening, but he wasn't certain he could make that happen.

She'd done her best at their morning meeting—she'd given all of them tasks that would hopefully point them in the right direction—but she couldn't be sure their inquiries would yield results that were useful at all. As another gust of wind slammed into her, her eyes watered, so she reached into her pocket, pulled out her handkerchief, and gave them a quick wipe. From the far side of the garden a dog barked and she winced, hoping it wasn't Mrs. Betts and her spaniel out for a morning walk. Mrs. Betts dearly loved a nice chat, and this morning, she needed to think.

What, if anything, did the red cord mean? Where had it come from? Had the killer picked it deliberately or was it just a weapon of convenience? She came around the far side of the garden and was relieved to still be alone. Yesterday evening, the inspector had reported that none of the servants at the lodging house had ever seen the cord, so perhaps it hadn't come from there. In which case, did that mean the killer wasn't someone from Durant's immediate circle, but was instead an old enemy from the past? But even if none of the servants had seen a red cord, that didn't necessarily mean that someone at the lodging house wasn't the killer.

Her shoulders sagged and her footsteps slowed as she realized this was the most difficult case they'd ever had. She couldn't make sense of any of it. Perhaps the others would find out something useful today, but she rather doubted it. Her instructions this morning had been born more of bravado and desperation than logical deduction. To begin with, they'd have very little chance of finding out very much. She winced guiltily and she wished she'd not sent poor Phyllis off to "find out anything there was to know about the victim." Yee gods, that was an impossible task. Edith Durant hadn't mixed with her neighbors and had very few servants, nor had she been the subject of local gossip, so what could Phyllis possibly learn? She stopped as she realized that wasn't true. Durant had had a screaming match with one neighbor, was carrying on an affair with one of her tenants, and had an argument with someone in her room the night before she was killed. She was also sociable enough to have tea with Lavinia Swanson. The inspector had smiled as he'd told her about Mrs. Swanson's reaction to learning Alice Robinson's true identity. She was horrified to realize she'd served her tea and let this suspected murderess pet her cat. No, she told herself, there was plenty to learn about both the victim and her tenants. To begin with, why did supposedly smart businessmen pay double the going weekly rate for lodgings to live in what the inspector had described as a "slightly rundown lodging house"?

She saw that the benches under the oak tree were empty so she wandered off the path, stepping gingerly over the spots in the soggy ground and finding to her delight that the seats were dry. There were so many things she ought to have already found out: Did the fact that the murder took place at Highgate Cemetery have any significance, and if not, why was Edith there? Did she have someone buried there? If not, how had Edith been lured to that particular place? Why had the killer tucked the clipping into the dead woman's hand? Was it only to insure that Witherspoon was called to the scene or had there been another purpose?

She sat for a long time, going over every little detail they had learned thus far in a logical and, she hoped, analytical fashion. Then she gave in to the urge to let her mind do its own sorting; closing her eyes, she let her thoughts come as they would. Ideas, images, and bits of conversation drifted in and out of her consciousness as she sat on the bench.

She was jerked out of her reverie by the barking of a dog. She turned and saw Mrs. Betts and her spaniel, Sugar, as they hurried toward her.

Experience had taught Betsy a bit of liquor could often loosen a reluctant tongue. She smiled at the woman pouring out two glasses of gin and hoped that was the case in this instance.

"Here you are, ma'am." The barmaid put Betsy's glass in front of her and then lifted the one she'd poured for herself. "This is decent of you, ma'am. Usually the ladies that come in here don't have enough coin to spare for buying me one." The barmaid was a tall, buxom woman with brown hair twisted into a knot at the nape of her neck and a curly fringe at the front.

"My newspaper is paying for it." Betsy took off her navy blue leather gloves. After leaving their morning meeting, she had nipped back to her flat and changed into one of her best outfits, a fitted blue suit with navy piping on the sleeves and cuffs and a high-necked white blouse. She hoped the ensemble would convince the barmaid that she was a journalist out for a story.

As she sipped her drink, she surveyed the saloon bar of

the White Hart, the pub she hoped was the one Edith Durant's servants popped into when their work was done each day. If it wasn't, she'd wasted both her time and money. It was a good working-class pub with a public bar on one side and the saloon bar on this side. The stools here were padded in red leather, there was a large mirror on the wall behind the counter, and the tables had proper chairs and not stools. Still, it wasn't a posh place. The black wooden floors were scuffed with age, the pink and red patterned wallpaper had faded in spots, and the ties on the old-fashioned drapes framing the front window were missing most of their fringe.

"What paper did you say you worked for?" The barmaid took a sip and leaned on the bar.

"Does it matter?" Betsy asked. "I'm willing to pay for information. My name is Jane Grant. What's yours?"

"Minnie McNab." She glanced over her shoulder toward the wall that served as a partition between the public bar and the saloon bar. "The guv wouldn't like me talking about his customers, so you've got to make it worth my while."

"Let's not tell the guv, then," Betsy replied. "And I will make it worthwhile for you."

"It's about that murder in Highgate Cemetery, right?"

"That's right. The woman who was strangled was wanted for murder so my editor thought that she must be a pretty colorful sort of person," Betsy explained. She was making it up as she went. "Did she come in here?"

Minnie shook her head. "Wish I could say she did, but that would be a lie. But some of her servants did and they still do. Leastways the cook comes in, and when she's in her cups, she does like to talk."

"Is she in her cups often?"

Minnie smiled slyly. "Often enough. What's it worth to you?"

Betsy knew this was the tricky part of her pretense. If she named a figure that was too high, Minnie might get suspicious about her, but if she aimed too low, the woman might decide it wasn't worth the risk. The barmaid was already uneasy about her guv finding her talking about the customers. "What do you think it's worth?"

Minnie's eyebrows shot up and then she grinned. "Half a crown."

Betsy pretended to think about it. "Alright, but what you've got to say had better be worth it."

"It will be." She stuck her hand out. "But I want it now." Again, she glanced in the direction of the public bar. "He'll have my guts for garters if he catches me."

Pretending reluctance, Betsy opened her small purse and drew out a coin. "Right, then, tell me what you know." She held out the half crown and Minnie grabbed it.

"I know that Mrs. Fremont and the other housemaid both thought there was something odd about the tenants in the lodging house." She tucked the money in her apron pocket. "Mrs. Fremont said sometimes when the tenants came in late at night, they weren't dressed in their fancy business suits but in dark clothes. She said it was strange because the reason that Annie and now that other maid had to sleep downstairs was to let them in when they came back from taking out their customers and clients." She leaned close to Betsy. "Now I ask you, who changes out of a proper business suit into black coats and trousers to take a customer out on the town? No one does."

The questions popped into Betsy's head so fast she wasn't sure what to ask next. "How often did this happen?"

"According to Annie—she's the girl who had the job before the one that's got it now—it was most of the time."

"Did all of the tenants change their clothes?"

Minnie shook her head. "Only three of them. There was one that never come in late but I don't remember his name. But Annie thought it was right strange and I do, too."

"Did she ever ask Mrs. Robinson about it?"

"'Course not." Minnie drained her glass and put it down on the counter. "Mrs. Fremont and Annie were both scared of their mistress. They'd not have risked asking any questions of her."

"But Mrs. Robinson let them come here in the evenings."

Minnie looked pointedly at her empty glass and then at Betsy, who nodded quickly. The barmaid reached under the bar, grabbed a bottle, and gave herself a refill. "That was another thing that was strange. Most times servant women have to sneak in here and pray to God that no one from their households gets wind of it. But not those two. As long as they did what Mrs. Robinson told them and got back by nine when the front door was locked, they could come as often as they liked."

"Mrs. Fremont and Annie didn't have any duties in the evening?" Betsy found that hard to believe. There was always something that needed doing in a big house.

"Not that they ever said." She took a long drink and sighed happily.

"What about now? Is it just Mrs. Fremont who comes here? What about the other servants?"

"There's just the two housemaids and neither of them

drinks. But Mrs. Fremont isn't alone. Mrs. Riddle comes in sometimes and the two of them have a right old natter."

"Who's Mrs. Riddle?" Betsy asked, though the name sounded very familiar.

"She's the cook in one of the neighboring houses." Minnie chuckled. "She comes in sometimes, too."

"So there's another household that lets their female servants out at night." Betsy picked up her gin and took the smallest sip possible.

"Whether they're allowed out at night or not makes no difference." Minnie swept her arm in an arc around the room. "If it did, this part of the pub wouldn't be here. Who do you think we cater to? It's not the gentry or the gents, that's for certain. It's shopgirls, Remington ladies, hotel maids, and lots of house servants. People find a way to get out and enjoy themselves some. As for Mrs. Riddle, her mistress is a skinflint and the only way she keeps a cook of Mrs. Riddle's ilk is to let her do what she pleases."

"Seems to be a lot of that in this neighborhood," Betsy muttered. "Do you have anything else to tell me?"

"Let me think a minute." She turned as the door opened and two bread sellers carrying empty baskets stepped inside. "Do you want your usual?" she yelled as the two women headed for a table. One of them nodded and Minnie grabbed the gin bottle out from under the counter, twirled around, and got two glasses and a wooden tray off the shelf behind her. She poured their drinks.

Betsy had a feeling she'd gotten all she was going to get out of the woman. She got up from her barstool. "Thanks for your time, Minnie. I'll be off, then."

She shrugged and put the two gins on the tray. "That's

really all I've got for you," she admitted with a grin. "And you've been real decent about it—you've paid me a fair bit and bought me two drinks." She picked up the tray and lifted the hinged counter bar. "Not like some that come around asking questions about Alice Robinson. That silly cow wouldn't even buy me a drink."

Wiggins barreled through the back door, out of breath because he'd gone to great lengths to make sure the toughs hadn't followed him. He'd even changed trains twice to make certain they weren't on his trail. He wasn't having the likes of those thugs near the people he cared about, and if that made him a bit late for the afternoon meeting, so be it. But he needn't have worried; he was actually the first one back.

Fred met him as he came into the kitchen. "Hey, old boy, you'll have to wait till after the meeting for your walkies." He reached down and petted the dog's fur.

"What's wrong?" The cook put the teapot on the table and studied him. "You've been running. Why? You're not late."

He gave the dog a final scratch behind his ears. "I thought I was," he lied. He didn't want them to know the whole truth about today. It would only worry the women and he had a feeling that Smythe might not take too kindly to it, either. In truth, he was grateful to be home. He'd tell them some of what happened but not all of it. Fred butted his head against Wiggins' knees and then trotted off to his warm spot by the cooker.

Wiggins went to the table and took his usual seat. "I hope I don't 'ave to wait long for my tea. I'm thirsty."

"Go ahead and pour yourself a cup." The cook put a seedcake and a plate of scones next to the teapot.

"I do believe some of them are coming now," Mrs. Jeffries said as she slipped into her chair at the head of the table just as the back door opened. Within minutes, the others arrived and they tucked into their tea.

"Who would like to go first?" Mrs. Jeffries asked.

"I'll have a go," Wiggins volunteered, and when no one objected, he plunged ahead. He told them about his trip to the Black Swan. "But when I started askin' questions, the barman got right nasty. He told me to get out and mind my own business, that they didn't like nobs comin' round and stickin' their noses into that which didn't concern them."

"I hope you left at that point." Mrs. Goodge shoved the plate of scones toward him. "Doing our duty for justice is right and proper, but you were on your own over there and it's not in the best part of the city, is it."

"Uh, I did," Wiggins muttered. "I left."

"Did you go to find out about Gordon Redley, then?" Smythe asked. He knew the footman was telling only part of the tale. He'd seen Wiggins coming out of the Shepherd's Bush Station and followed him, hoping they could come back here together. But within a few seconds it was obvious something was wrong. The lad couldn't go ten steps without stopping and looking over his shoulder. The only reason he'd not seen Smythe was because he'd ducked behind a mover's cart. After that, Smythe had deliberately tried to stay out of Wiggins' line of sight. He'd seen the lad scurrying across the roads and dodging in and out of traffic as if he were being chased by the devil himself. Something or someone had scared the young man.

After his own experience today, Smythe could come to only one conclusion. This case was getting dangerous. He glanced at his wife, who was sitting serenely next to him and drinking her tea. Thank goodness her assignment had been safe. All she'd been asked to do was to find out a bit more about the woman Durant had threatened. Amanda was at home with their neighbor so he had no worries about his little one. Mrs. Cullins knew better than to let anyone into the house.

"Yeah, I did, but it was odd because . . ."

"Tell us what really happened," Smythe interrupted impatiently. "I know something did, Wiggins, because I followed you from the train station and you were actin' as skittish as a tomcat in a roomful of howling bulldogs"

Wiggins could tell by the determined expression on the coachman's face that he'd keep at it till he found out the truth. Maybe that was best. "I wanted to make sure I wasn't bein' followed," he blurted. "I didn't want them comin' 'ere and seein' where my people live. They're a bad lot at the Black Swan and I don't want them near any of you."

"Oh dear Lord." Mrs. Goodge's hand flew to her mouth. "Are you alright?

"I'm fine." He smiled at the elderly cook. They'd become close over the years and he didn't want her upset for no reason. But the best way to keep her safe, to keep them all safe, was to tell the truth. He understood that now. He needed for them to be on their guard. "I got away from 'em."

"What happened, Wiggins?" Mrs. Jeffries asked.

For a brief moment, Wiggins wasn't sure how to start, so he took a quick sip of tea. "Like I said, I went to the Black

Swan and I got there right after it opened. I looked about a bit and kept my ears open, hopin' that someone would mention this Mr. McConnell by name or something like that. But no one did and that's when I made my first mistake. I asked the barmaid if he was about the place." He smiled briefly. "I thought I was bein' clever, you know, pretendin' I knew 'im, but I wasn't sure if it was him because I'd not seen him for years. That sort of thing. But it didn't work. The girl just give me a funny smile and then sort of sauntered away. She didn't even ask me if I wanted a drink."

"What happened then?" Ruth prodded.

"You know 'ow you get a funny feelin' when something isn't right? I saw the girl go up to the barman and point at me. He said something to the men at the bar. I knew I 'ad to get out of there. So I left. I nipped out the back door of the saloon bar and thought I'd take a shortcut to the station through the mews behind the pub, but when I got back there, I saw a gang of toughs comin' at me. So I made a run for it and got away."

Everyone, save Mrs. Jeffries, started talking at once.

"Oh, Wiggins, how awful," Phyllis cried.

"I'll have their guts for garters," the cook yelled.

"Thank goodness you're a fast runner." Betsy blinked hard to hold back her tears.

"Clever of you to know when to make your move," Hatchet said.

"Nell's bells, maybe I oughta give you my peacemaker," Luty offered.

"I'm fine." Wiggins smiled self-consciously. "But I don't mind admittin' I was scared. There was four of them and only one of me."

"What time did this happen?" Mrs. Jeffries asked.

"Midmornin', right after the pubs opened," Wiggins said. "I've spent the rest of the day makin' sure that no one followed me back 'ere. I don't want any of them thugs knowin' where we live."

"We can take care of finding out about Gordon Redley some other time." Mrs. Jeffries spoke calmly but her heart was thumping so loudly she was surprised no one else could hear it. Wiggins could have been badly hurt or worse. Oh dear God, what had she done? She never meant for any of them to be at risk.

"But I did find out about 'im," Wiggins insisted. He grinned proudly. "Mind you, I kept lookin' over my shoulder, but even with doin' that, it didn't slow me down much. I went to that address on Pelham Road, and it's a proper office building. But you'll never guess what I found out."

"They'd never heard of him," Hatchet said softly. "The address was a fake."

"'Ow'd you know that?" Wiggins exclaimed.

"Because no one at the building where Andrew Morecomb supposedly works has ever heard of him, either."

CHAPTER 8

Edith Durant's solicitor had offices on the second floor of a commercial building in Islington. "Let's hope Mr. Neville can give us a few facts that might prove helpful," Witherspoon murmured to the constable as they followed Franklin Neville's clerk into his office.

"The police, sir," the clerk announced.

Franklin Neville came out from behind his desk with his hand outstretched. He was of medium height with thinning brown hair sprinkled with gray, hazel eyes, and a long, rather sharp nose. "Inspector Witherspoon, I presume," he said as they shook hands.

"I am, sir, and I take it you are Franklin Neville, the late Alice Robinson's solicitor."

He nodded. "I've been expecting you, sir. Had you not come today, I was going to go to seek you out."

"This is Constable Barnes," Witherspoon said.

Neville shook his hand as well and then motioned to the chairs in front of his desk. "Please sit down, gentlemen," he invited before taking his own seat. "I'm sure you've a number of questions for me."

Barnes laid the file box containing the ledger and the most recent witness statements onto the corner of the desk, sat down, and took out his notebook.

"Mr. Neville, you appear to know why we're here today, so I'll get right to my questions," Witherspoon began. "As you may know, Alice Robinson was actually a woman named Edith Durant."

"I only knew her as Alice Robinson," he replied. "I learned of her true identity when I read about her murder in the newspaper, and I must say, I was very surprised."

"What kind of legal work did you do for her?" Barnes asked.

"I handled the purchase of her property on Magdala Lane. It was a very straightforward transaction." He leaned forward, put his elbows on the desk, and clasped his hands together. "Actually, I only met her a few times so there's really not much I can tell you about her."

"How did you come to represent her?" Witherspoon asked. "Had you been recommended by someone she knew?"

"Not that I'm aware of, Inspector. She never said why she wanted me to represent her, she simply walked into the front office one day and asked my clerk for an appointment. As I said, the property purchase wasn't complicated so my contact with her was somewhat limited."

"Did you do any other legal work for her?" Witherspoon asked.

"No, I'm afraid not."

Barnes looked up from his notebook. "She didn't have a will?"

"I can't say for certain, Constable. All I can tell you is she never asked me to do one for her." He leaned back in his chair. "But that isn't to say she doesn't have one. She may have had another solicitor. Perhaps I shouldn't say this, because I didn't know her well at all, but in the few times we did meet, she struck me as a woman who was very self-reliant and somewhat protective of her privacy."

"How so?" Witherspoon asked.

"She didn't like to answer questions," he replied bluntly. "When she first approached me, she refused to give me her address. She only relented when I insisted. I must say, Inspector, I found her odd, to say the least. When she actually paid for the property, she walked in here with a suitcase full of money."

"You didn't find that suspicious?" Barnes asked incredulously. "Most people use a building society."

"That's true, but she wasn't the first of my clients to buy a property with cash," he admitted, "and as I said, she'd already made it clear she was in charge and that I was merely the hired help."

Witherspoon didn't know what to make of this. "You said, sir, that if we'd not come to see you, you were going to contact us. Did you have a specific reason?"

Neville frowned and glanced at the shelves of file boxes and law books on the wall by the door. "I'm not sure I ought to even mention this. It's probably nothing but it's bothered me ever since I read about her murder."

"What has, sir?" the inspector pressed.

"It wasn't really a legal matter, but she did come to see me once after the property matter was over and done with. It was sometime in February, probably close to the twentieth."

"Of this year?" Barnes asked quickly.

"Yes, she arrived without an appointment and demanded to see me. My clerk won't have her name in the book so I can't give you the exact day she was here. I had a few moments so I agreed to see her. She came into my office and it was obvious she was very upset. You must understand, the other times I'd seen her she was always very poised and self-confident, very much in control of her emotions."

"I take it that wasn't the situation this time," the inspector said.

"No, to put it bluntly, she was in a state. When I asked her what was wrong, why she'd come to see me, she began . . . well"—he shrugged—"there's no nice way to put it. She began babbling that someone in her house was trying to ruin her."

"Ruin her?" Barnes repeated. "How?"

"She claimed someone was playing malicious tricks on her. She was so upset that it took almost fifteen minutes to get her to calm down enough to explain what she meant."

"Had something specific happened that day?" Witherspoon guessed. "Was that why she was distraught?"

"Oh yes, Inspector, I'll get to that. This will make much more sense if I start from the beginning." He paused, and at Witherspoon's nod of assent, he continued speaking. "I first offered her a cup of tea—that generally helps people bring their emotions under control; it's difficult to be hysterical when you're sipping a nice cup of Assam—but she asked if I had any whiskey." He smiled, somewhat sheepishly. "I do. I keep a bottle in my desk for the occasional celebration with a grateful client, but you're not interested in my business practices. I poured her a whiskey and she tossed it back like a sailor, but it did the trick. She said the first time it happened, it never occurred to her that it wasn't some sort of mistake."

Barnes interrupted. "The first time what happened?"

"One of the tricks. The first time it was a theft at the house. Right after Christmas one of the tenants claimed his brand-new umbrella had been stolen, a few days later, another tenant claimed his watch was missing, and then Mrs. Robinson began receiving letters from the gasworks and the bank that she was past due on her monthly accounts yet she was certain she'd sent off letters with the payments. Then one of the tenants didn't pay his weekly rent, and when she confronted him about it, he claimed he had paid. Now let me explain, Mrs. Robinson had a very specific method for receiving her rent. She kept a stack of envelopes on the table in the foyer, and every week, the tenants were instructed to pay their rent in cash, put it in the envelope, and slip it under the door to her private quarters. The tenant claimed he'd done just that but she insisted she never got it. This was in the middle of January. Three weeks later, it happened again, and again the tenant swore he'd put the money under her door. The day she came to see me it had happened yet again only this time, all of the rents were gone yet every tenant claimed they'd paid. What's more, one of the tenants had a witness that he slipped the envelope under the door."

"Who was the witness?" Witherspoon asked.

"One of the maids. She verified the tenant's account of the matter and I suspect that's when Mrs. Robinson realized she was the victim of deliberate malicious mischief."

"Did she have any idea who might be responsible?" The inspector thought this case couldn't get any more difficult, but he'd been wrong.

"She didn't name names but she did tell me that she was certain it was either her neighbor or one of her tenants. Odd. When you think about it, most people always try to blame the servants when things go missing in a household."

"So now we know that at least two of the lodging house tenants weren't what they claimed to be," Mrs. Jeffries murmured.

"Three," Smythe said. "John Erskine is no more a respectable businessman than I'm the king of Siam."

"Cor blimey, what's goin' on 'ere?" Wiggins exclaimed. "None of 'em is what 'e's supposed to be."

"That's not quite true," Hatchet said. "Norman Teasdale is exactly what he appears to be. I spoke to the porter at his office building."

"That don't mean he ain't as crooked as the rest of them," Luty declared. "That's what we're all thinkin', isn't it. They're a bunch of criminals and Edith Durant was chargin' them an arm and leg to hide out at her lodgin' house."

"That would explain why they were willing to pay more than double the going rate for the accommodations," Ruth murmured. "And why there were so few servants there."

"Teasdale is exactly what he claims to be. I didn't just

take the porter's word, I spoke to the lad that takes his daily order to the telegraph office, and I also had a quick word with one of the clerks at the customs house." Hatchet shot Luty a triumphant grin. "So even if Durant's other tenants are part of some sort of criminal gang, and I'm not sure I agree with your assessment of that matter, I very much doubt that Teasdale is part of it. From what I learned today, he simply wouldn't have time—he works too hard."

Luty's eyes narrowed. "There ain't nuthin' wrong with my *assessment of that matter*, there's only one reason people ain't who they're supposed to be: They've got somethin' to hide."

"They're crooks, that's for sure," Smythe interjected. "Wiggins isn't the only one who 'ad a spot of trouble today."

"Oh God, are you alright?" Betsy swiveled in her seat and began to run her hands up and down her husband's arms. "Were you hurt?"

"I'm fine, sweetheart." He grabbed one of her hands and gave it a squeeze. "Stop your frettin' now. I'm right as rain."

Betsy took a deep breath and sat back. But when he went to pull away, she clasped his fingers and held them tightly.

"Are you certain you're alright?" Mrs. Jeffries sucked in a lungful of air as her stomach contracted in fear. Dear God, first Wiggins and now Smythe. She'd never forgive herself if any of them were hurt because she sent them out on the hunt.

He gave her a cheeky grin. "'Course I am. I wasn't ever in any real danger," he lied. He told them about following Erskine and being surprised when he wound up in Whitechapel. When he got to the part about the pub, he skipped

90 percent of the specifics and merely said he'd needed to get out of there fast and that he'd been followed.

Mrs. Goodge frowned in confusion. "Who followed you? Erskine?"

Smythe shook his head. "No, it was a thug he'd paid."

"So both of us 'ad to make a run for it today." Wiggins seemed quite cheered by the news.

"You could say that." Smythe laughed.

Mrs. Jeffries knew he'd left out a number of pertinent details and she'd most certainly tax him about them later. "So now we know that at least three of Durant's four lodgers aren't respectable businessmen."

"Clever of you to have us take a closer look at them," Luty declared.

"How did your day go, madam?" Hatchet inquired. "Find out anything useful about the neighbor?"

"Not yet, but I'm hopin' tomorrow will be a better day." She turned to Mrs. Jeffries. "I didn't have any luck findin' out about that Mrs. Travers."

"Neither did I," Ruth added.

"I'd like to believe that she isn't important," Mrs. Jeffries said. "But she might be. Even with all we've discovered about the lodging house tenants, Mrs. Travers is the only person who we know had a direct confrontation with the victim. Edith Durant threatened to kill her, and we don't know that Mrs. Travers didn't take her seriously and decide to strike the first blow. I don't think it's likely, but it is a possibility, and right now, we've got to investigate every aspect of this case."

"I'll keep at it," Luty promised.

"As will I." Ruth glanced at the clock on the pine

sideboard. The Reverend Pontefract was coming to dinner tonight and she wanted to get home soon. She had some very specific instructions she wanted to give her butler.

"My bit's not near as excitin' as Smythe and Wiggins." Mrs. Goodge gave the footman a good frown. The lad should know to be more careful. If one of those ruffians had hurt him, it would have broken her heart. Smythe caused her a bit less worry. He was a strong man and could hold his own in a bout of fisticuffs, but he needed to take care as well. As soon as she could get either of them alone, she'd give them both a piece of her mind. "I had a chat with one of my old colleagues, Letty Sommerville. She was the one that used to have tea with Mrs. Nimitz, the Christopher housekeeper. Now I know that those original murders were solved, but I thought that maybe Letty would remember something useful about Edith Durant, you know, something that might help us figure out what she's been up to all these years."

"Did she remember anything?" Wiggins asked eagerly.

The cook made a face. "Not really. All she said was that the Christopher family sold the house to pay the legal bills, and there was gossip that Karlotta Christopher had used the money to bribe a clergyman to write a letter to the Home Office in an attempt to get his sentence commuted to prison rather than hanging."

"You can do that?" Wiggins looked scandalized. "You can really do that?"

"You can indeed," Mrs. Jeffries said. "Why do you think so many more poor people get hung than rich ones? Once the public scrutiny is over, the Home Office frequently commutes sentences."

"But Christopher was 'ung." Smythe took a quick sip of tea. "And his family weren't peasants. They were related to the aristocracy."

"But like many in the upper class, they had no money, which was one of the reasons Christopher was legally married to Hilda, not Edith. What's more, if you'll recall, one of his victims was a clergyman," Mrs. Jeffries reminded them. "So I doubt the clergyman's letter was very effective." She didn't want to undermine the cook's information, but she wanted to concentrate on the here and now, not the past. "Is there anything else?" she asked Mrs. Goodge.

"Only that Karlotta Christopher had hysterics when her brother was sentenced and screamed at the judge that she'd have her revenge. Mind you, I've not heard of any judges being murdered in the last few years so I doubt anyone took her seriously."

"Well, it is getting late and we must move on," Mrs. Jeffries said. "Who would like to go next?"

"I found out something." Phyllis told them about her meeting with Annie Linden. As usual, she repeated the conversation almost word for word, taking care not to leave out anything no matter how insignificant it might seem. "I felt sorry for the poor girl. Even though she didn't like Edith Durant much, she really needed her job."

"Maybe she shouldn't 'ave drunk all that gin," Wiggins suggested. "A whole bottle? Cor blimey, maybe that's why she slept through the bell."

"She claims she didn't drink it all at once," Phyllis said. "Besides, from the way she talked about her life, I don't think a few drinks would put her to sleep."

"Poor thing," Betsy said softly. "It's hard to be out on your own like that."

"I felt sorry for her, too." Phyllis reached for the teapot and helped herself to another cup. "That's all I learned today,"

"You're right about her," Betsy said. "Annie was used to drinking. I didn't find any of Edith Durant's previous servants to talk to, but I did have a chat with the barmaid at the pub where Annie Linden and Mrs. Fremont did their drinking." She told them about her chat with Minnie McNab.

"Annie never mentioned the lodgers coming home in different clothes to me," Phyllis interrupted.

"She probably wouldn't when she was sober," Betsy said. "According to Minnie, both Mrs. Fremont and Annie were scared of their mistress. The only time they talked about the strange goings-on at the lodging house was when they'd been drinking. But that's not all I found out. Just as I started to leave, Minnie told me that right before Christmas, there was another woman who went around the neighborhood asking questions about Alice Robinson."

There was a nudge in the back of Mrs. Jeffries' mind, but it was gone as quickly as it had come. "A woman? What did she look like? What kind of questions did she ask?"

"Minnie said she was very ordinary, well dressed, and well-spoken. She had brown hair and looked to be middle-aged. She gave Minnie some story about looking for a long-lost cousin as she asked her about the lodging house and the woman who owned it. When she left, Minnie remarked to one of her regulars that she didn't believe the woman's story, and he told her this woman had been around the neighborhood for a couple of days asking questions about Alice Robinson."

"Would she recognize the woman if she saw her again?" Ruth asked.

"I don't know. Just then her boss came in so she stopped talking."

"Maybe it was someone from Edith's past," Mrs. Goodge speculated. "Carl Christopher probably wasn't the only person who ended up paying the price for her crimes."

"I'll bet there are dozens who wanted to see her six feet under," Luty added.

Ruth glanced at the clock again. "If no one has anything else to report, I really must get home. I've guests coming for dinner," she said. She told herself it really wasn't a lie; nonetheless, she felt terribly guilty because the only guest was Reginald Pontefract and she'd deliberately intimated she had guests plural rather than singular. But she didn't want dear Gerald finding out she'd invited him. "And I must have a word with my cook and butler." She was going to make sure Everton, her devoted butler, stayed close tonight.

Mrs. Jeffries looked around the table, but no one spoke up so she said, "I think we're done. We'll meet again tomorrow at our usual time. I'll be able to give all of you a full report. Let's hope the inspector and Constable Barnes have had as interesting a day as we have."

Everyone scraped back their chairs and prepared to leave. Hatchet helped Luty on with her cloak, Betsy and Smythe bundled themselves up in their coats, and Wiggins got Fred's leash and clipped it on his collar. He straightened up and looked around the room for Ruth. "I'll walk you home," he offered.

But she'd already disappeared down the hall and out the back door. "Cor blimey, Lady Cannonberry was in a 'urry. I guess her company must be right important."

Witherspoon came in the front door a few minutes after the meeting ended. "To be honest, Mrs. Jeffries"—he handed her his bowler—"I simply couldn't face going back to the lodging house and asking more questions. It's been a very distressing day."

"Oh dear, sir." She quietly tried to catch her breath. When his hansom pulled up just as Luty and Hatchet were slipping out the back door, she'd raced up the back steps and, at her age, there was a price to be paid. "You could really do with a glass of sherry. What's that under your arm, sir?"

"It's the ledger we found in the secret compartment of Edith Durant's wardrobe." He handed it to her as he unbuttoned his coat. "Thus far no one can make heads nor tails of it. Chief Superintendent Barrows had some of his brightest chaps take a look, but none of them had any idea what it meant nor did Inspector Rogers or his lads. We were going to drop it off at the Ladbroke Road Station to see if any of our constables might have an idea, but then it got so late and Constable Barnes pointed out that the evening hours are the busiest at the station, so we thought we'd wait until tomorrow." He took off the coat and tossed it onto the peg under his bowler. "We even had Edith Durant's solicitor take a look at it, but he had no idea what the entries meant. A nice glass of sherry sounds wonderful."

She tucked the book under her arm and led the way to the drawing room. "You're early, sir, so it'll be a while before dinner is ready."

"Excellent. Perhaps after I've had a sherry, I'll nip over to Lady Cannonberry's and spend a few moments with her. I've not seen her in several days." He followed her into the room and flopped into his chair.

Mrs. Jeffries put the ledger on a corner table and went to the liquor cabinet on the far side of the room. She didn't like the sound of that. She had the distinct feeling that Ruth wouldn't welcome the inspector's company tonight. There had been something in Ruth's expression today that suggested she was worried or anxious about her mysterious dinner companions. But then again, perhaps she was imagining things. Perhaps she'd misinterpreted Ruth's face, and instead of anxiety, she'd seen anticipation.

On the other hand, why hadn't Ruth invited the inspector? Since the two of them had become close, Ruth always asked him to play host when she entertained at home and to escort her if she'd been invited out. But she'd not done that this time.

Pouring their drinks, she turned back to Witherspoon. "I saw Lady Cannonberry in the garden this afternoon and she mentioned she was having dinner guests tonight." She handed him his glass and took the chair across from him.

His smile disappeared and his shoulders slumped. "Perhaps it is best not to barge in, then. I wonder who her guests might be? She generally invites me when she's having a dinner party."

"It might be the ladies from her women's group," Mrs. Jeffries said quickly. She hated seeing the hurt look in his eyes. "You know how Lady Cannonberry seeks to insure you're never embarrassed by her, uh, political activities."

"But there is nothing wrong with her working for

women's suffrage," he replied. "I think women ought to vote and have the same rights as men. Still, I understand what you're saying. If it's a party of ladies, it would be awkward for me to turn up unannounced—not that I'd ever do such a thing."

"Of course you wouldn't, sir," she said. "Tell me about your day, sir. Any progress?"

Witherspoon took a sip of his sherry. "It's difficult to determine," he replied honestly. "The day started out well enough. We went back to the lodging house and spoke to Norman Teasdale."

Mrs. Jeffries listened carefully and occasionally broke in to his recitation to ask a question or clarify a point. "So he was reluctant to give you the name of his customer so you could verify his whereabouts?"

"Yes, but he finally told us he was at the Armitage Hotel. Before we went off to the Yard, I sent Constable Griffiths over to confirm his story so we'll know one way or another by tomorrow."

"It would be useful for you to have one person from that household that you can strike off your suspect list," she murmured. After what Hatchet had told them today, she was fairly certain that Teasdale was exactly who he claimed to be, not that that meant he was innocent of murdering Durant. But she needed a way to get the inspector to look at the other three tenants, the ones who definitely weren't what they appeared to be.

"That would be very useful indeed."

"Were you able to speak to the other tenants? I know you wanted to find out where they were at the time of the murder."

"No, unfortunately, we were summoned to the Yard." He sighed. "Chief Superintendent Barrows wasn't in a very good mood."

"But surely he didn't expect you to have it solved in three days?"

"He was hoping we would." Witherspoon smiled faintly and told her about his visit to New Scotland Yard.

Across the garden, Ruth was in earnest conversation with her maid, Abigail, and her butler, Everton. "Do you both understand what I need you to do?"

Abigail nodded. "Yes, ma'am, Dulcie will bring the courses up on a cart, and I'm to serve from the cart, not from the kitchen."

"That's correct, and what else?"

"I'm to stand inside the dining room by the sideboard while you and the gentleman dine."

"Excellent, Abigail. I know it's burdensome but I'd rather not be alone with my dinner guest."

"I'll be serving the wine with each course, madam," Everton said somberly. "And I shall make sure you're not alone with this gentleman."

Ruth knew her servants must think her behavior odd, but she really didn't want to be alone with the Reverend Reginald Pontefract. He might be a man of the cloth, but she didn't trust him. More important, having people in the room while they had dinner made it seem less disloyal to her dear Gerald. "I know this must sound strange."

"Nonsense, madam." Everton's austere face cracked into a smile. "We're here to do what you ask of us."

"But I hate taking you away from your own dinner."

Ruth didn't stand on ceremony, and when she took her meals, she didn't insist her servants serve course after course. Instead, her food was brought up to her morning room and put under chafing dishes on the cabinet while her household staff enjoyed theirs downstairs. "You've both worked hard and I'm sure you're tired."

"It's no trouble, ma'am," Abigail said quickly. "We'd do anything for you. Should I put the sugar hammer in my apron pocket just in case?"

"In case of what?" Ruth wasn't sure she wanted to hear the answer. She'd taken Abigail in and trained her as a maid to keep the girl from being sold to a brothel in Stepney, and for the most part, it had been a successful enterprise. However, there were moments when Abigail's less-than-perfect upbringing on the streets of the East End superseded all of Ruth's patient instructions on how a young woman should behave.

"You know, ma'am, in case he tries to get too familiar with you. I can clout him on the back of the head. The sugar hammer'll be good for that. Stop him right in his tracks."

"Chief Superintendent Barrows confirmed that none of the victim's family had a connection to Highgate Cemetery?" Mrs. Jeffries exclaimed.

"Yes, it was rather embarrassing that we'd not checked that ourselves, but none of the Durants, the Claypools, or the Rileys have anyone buried there. So it appears the killer somehow lured her there. But the question is, how? Neither the servants nor the tenants reported a telegram or a letter or even a note being delivered."

"Perhaps it has something to do with the person that was heard arguing with her the night before the murder?" she suggested.

"That's possible, I suppose." He took another sip. "I just wish we knew that individual's identity."

"But you do believe that the report is correct?" Mrs. Jeffries asked. "You believe that Mr. Erskine was telling the truth when he claimed to have heard the argument? You don't think he might have been lying? No one else in the household seems to have heard the quarrel." She wanted to sow a few seeds of doubt about John Erskine. As far as she was concerned, after what had happened to Smythe, nothing the man told the police could be trusted. Muddying the waters was an easy tactic when you were trying to get the police to focus their attention elsewhere.

He paused for a moment, his drink halfway to his mouth, and then took a quick sip. "I'd not thought of that. Even if the other tenants were out, surely one of the servants should have overheard the argument." He put his glass down. "I think we'll need to have another chat with Mr. Erskine tomorrow."

"Will you be speaking to him at his office?" She was fairly certain the High Holborn office address was as false as the ones supplied by Morecomb and Redley. "As you always say, sir, always confirm before you accuse."

His eyebrows lifted a fraction. "Yes, yes, I do."

She could see he was confused and struggling mightily not to show it. "It's good of you, sir, to spare the servants any embarrassment by confirming with them before going to his office to confront him. They're stuck living there so it might make it a bit awkward for them if Erskine got nasty about it. Unless, of course, one of them did actually overhear the argument."

Relief was evident in his eyes. "I try to be sensitive about this sort of situation. The servants are nervous enough about what's going to happen to them. Carrie Durridge, the housemaid, has dogged my footsteps whenever I'm at the lodging house."

"What about the other tenants, sir?" She got up, picked up his glass, went to the cupboard, and poured him another drink. "Have you been able to confirm their accounts or their whereabouts at the time of the murder?" She needed him to come to the same conclusion that she and the others had reached today, namely, that three of the four men weren't what they appeared to be. She'd make sure to tell the constable tomorrow morning, but it never hurt to nudge the inspector in that direction as well.

"The tenants all claim they were with customers that morning, which makes it very awkward. One doesn't want to unduly embarrass innocent businessmen by barging into places where they do business and asking questions, but I'm afraid it can't be helped. I'd have done it today but we were interrupted by being called to the Yard."

She handed him his sherry and took her seat. "I'm sure you'll be very discreet when you interview their customers."

"After we left the Yard, we went to see the solicitor, Franklin Neville." He took a sip. "She didn't have a will."

"Who will inherit her estate? Oh, silly question. It'll be her relatives, won't it. "

"Mr. Neville was very pleased when we told him that Edith Durant did indeed have relatives. We passed along the names of her cousins, which, I suspect, are the only family she had left. Having the information will save him a great deal of time and effort. He won't have to advertise now. He also told us something else, something very interesting. Neville didn't do any additional legal work for the woman he knew as Alice Robinson, but she did come to see him last month." He described the last meeting the solicitor had with the victim.

Mrs. Jeffries listened carefully, forcing her mind to stay still as she absorbed all the details of his narrative. When he finished, she said, "She told him she suspected whoever was behind the tricks was one of her tenants?"

"Or her neighbor, Mrs. Travers, though I find that difficult to believe. Mrs. Travers would have no way of knowing when the tenants paid their rent, nor did she have a way into the house."

"She could have had a key," Mrs. Jeffries suggested. "Were the locks changed when Edith Durant bought the house? Neighbors sometime have keys to one another's homes."

"We'll definitely have another word with her," he replied. "But I find it difficult to believe that she's the culprit. Of course, stranger things have happened."

Ruth forced herself not to flinch as Reginald Pontefract took her arm and escorted her into the dining room. She was finding it more and more difficult to be civil to the man. For the past hour, they'd been in her drawing room while he drank far more sherry than was considered polite. She'd assumed their predinner drink would last ten minutes and hadn't thought she'd need Abigail or Everton. But she'd been wrong. Reginald Pontefract liked his liquor and one glass of sherry wasn't enough.

She wouldn't have minded him having as many as he liked except that he'd spent the whole time lecturing her on a woman's place. Attempting to argue with him was useless; he'd barely let her get a word in edgewise. He quoted Scripture, he cited allegedly expert medical doctors and their absurd theories about female hysteria, and he had the gall to insinuate that it was a man's duty to make sure women were treated with "a firm hand and corporal discipline when they strayed." Worst of all, he did it all while fawning all over her. Patting her hand, touching her arm, moving so close she had to duck to one side to avoid bumping his nose. Luckily Everton, realizing something was amiss, had barged in rather unceremoniously and announced that dinner was served.

As he seated her, she ducked her head to hide a smile. It was her turn now, she thought as Pontefract took his seat.

"What a lovely room, Lady Cannonberry," he exclaimed.

Dinner was being served in the cavernous dining room that she used only if she was hosting a dinner for her women's suffrage group or some of her late husband's relatives. When she and Gerald dined together, the meal was served in front of a roaring fire in her cozy and intimate morning room. But cozy and intimate were most definitely not on the agenda tonight. Not after what she'd just endured. This dinner would be impersonal, formal, and chaperoned by both her maid and her butler.

The long table was covered in stiff white damask and two places were set with elegant blue and gold china, crystal water and wineglasses, and heavy silverware that dated from the previous century.

"Thank you, Reverend Pontefract." She nodded at Abigail to serve the first course.

"You mustn't be so formal." He clasped her wrist. "We're old friends and I've told you to call me Reginald."

"Of course." She smiled stiffly as she extricated her hand from beneath his fingers. "I hope you like potato and leek soup."

"I'm sure it will be delicious." He hiccupped softly and then giggled. "Do forgive me, my dear. It was that excellent sherry."

She said nothing as the soup was served and the wine poured, and then Abigail and Everton took their places on each side of the huge mahogany sideboard.

Pontefract watched them with a slight frown but said nothing as he picked up his spoon.

He scooped up the soup and ate it greedily. The moment his mouth was full, Ruth pounced. "I was so disappointed to find out that you knew nothing about the woman who was murdered in Highgate Cemetery. I'd so hoped we could talk about it."

His eyebrows rose and his Adam's apple bobbled as he hastily gulped his food. "I hardly think that's a suitable subject," he began but she cut him off.

"Don't be silly, of course it is," she insisted with a bright smile. "You're a clergyman and murder is a sin. I should think you'd not only want to discuss it, but speak to your flock about it as well."

"That's not a fitting topic for church."

She interrupted. "What, sin isn't a fitting subject?

Honestly, Reginald, what kind of clergyman are you? My father never shied away from a good, heartfelt sermon on sin and its consequences." She tut-tutted disapprovingly. "Really, Reginald, this happened in your community. I find it alarming that you're not more interested. Surely you have an obligation to know what's happening in your neighborhood. How can your congregation understand evil if you shy away from the subject?"

His mouth opened in shock, and he put his spoon down, then quickly retrieved it, scooped up another spoonful of soup, and shoved it in his mouth. "I'm not shying away from evil and I didn't say I wasn't interested," he finally snapped. "I merely don't think it suitable conversation."

"Why not? Murder is certainly more interesting than the weather." Turning the tables on him, she reached over and patted his arm. "But I do understand if you're not comfortable discussing important social issues like murder and their effect on our community. I should have guessed, of course. You have such a quaint, old-fashioned understanding of both the Scriptures and the current social ideas about half the human race."

"You mean women?" His face was red and his mouth a flat, angry line. He grabbed his wineglass and took a huge gulp.

Ruth wasn't sure, but she thought she heard a stifled snicker and wondered if it was Everton or Abigail. She knew she wasn't turning the other cheek and loving her enemy, but at the moment she didn't care. She'd ask the Almighty for forgiveness later. Right now, she wanted Pontefract so riled he'd forget his ridiculous sensibilities and talk about the people in his congregation. Someone had to know something. His church was the closest to the lodging house and she was determined to find at least one useful fact from this miserable evening.

She ignored his comment about women and focused on the matter at hand. It was obvious he'd like nothing more than to take control of the conversation and she wasn't going to let him. "I'm not being critical of you." She smiled sweetly. "Some men are simply too delicate to discuss such things."

"I'm not delicate just because I'm a clergyman." He took another gulp of wine, and this time he drained the glass. He waved it in the air.

Everton lifted the wine bottle out of the ice bucket and took his time coming to the table. He refilled the glass and went back to his spot.

"Of course, it's not because you're a clergyman." She laughed. "As you know, my father was a clergyman and he had a most robust, manly constitution."

"I do, too," Reginald cried. "I'm robust and manly."

"My neighbor, Inspector Witherspoon, and I talk about his cases frequently. I do apologize, Reginald, I shouldn't have brought the matter up. You're not the sort of vicar who gets involved with his congregation, so I shouldn't have expected you to know anyone who had a connection to Alice Robinson's lodging house."

"I didn't say I didn't know anyone who had a connection to that poor, sinful woman," he insisted. "I do, I do know someone."

"Really, Reginald, you don't have to say such things to impress me." She took a delicate spoonful of soup and ate it.

"But I do know someone. Her name is Lavinia Swanson and she was the last person to see Alice Robinson alive."

Mrs. Jeffries put the lantern and the ledger on the kitchen table. She debated making herself a cup of tea but then thought better of it. She didn't want to wake Mrs. Goodge. The cook was a light sleeper and would insist on trying to help. She knew the door to Mrs. Goodge's quarters was ajar because Samson was sitting on Fred's rug by the cooker. The fat old tabby usually stayed with the cook, but sometimes he liked to roam at night.

She wanted to examine the ledger uninterrupted, so she'd waited till the house was quiet. Sitting down, she opened it to the first page and began to read.

It didn't take long to reach the end, so she went through it again and then again, hoping that something would make sense. But it didn't. Some of the entries were obvious references to nursery rhymes, but other than that, she hadn't a clue what it meant.

Closing the cover, she stared across the room at the window over the sink to give her tired eyes a rest. This case wasn't going well at all. She couldn't decide whether they had too many facts or not enough. Fact: Three out of four of the lodging house tenants weren't what they appeared to be. Ordinary businessmen didn't set thugs on people they thought were following them nor did they have fake office addresses.

Fact: Edith Durant had threatened to kill her neighbor whom she accused of spying on her while she was in her garden. Fact: She'd been murdered with a red cord. Fact: She'd been murdered in broad daylight in a public cemetery.

Fact: She went to Scotland once a month to see a relative who didn't exist. Fact: She charged double the going rate for her rooms and then let them sit empty if she didn't like the applicant.

But facts alone are useless, she thought. They are nothing but a list unless they come together in some sort of discernible pattern or theory. She was missing something, something that was right under her nose. But what was it?

CHAPTER 9

———

"I hope the constable isn't overwhelmed by all the information." Mrs. Jeffries put a pot of tea on the table. "This time might be very difficult for him. No matter how many informants he has, he couldn't possibly have found out everything we passed along to him this morning."

Mrs. Goodge put the empty kettle back on the cooker top. "Don't worry so about it. He's a sharp one is our constable. He'll find a way. Were you able to understand what was written in the ledger?"

"No, the best I could come up with was the nursery rhyme names must refer to individuals, but the rest of the entries were meaningless"

"She wasn't murdered for the ledger, then," the cook mused.

"What makes you say that?"

"If Scotland Yard, Y Division, Inspector Witherspoon,

Constable Barnes, and even you can't make sense of it, then it's useless to anyone but the dead woman. If no one knows what the entries mean, it couldn't be used for blackmail, and if you can't understand the entries themselves, then even if they point to a pot of gold, no one but Edith Durant could find it." She draped a clean tea towel over a bowl of dough and put it on the counter next to the cooker to let it rise.

"That's possible, I suppose, but perhaps the killer would have understood the entries," Mrs. Jeffries suggested. "In which case, acquiring the volume would be a reason for murder. Oh, bother, I don't know what I'm on about." She flopped down in her chair. "I simply can't seem to come up with any reasonable ideas or theories about this case. I'm afraid that in one real sense Edith Durant will be the one who genuinely got away."

"Nonsense. You say this sort of thing in every single one of our cases." She yanked out her chair and sat down. "So stop your fretting and wait for it to happen. It always does, Hepzibah."

Mrs. Jeffries would have argued with her but they heard Wiggins and Phyllis coming down the stairs just as the back door opened.

Betsy, holding a smiling Amanda Belle, appeared under the archway in the kitchen. "Smythe is going to be a bit late." She advanced toward the table, holding the baby out to the cook. "He had an unexpected visitor and he shuffled me off because he said it was one of his sources. Here, you better take her for a cuddle because I saw Luty and Hatchet coming in the back gate."

"Of course I want my darling." Mrs. Goodge settled the child on her lap as the others arrived and coats, scarves, cloaks, and hats were hung up on the coat tree.

"You'd better make sure I git my turn with the baby," Luty warned them as she sat down. Amanda gave her a huge grin and the elderly American laughed in delight. "She's happy to see her old godmother."

"You're not old, Luty," Betsy said. "And she's always delighted to see you. Smythe won't be here until later, but he said to go ahead and start the meeting."

"Oh, good." Ruth poured herself a cup of tea. "I've a meeting this morning that I must attend, but I have news for all of you as well."

"You found out something last night?" Mrs. Jeffries said.

"From my gu . . . er . . . one of my dinner guests," she corrected quickly.

"I found out somethin', too," Luty declared.

"Excellent, ladies, but do let me share the information I heard from the inspector last night," Mrs. Jeffries said. She looked at Betsy. "I hate starting without Smythe, but it appears we've a lot of territory to cover this morning."

"Go ahead, Mrs. Jeffries. He might be a long time."

Mrs. Jeffries gave them a complete report on everything she and Mrs. Goodge had learned from both Witherspoon and Constable Barnes. "Alright, Ruth, you're the one with an appointment this morning, so why don't you go first."

"I don't know if it is particularly useful information," Ruth began, "but I found out something about the woman who was the last person to see Edith Durant or, as she knew her, Alice Robinson alive."

"Lavinia Swanson," Phyllis murmured. "She's the one who saw Edith Durant just before she went into the cemetery, right? She's a neighbor of some sort."

"And she's the only person we know of in the neighborhood who had a social connection to Edith Durant," Mrs. Jeffries said. "They had tea together."

"They did and it was always at Lavinia Swanson's home," Ruth continued. "Mrs. Swanson is a member of St. Peters, and the vicar told me that she, well, I'm not sure how to describe it, but she earns a bit of money by taking care of houses for people who have gone on holiday."

"Wouldn't they have servants to do that sort of thing?" Betsy asked. "I mean, I'm assuming that she only does this for people who can pay her."

"Your assumption is right, but these days, so many households take their servants with them when they leave or the servants take the opportunity to go home and visit their own families."

"What does she do for 'em?" Wiggins asked.

"A variety of tasks." Ruth wanted to explain it so it made sense to them. She'd come up with a theory last night, but in the cold light of day, she was losing confidence in her idea. "She goes in to water their plants, check to make certain the windows are locked and haven't been disturbed, and then when the family is ready to come home, she goes in and opens up the house and restocks the larders."

Mrs. Jeffries smiled slowly. "You think the reason that Edith Durant befriended this woman was so she could know which house in the neighborhood was empty?"

Relieved, Ruth nodded. "That was my idea. Reverend

Pontefract mentioned that Mrs. Swanson wasn't a particularly interesting person and was a bit of a busybody."

"Not the kind of person you'd think Edith Durant would pick for a friend," the cook agreed. "So that means that she must have had a reason for cultivating Mrs. Swanson."

"Was Edith Durant breakin' into the empty 'ouses and stealin'?" Wiggins asked.

"I don't think so," Ruth replied. "But from what we learned yesterday about most of her tenants, I suspect it was the sort of information she'd pass along to them."

Mrs. Jeffries wanted to call a halt to their speculating, but in truth, it made sense. "That whole neighborhood has been plagued with burglaries," she said. "But we mustn't assume it's the tenants that are responsible."

"We can't assume they aren't, either," Hatchet said

"And it does fit together nicely," she agreed. "A falling-out amongst thieves would explain her murder, if, of course, we can ascertain which thief she fell out with." Yet even as she said the words, there was something about the whole situation that rang just a bit hollow.

"Before you all go solvin' this case now, can I tell ya what I found out?" Luty grumbled. She glanced at the cook. "And are you goin' to hog the little one during the whole meeting? I want to hold her, too."

"I've only had her for a few minutes," the cook complained. "But if you're goin' to make a fuss, you can take a turn." She handed Amanda to Wiggins, who chucked her under the chin before settling her in the elderly American's lap.

"Good, now I can talk without worryin' about missin'

time with my sweetie pie." Luty dropped a quick kiss on
the baby's head.

"Do get on with it, madam." Hatchet frowned impatiently. "Time is getting on and we've a lot to do today."

"Alright, alright, keep your shirt on, Hatchet. Last night I
was out at a dinner party, and luckily, one of my sources was
there, too. Even better, he had some right good news for me."

"Oh, do tell, madam," Hatchet muttered. "We're all waiting with bated breath for your no doubt important revelation."

"You're jist jealous 'cause I found out somethin' last
night and you didn't." Luty cackled in delight.

"What did you find out, Luty?" Mrs. Jeffries asked quickly.

"You know how you just told us that the victim didn't
have a will? Well, maybe Alice Robinson didn't have one,
but Edith Durant sure did and you'll never guess who gits
her estate." She paused dramatically for a moment. "She
left everything to Carl Christopher."

Carrie Durridge was dusting the spindles on the staircase
when Witherspoon came up from the kitchen. "Mr. Redley's waiting in the drawing room for you." She poked her
feather duster toward the closed doors. "He's in a bit of a
state, sir."

"Thank you, Miss Durridge." He went inside.

Gordon Redley was sitting on the settee. He gave With-
erspoon a steely glare. "How long is this going to take,
Inspector? I've an appointment this morning. Furthermore,
I don't appreciate the servants ordering me about."

"It wasn't the servants ordering you about, sir." Witherspoon sat down across from him. "It was the Metropolitan
Police. We're the ones that asked Miss Durridge to tell you

to be available for questioning. I thought you'd be more comfortable here, Mr. Redley. However, if you'd like, we can go to the station."

"Get on with it." Redley leapt up and stalked to the fireplace. "Just get on with it. Though I don't know what you expect to find out, I've already told you everything I know about that woman."

Witherspoon studied him for a moment. Redley didn't look good. The lines around his mouth seemed to have deepened overnight, his face was gaunt, his tie was crooked, his shirt bulged out over the top of his waistcoat, and there was a definite tic in his right eye. "Mr. Redley, the last time we spoke, you claimed you overheard an argument between Mrs. Robinson and her neighbor, Mrs. Travers."

"That's right. What of it?"

"There's no nice way to put this, Mr. Redley, but your account of that dispute differed substantially from what Mrs. Travers told us. Would you care to amend your earlier statement?"

His eyes narrowed suspiciously. "I may have been mistaken in one or two of the details, but I stand by what I said earlier."

"Mrs. Travers claims she made no mention whatsoever of dragging Mrs. Robinson through the court. Yet in your account, you mentioned you'd heard it twice."

He moved back to the settee and sat down. "Has it occurred to you, Inspector, that it might be Mrs. Travers who needs to amend her statement? Why would you believe her and not me?"

"Because her account of the incident was verified by other witnesses."

"You mean her maid." He snorted derisively. "Servants will say what they're told to say by their masters."

"It wasn't just the maid, it was also the man from the gasworks," Witherspoon said, "and he'd have no reason to lie to us. So I ask you, again, Mr. Redley, would you care to amend your statement?"

Redley's eye jerked furiously. "Alright, you've made your point, Inspector. I didn't overhear the argument."

"Why did you lie about it?"

"Because I knew she'd had an argument with Mrs. Travers, and I didn't wish to embarrass myself by admitting how I actually learned about it. It seemed more dignified to pretend I'd overheard the quarrel."

Witherspoon didn't believe him. "How did you find out about it?"

"I was eavesdropping, Inspector. I heard them talking about it," he admitted. "Her and Norman Teasdale. They were in Teasdale's room and the door was open an inch or two. I spied on them through the crack and I saw her pacing like a madwoman back and forth. Teasdale kept trying to calm her down, but she was beyond reason. She kept babbling that now she knew who'd been playing such malicious tricks on her and she'd make her sorry. She'd make her pay."

"You mean the thefts and the rent envelopes that disappeared from her room?" Witherspoon said. "Why didn't you mention any of this before, Mr. Redley? We specifically asked if anything unusual had been going on, and no one in the household thought to tell us that an umbrella, a watch, and a substantial amount of money had been taken."

Redley rubbed his face. "That was stupid. I should have told you."

"Again, sir, why didn't you?"

"Because once she was dead, I didn't think it mattered. I thought she was the one doing it. For God's sake, Inspector, everyone in the house thought she was lying about tricks being played on her. The woman was incredibly greedy. She was quite capable of stealing from her tenants and then pretending she'd not got the rent money."

"Then why did you stay here?" Witherspoon pressed. "She charged double the going rate for very mediocre accommodations, her housekeeping was certainly below standards, and you've admitted you thought her capable of thievery."

"I stayed for the same reasons the others did. She left us alone to do our work." He got up again. "My work takes me all over Europe and I needed a room where I could come and go as I pleased. Someplace that could accommodate my late evenings with customers."

"Where were you on the morning the woman you knew as Alice Robinson was murdered?"

"I was with a woman, Inspector, a married woman."

"I take it your relationship with this person is, uh . . . intimate?" Witherspoon knew he was blushing.

"If it was innocent, I wouldn't have found it necessary to try and hide it." Redley sighed. "I didn't want to cause her any difficulties. Her husband has a terrible temper, and if he found out about us, he'd . . . he'd . . . oh dear God, I don't even like to think what he'd do."

"We'll be as discreet as possible, Mr. Redley, but I must have her name and address."

"Can you go there in the afternoon? He's gone then," Redley pleaded. "Please, it could be a matter of life or death."

"I've a very reliable constable I can send."

"A constable," he cried.

Witherspoon held up his hand. "Don't worry, Mr. Redley, Constable Griffiths will be extremely tactful."

He thought for a moment and then nodded. "Her name is Samantha Kemp and she'll be at the Plough Inn. It's just off the high street where the road curves round to Clapham Common."

"Constable Griffiths will instruct the lady that if anyone asks what he was doing in her pub, she can say that he was looking for a missing person, an elderly senile man. Will that do?" Witherspoon asked.

"Yes, Inspector, but please, make your constable promise that if he sees a burly, black-haired brute behind the bar, he's not to ask for Sammi. I'll not put her in danger."

"Why didn't you tell me any of this before, Mr. Redley?" Witherspoon honestly didn't understand why people found it necessary to lie to the police.

"Why do you think, Inspector? I love Samantha and I didn't want either her reputation ruined or her life threatened by that monster she married." Redley shrugged. "Secondly, I didn't like my landlady nor did I think much of her character, but she was dead and I didn't wish to speak ill of her."

Downstairs, Constable Barnes frowned at Etta Morgan and Mrs. Fremont. "Why didn't either of you mention that in the month prior to the murder things had been stolen from the house?"

Etta licked her lips and cast a quick, worried glance at the cook. "I wasn't sure I ought to," she muttered. "I mean, you asked us if anything unusual had happened about the time of the murder, and we'd not heard the mistress shouting about tricks bein' played for a couple of weeks. I didn't think of it."

"Neither did I." Mrs. Fremont crossed her arms over her chest. "And what's more, none of us below stairs here was all that certain the mistress wasn't makin' the whole thing up."

"You think she might have stolen an umbrella and a watch from her tenants?" Barnes looked doubtful. "Really?"

Mrs. Fremont unfolded her arms and leaned across the table toward him. "We didn't say anything about it because we were scared."

"Scared? Of what?"

"Of the tenants," Etta exclaimed. "They're a right odd lot, and if one of them was stealin' and killin', we didn't want to be next. Mrs. Robinson was already dead, and if they got wind that we'd told the police anything untoward, we might be next."

"Stealing and killing?" Barnes stared at them in disbelief. "But we're the police. We stop that sort of thing from happening."

"You're going to station a constable here in my kitchen? Or maybe on the landings?" Mrs. Fremont laughed softly. "We know who you are, Constable, and you look like a decent sort, and you and that inspector would be right upset if one of us was found with our throat slit, but we'd still be dead, wouldn't we."

"If you'd told us everything from the beginning, we might have found Mrs. Robinson's killer," he protested.

"But what if you didn't?" she demanded. "What if he's still here and just waitin' for you lot to clear off before he heads for the hills? None of us has anyplace to go so we're stuck here with them. You should have heard the screamin' and shoutin' and the threats when her nibs accused them of not payin' their rents. They went mad."

"And when Mr. Erskine's watch went missing, he called her a terrible name and threw the umbrella stand at her," Etta said. "That's why it's so battered in places."

"And the next night, his umbrella was taken," Mrs. Fremont added. "He was so furious he stormed out and slammed the front door so hard it almost broke the window in the drawing room. So you tell me, Constable, if you was trapped in a house with people like that, wouldn't you be careful about what you said?"

"Tell me about the time that all the rent envelopes went missing," the constable said.

"It was in February." Mrs. Fremont picked up her teacup and took a quick sip. "Her nibs had been gone the night before."

"Where had she been?" Barnes picked up his pencil and flipped to the next page in his notebook.

Mrs. Fremont gave a short, contemptuous laugh. "She wasn't one to explain herself to us, Constable. The only reason we knew about her monthly trip to Scotland was so Carrie or Etta would be sure to have her shoes shined. But sometimes, she went off alone and all she ever said was that she'd be back the next day."

"Go on, what happened when she came home that morning?"

"She dropped her suitcase in the foyer and stuck her head in the dining room to tell Carrie to bring her a pot of tea and then she went upstairs. Etta was down here helpin' me and Carrie was servin' breakfast," Mrs. Fremont continued. "I set about making the tea but then Mrs. Robinson came back downstairs and charged into the dining room. She demanded to know why there weren't any envelopes in her room, why they hadn't paid their rent."

"Carrie said she looked like a madwoman," Etta put in. "Poor Carrie was so frightened she dropped the toast rack."

"The tenants weren't scared," Mrs. Fremont said. "They all claimed they'd slipped the envelopes under the door, just like they did every Friday evening. By this time she was shoutin' loud enough to wake the dead. She said she wasn't goin' to stand for it and for them to pay up. Mr. Erskine told her he wasn't falling for her tricks, that he'd paid his rent, and that he had a witness who'd seen him shove the envelope under the door."

"He pointed at Carrie," Etta said, "and that's when she dropped the toast rack. She was scared, but she told the truth. She had seen Mr. Erskine push it under."

"What happened then?"

"Mrs. Robinson went real quiet for a minute, then she stomped into the foyer, grabbed her coat, and stalked out of the house."

Barnes had one more thing he needed to know. "Mrs. Fremont, Etta, did either of you hear Mrs. Robinson arguing with someone in her room the night before she was killed?"

"They 'urt like the very devil," Blimpey Groggins complained. "But you and your lot did me a good turn once, so shingles or not, I wanted to pass along a bit of information."

They were out on the street and heading toward Upper Edmonton Gardens. Smythe glanced at his companion as they rounded the corner. "That's right good of ya, but are you sure you don't want to go back to the flat so ya can sit in comfort? Ya don't look well. You're pale as a sheet and shingles shouldn't cause that."

Blimpey waved his hand impatiently. "I'm fine. There's a reason I look like death warmed over but I'll get to that after I tell ya what I know. Don't worry, I'll only charge ya my usual rate even if I was the one that come to you."

Smythe snorted. "I went to you first."

He noticed that despite Blimpey's slow gait and pallor, he was dressed a bit nattier than usual. His shirt, usually the color of dirty water, was now a pristine white, his dark blue jacket and matching suit trousers appeared to be brand-new, and he wasn't wearing his old red scarf, but a perfectly clean maroon one was wound around his throat.

"True, true, but let's not haggle over trifles." Blimpey stopped as they reached the busy Holland Road. They waited for a break in the traffic and then started across. "I wanted to pass along some rumors that might have a bea-rin' on your inspector's latest case."

"What kind of rumors?" Smythe pulled his coat tighter as a blast of wind ripped into them. Beside him, he heard Blimpey gasp. "You alright?"

Blimpey grimaced. "These ruddy shingles are so sore that even a puff of blooming wind hurts. Anyway, what I've 'eard is that there's a new criminal enterprise 'ere in town."

"What kind?"

"That's the 'ard part. I'm not sure there's a name for what they're doin'. Mind you, there should be. I guess you could say that crime 'as caught up with the modern world we live in."

Smythe came to a complete stop and stared at Blimpey, who'd also halted. They were in front of an estate agent's shop. "What on earth are you on about?"

"There's a criminal gang operatin' 'ere. They've been workin' London for the last two years or eighteen months—my source wasn't sure of how long exactly they'd been here."

"And you're just now findin' out about it?" Smythe found that hard to believe. "Come on, Blimpey, pull the other one. Your business is knowin' what's goin' on."

"Alright, alright, don't get all het up. I'll admit, I've heard rumors about it. But it's only been recently that I could find out anything solid." He had the good grace to look embarrassed. "But in my defense, there's a reason I don't know as much as I should. They've done a good job of keepin' the local bad lads from finding out about their operation."

"And why would that be?"

"Competition, Smythe. Criminal enterprises are just like any other business and this lot has come up with a good method for moving goods that reduces the risk of them bein' nicked. To be fair, it's a pretty smart method."

"What kind of method?"

"From what I 'ear, an experienced burglar comes to London, picks his territory, and then helps himself to the goodies. Now you've got to understand, Smythe, the police never catch burglars in the act. They get 'em through informants or by leanin' hard on the local fences. You know what a fence is . . ."

"I do," Smythe interrupted. "'E's the one that buys the stolen goods. Go on, we're almost there. Tell me the rest."

"So the burglar's got his goods, but instead of fencing them through one of the local channels, there's supposedly a person who takes the stuff out of England and fences it there."

"What good would that do? The police could still track it. They've got telegrams and even them new instruments, telephones." Smythe kept up on all the new inventions that were available. The telephone looked like it might be a useful one to have as well.

"You're not understandin' how it works, Smythe." Blimpey sighed theatrically. "The police don't go lookin' that far afield for stolen goods. Like I said, they make arrests by leaning hard on fences or their informants. If none of the locals know anything, then they can't tell the police, so a clever sort of burglar, someone who was good at his job, could come into a neighborhood, lift a few pretty bits and pieces from an empty house, and take his share of the lolly when it was fenced somewhere far away."

"Do ya 'ave any idea who this person is, the one who takes it out of the country?"

Blimpey grinned broadly. "That's the interestin' bit, Smythe. My lads tell me the rumors are that this ring is run by a woman."

"A woman," Smythe repeated. "Blast a Spaniard, are you sure? Tell me you're sure, Blimpey. It could be bloomin' important."

"You mean if that woman was Edith Durant?" He shrugged. "I've got some people workin' on it, Smythe, but I can't tell you she was the one for sure."

By this time, they'd reached the back gate to the communal gardens. "Thanks, Blimpey, this helps a lot. I appreciate you comin' to see me."

"I'd like to say this was the only reason I got off my sick bed." A red flush climbed up Blimpey's chubby cheeks. "But there's something else I wanted to ask ya."

"Go ahead." Smythe stared at him curiously; it took a lot to make someone like Blimpey blush.

He cleared his throat. "We both married younger women, Smythe. Your Betsy is a good twenty years . . ."

"Seventeen," he interrupted. "She's seventeen years younger. Don't make me older than I am."

"Right, well, that's as may be, but my Nell is fifteen years younger than me." He stopped and took a deep breath. "I don't quite know how to say this. I never thought it would happen to me, to us."

"What's 'appened?" Smythe's heart sank. Something was wrong, seriously wrong.

"Ya hear about it happening to others, but never to yourself, if you know what I mean." Shaking his head, he looked off into the distance.

"But I don't know what ya mean," Smythe objected. "You've not told me."

"I'm not sure 'ow to put it in words."

"Are ya sick, Blimpey? Are ya dying? If you need someone ya trust to keep an eye on your Nell, Betsy and I can do it for ya. You've only to ask. You can tell me. You're a good friend, and if somethin' is troublin' you, I want to 'elp."

He turned back to Smythe and the faraway expression in his eyes sharpened. He broke into a wide grin. "I'm not dyin' but I might need your Betsy to have a word with my Nell."

Smythe was confused. "Then what's this all about?"

"I'm goin' to be a father, Smythe, and I'm more scared than I've ever been in my entire life. My Nell and I are goin' to have us a baby."

Constable Griffiths yanked open the front door and turned to look at Witherspoon. "I'll stop back here with a full report and I promise, sir, I'll be very discreet."

"I know you will, Constable, that's why I'm sending you and not one of the local lads," he replied. "Regardless of what one may think about a liaison between a married woman and a man that isn't her husband, we don't want to do anything to put her directly in harm's way."

Griffiths nodded respectfully and closed the door. Witherspoon turned and almost knocked over Carrie Durridge. "Oh dear, I'm so sorry."

"It was my fault, sir." She smiled apologetically. "I was going to ask if you and the other constables want tea?"

"You needn't go to any trouble on our account." Witherspoon moved past her toward the drawing room. John Erskine was waiting for him.

"It's no trouble, sir." Carrie dogged his footsteps. "I've got to go downstairs anyway. Constable Barnes wants to ask me something."

"In that case, I'd love a cup of tea."

"I'll take one, too," Erskine called through the open door.

Carrie frowned in his direction and then gave the inspector a quick smile as she hurried toward the back stairs. Witherspoon stepped through the oak double doors

"I understand you wish to speak to me." Erskine was leaning against the unlighted fireplace. "Was there something in particular you wanted to ask?"

Witherspoon advanced into the room. "Mr. Erskine, in your original statement, you said that you overheard a rather heated argument between the victim and some unknown person."

He pushed away from the fireplace and sat down on the settee. "That's correct. Why?"

"Would you care to amend that statement, sir?" Witherspoon asked politely. As soon as they arrived today, he and Barnes as well as Constable Griffiths had inquired if any other member of the household had heard the argument. None of them had.

Erskine drew back slightly, his face darkening. "Why should I? I've told the truth. The woman was having a bloody row with someone."

"There were a number of other people here that night and none of them overheard this alleged quarrel."

"Alleged," he blustered. "There was nothing alleged about it. I know what I heard and she was shouting her head off."

"Neither Mr. Redley nor Mr. Morecomb heard anything and they were both home."

"Did they tell you that?" He sneered. "I shouldn't believe them if I were you. They've no great love for me and would like nothing more than to see me embarrassed."

"That's hardly a reason for respectable businessmen to lie to the police," Witherspoon continued. "The servants didn't hear anything, either. Why was that?"

"Of course they didn't. The cook was out at the pub, the

scullery maid sleeps like the dead, and Durridge wasn't in her room when I popped in to ask her to find me a head-ache powder," he protested. "Surely, Inspector, you've seen enough about this household to know that it's peculiar. Alice Robinson or Edith Durant, whatever the woman was calling herself, was incredibly cheap. What few servants she had were worked to death and the only way she could keep anyone here was to let them do as they pleased in the evenings. So it's no wonder that no one overhead the argu-ment, but I know what I heard."

Witherspoon changed tactics. "Where were you on the morning of the murder?"

Erskine's hands balled into fists. "I was with a cus-tomer. You know what I do, Inspector, and it'll ruin me financially if the people I depend on for my livelihood sus-pect for an instant that I can't be trusted."

"You sell furs." Witherspoon smiled slightly as he saw the door start to slide open. "You claim to have offices in High Holborn. Is that correct?"

"You know all this." He got up and began to pace. "Can we move this along, please? I don't want to be late."

"Perhaps you'd be so good as to explain, Mr. Erskine, how you can work for a company that went out of business four years ago," Barnes asked as he stepped into the room.

Erskine stared at the constable, his expression stunned.

"Well, Mr. Erskine, can you explain this matter?" With-erspoon pressed.

"I must have made a mistake," he muttered. "I gave you the wrong name."

"You also gave us the wrong address for your business

and the wrong name of the Canadian firm you claim you represent," Barnes said. "Can you explain those mistakes as well?"

Even before Constable Barnes had found out about Smythe's and Wiggins' respective spots of trouble, he'd been suspicious about the tenants and had followed established procedure by sending off inquiries to confirm their statements. Inspector Rogers had sent a constable from Y Division over this morning with a telegram from the High Holborn division, and Barnes suspected that if Erskine was lying about his business, he was lying about the office address. If two of the other three tenants' occupations were bogus, there was a good chance that Erskine's was a sham as well.

"Alright, I lied about them. I'm actually unemployed, but I didn't want anyone to know that, because when a man is out of work, people tend to regard him as a failure," he said defensively. "Besides, it's much easier to obtain employment if prospective clients think you're already successful."

"Where were you at the time of the murder?" Witherspoon asked again. "Please don't waste our time, Mr. Erskine, we're going to verify your story immediately, and if you weren't where you claim to be, we're going to ask you to come to the station to help with our inquiries."

The meeting was breaking up by the time Smythe arrived, but they'd quickly gone back to their seats when he told them who his source was and that he'd learned something important.

He told them about the baby first. "I wasn't sure whether to offer him condolences or congratulations." He laughed. "But then I saw him grinnin' like a madman and that settled it for me. He's 'appier than a cat that's got the canary."

"He's just nervous about becoming a father." Betsy patted her husband's arm. "That's understandable. You were, too."

"It was good of him to seek you out," Hatchet said.

"Especially as he's still got shingles." Luty winced. "My late husband had 'em twice and they like to have killed him."

"This Mr. Blimpey Groggins person—he's a source?" Phyllis had been under the impression that the household didn't share the names of the people that they mined for information.

Smythe knew he was on delicate ground here. Everyone knew how Blimpey made his living. "'E's not really a source," he explained slowly. "But I do use 'im occasionally to find out a few things. But that's not why 'e came to see me this mornin'."

"I expect he came because he wished to do us a good turn," Mrs. Jeffries interjected smoothly. She'd long suspected that Smythe frequently used Blimpey's rather expensive services, and she was most grateful he was willing to spend his own money to assist in their investigations. Helping the coachman out of an awkward explanation was the least she could do. She looked at Phyllis. "Before you came here, we once helped Blimpey with a problem, and he's always looked for a way to repay the favor."

"What did he tell you?" Betsy asked. Like Mrs. Jeffries, she thought the less said about Blimpey being a source, the better.

"He 'ad some information about the burglaries in the neighborhood of the lodgin' house," he began. He repeated what Blimpey had told him. "Mainly, the thieves are takin' small but expensive items like silver, jewelry, coin collections, even small pieces of art and ceramics."

"But they're not being fenced here in London?" Mrs. Jeffries mused. "That certainly fits."

"He was sure that it was a woman who was the ringleader?" Ruth asked.

"She's the brains behind the operation." Smythe took a quick swig of tea. "And what's more, the rumor is that she's been doin' it for eighteen months or more."

"But most of the current tenants haven't been there for more than a few months," Mrs. Jeffries exclaimed. "Norman Teasdale's been there the longest and that's just six months, and he's the only one who appears to be a legitimate businessman. So how could Edith Durant have been doing this for eighteen months?" The moment the words left her lips, Mrs. Jeffries knew the answer. "Oh gracious, they're not the first, are they?"

"No, there were others before this lot," Smythe said. "Some were from the Continent and some from America."

"Let me see if I understand what we're gettin' at here." The cook looked from Smythe to Mrs. Jeffries. "Are you sayin' that Edith Durant was the ringleader of an international band of thieves?"

"I think she was more like an administrator than a ringleader," Mrs. Jeffries explained. "I'm not certain, but I think that when Edith Durant fled London when Christopher was arrested, she got in touch with her old contacts on the Continent."

"And most of them was criminals," Luty added.

"She also made contacts in North America," Mrs. Jeffries continued. "I think she saw a need in the modern criminal world and realized she could make a substantial amount of money by providing a respectable haven for housebreakers and burglars as well as affording them a safer method of selling the goods they'd stolen."

"So you're sayin' Durant used her old contacts to let other criminals know that they could safely hide out at her boardinghouse and that for a fee she'd sell the goods for them miles away from where the crime took place?" Mrs. Goodge wanted to make sure she understood.

"That's very clever," Betsy murmured. "If she resold the goods that had been stolen in London to a fence in Scotland, the chances of her being arrested were small."

"But why would the thieves and burglars go along with it?" Phyllis asked. "They've taken all the risks by committing the crime so why would they pay to stay in her lodging house and a fee on top of that?"

"They'd do it to avoid getting caught and going to prison." Hatchet smiled at Phyllis. "Most burglars and thieves aren't caught in the act, they're arrested because the police put pressure on the locals who receive the stolen goods and sell them on."

"Either that, or they get caught because of informants," Smythe added. "So if you've nicked a diamond necklace in Paris, it'll be the French police that's huntin' you, not the English."

Something poked at the back of Mrs. Jeffries' mind, but it was such a soft nudge that it disappeared as quickly as it had come.

"So having someone here to move the goods would increase your chances of not getting caught." Phyllis nodded eagerly. "That makes sense. So Morecomb, Redley, and Erskine are thieves, and that's why they've been at the lodging house."

"That seems to make sense," Mrs. Jeffries muttered. "But which one of them would have a motive to murder her? That's the question."

"I still think Norman Teasdale might be in the mix," Luty declared. "He seems like a respectable feller, but he was the only one that was intimately connected with the victim."

"What should we be doing today?" Phyllis asked.

Mrs. Jeffries wasn't sure. "We've already nudged the inspector into taking another look at the tenants, and Constable Barnes was going to relay the information we've learned to both our inspector and Inspector Rogers. Rogers is the one investigating the local burglaries."

"What about the Black Swan and the Hanged Man?" Smythe inquired. "Someone needs to send some lads there to shake up the locals."

"Yes, but that's far too dangerous for any of us," Mrs. Jeffries said quickly. "We'll have to leave that to the police. Once Constable Barnes lets Rogers know what we've learned, he'll probably send some of his tougher young men over to have a word with the publicans." She looked at Phyllis. "See if you can make contact with Annie Linden and find out any details she might know about the Scotland trips." Then she turned to Wiggins. "Can you keep an eye on the lodging house today? If the inspector starts applying a bit of pressure to the tenants, one or more of them might attempt to leave."

"'Course I can, but what should I do if I see someone runnin' for it?"

"Don't chase after them," Mrs. Goodge ordered. "You stay well away from that lot. They're criminals and, like rats, we don't know what they'll do if they're cornered."

CHAPTER 10

"Do you believe him, sir?" Barnes asked the inspector as soon as Erskine was out of earshot.

"It's something we can easily check, so I don't know why he'd lie about it. He'd had to have registered and there would be plenty of attendants about the place. It wasn't that long ago, so if he was actually there, someone will remember him. But the more important question is why didn't he tell us the truth from the start?"

"There's nothing wrong with them, sir, but some men don't like admitting they use Turkish baths," Barnes replied.

"But the Jermyn Street Baths are perfectly respectable." Witherspoon didn't understand it. Life would be so much easier if people would only stop telling lies to the police. "Send Constable Shearing to the baths to verify Erskine's statement. He ought to have time to get there and back before we're finished here."

"Once Constables Griffiths and Shearing get back, we'll have confirmation of all three alibis," Barnes said thoughtfully.

"Yes, I suppose we will. We've already verified that Norman Teasdale was telling us the truth when he said he was at the Armitage Hotel"—Witherspoon held up his hand and ticked off his fingers as he spoke—"Erskine would have been at the Jermyn Street Baths, and Redley at the Plough Inn. The only one left, then, is Andrew Morecomb."

The door wedged open just enough to reveal Carrie shoving at it with her shoulder. She carried a tea tray holding two steaming mugs. Witherspoon dashed over and pushed the double doors apart.

"Thank you, sir." She smiled gratefully and put the tray on the table. "But where's Mr. Erskine? He said he wanted tea."

"He went up to his room," Witherspoon said. "But as you've very kindly brought up two mugs, Constable Barnes will have his."

"Very good, sir." She served Witherspoon first and then handed the other mug to Barnes.

"Now that you're here, Miss Durridge," he said as he took his mug, "can you answer a question for me?"

"Certainly, sir, what is it?"

"On the night before Mrs. Robinson was murdered, Mr. Erskine claimed he overheard her and some other person having a row in her quarters."

"That's what the constable asked me, sir, and like I told him, I don't remember hearing anything like that."

"Yes, I understand that. But Mr. Erskine now claims that when he heard this row, he went to the kitchen for a drink of water and that he then went to your room to ask for a headache powder but you weren't there."

She cocked her head to one side, her expression confused. "But I was there, sir. I'm always there in the evenings. I like to read. The only time I left my room was when I went upstairs to the box room to fetch another blouse out of my trunk."

"What time did you go upstairs?" Witherspoon recalled that someone, he couldn't remember who, had stated they'd heard someone in the box room that night. No doubt it was Carrie.

"I don't know, sir. I wasn't watching the clock, but it was before nine, I know that much." She pointed toward the hall. "The front door gets locked at nine sharp every night, so I've got to be in my room just after that time in case one of the gentlemen wants to be let in."

"Was it always Mrs. Robinson who locked the front door?" Barnes asked. "We've been told she was often out in the evenings."

"She was, sir." Carrie nodded vigorously. "But the door was still locked up good and tight. If she was out for the evening, either Etta or I locked up."

"Where was the key kept?" Witherspoon suddenly remembered they'd never found the key to either Durant's quarters or the passkey to the tenants' rooms.

"If she was going out, she put the key under the ivy plant in the foyer."

"And you let her in when she came home?" he clarified.

"No, sir, she let herself in. She had her own key, and when she was out, we didn't throw the top bolt—it was left unlocked."

"You've no idea where she kept her keys?" he pressed. "We've still not found either her passkeys or the keys to her quarters."

Carrie shook her head. "No, sir, I don't. I've kept my eyes open for them ever since you asked the first time, but I've not seen them. Will there be anything else, sir?"

"Do you know where Mr. Morecomb went today?" Barnes asked. "Or what time he'll return?"

"I've no idea when he'll be back, but he's gone to the train station, sir. He left before breakfast this morning." She picked up the empty tray and started for the door.

Witherspoon frowned in annoyance. "The train station. Did he mention where he was traveling?"

"No, sir, he didn't, but then again, he'd not say anything to me or the other servants. But he had his suitcase with him, if that's any help to you, sir. Oh, but he dropped his handkerchief as he was leaving and I took it out to him just as he was getting into a hansom cab. I overheard him tell the hansom driver to take him to Victoria Station."

"Do you think he's run, sir?" Barnes muttered as soon as Carrie was out of earshot.

"I don't want to believe it." Witherspoon closed his eyes as other, more painful memories almost overwhelmed him. He put his mug down on the table. "Surely I've not been foolish enough or incompetent enough to let another suspect slip through my fingers. Yee gods, that's exactly what I did the last time."

For a moment, Barnes thought he was hearing things. It wasn't like the inspector to turn maudlin this early in the day. His miserable moods usually hit him in the evenings when he was tired as a pup. "That's not what happened, sir.

If you'll recall, we were getting ready to arrest her when she went on the run. What's more, we'd no idea that the tenants here weren't exactly the respectable businessmen they appeared to be until you had the notion to take a closer look at them and at that ledger."

Witherspoon gave himself a small shake. "Yes, of course, you're right. I'm being absurd."

Relieved, Barnes let out the breath he'd been holding. "Not to be rude, sir, but you are." He took a huge gulp of tea. "You've too many irons in the fire now to worry about Andrew Morecomb. If he left from Victoria Station, we'll find him eventually."

"Of course we will," Witherspoon said. "Unlike Edith Durant, he has no idea we know what he's been up to."

"Do you want me to ask if Inspector Rogers can spare us a constable or two to search the back garden? He owes us, sir. We've passed along our suspicions that the tenants could well be involved in those burglaries he's under pressure to solve."

Witherspoon's face clouded. "Back garden?"

"As you said earlier, sir, there had to be a reason Durant was so upset at the thought of her neighbor spying on her while she was outside that she threatened to murder her."

"Yes, yes, indeed. Thank you, Constable, for reminding me, and we could certainly use all the help we can get. But there's no need to add to Inspector Rogers' burden. He needs his men. The garden isn't large—we can have a hunt ourselves, and if we find we need assistance, Constables Griffiths and Shearing can lend us a hand when they return." He went toward the hall. "The most likely reason was that she had something hidden out there."

* * *

Mrs. Jeffries pulled the inspector's bedcovers to the foot of the bed and straightened the sheets. Cleaning his quarters was Phyllis' job, but when they were "on the hunt," she took over as many of the maid's chores as possible.

Mrs. Jeffries stopped and thought about this morning's meeting. Once they heard what Smythe had discovered, everything fell neatly into place. Everyone, save herself and the cook, was now out and about, looking for evidence that would point to which of Durant's tenants had murdered her.

Why, then, was she so uneasy? Don't be ridiculous, she told herself as she went to the foot of the bed and grabbed the top sheet, all the evidence points to one of the tenants. Thieves fell out with one another all the time and someone obviously had taken serious issue with Edith Durant's overwhelming greed.

She made the bed, yanking the sheets and covers into place with such force that her arms hurt. Then she grabbed the dust cloth and the furniture polish from the workbox she'd brought up from the old butler's pantry and attacked the chest of drawers.

She let her mind go blank as she dusted and polished the elegant mahogany furniture. By the time she reached the wardrobe doors, the monotonous repetitive motions had done their magic and her mind had focused on what was troubling her.

Highgate Cemetery, that was the key to this murder but she couldn't for the life of her understand why. People were murdered in all sorts of odd places. But if a tenant was guilty, they had to lure her there, and what would be the point of doing that? The lodging house itself would have made a much more sensible place to kill the woman. If their recent assumptions were correct, the murderer should be a pragmatic thief willing to give up a good percentage of his ill-gotten gains for practical reasons such as avoiding prison.

She opened the right-side door and ran her cloth over the inside, taking care not to let the dust brush against the inspector's neatly starched white shirts. The most practical place to have murdered Durant was in the privacy of her bedroom or the lodging house attic. Strangling someone in a public place carried enormous risks. That's what she couldn't understand. She closed the right side and started on the left half of the door.

Because the killer wanted to make a statement, she thought. She went still as she realized what had just popped into her head. But she knew she was right. The place where Edith Durant had been murdered was significant. But significant how?

They knew that the dead woman hadn't any family buried there so how could it have any meaning for her whatsoever? Mrs. Jeffries continued cleaning and had the room done by the time she'd decided there was only one way to find out.

She tucked the cleaning supplies in the workbox, picked it up, and rushed downstairs. Mrs. Goodge was still deep in conversation with one of her old colleagues, so she slipped quietly into the tiny butler's pantry next to the cook's quarters, put the box away, and took off her apron. She dashed through the kitchen, grabbed her cloak off the coat tree, and smiled apologetically at the cook. "I'm so sorry to disturb you, but I'm going out for a while. I'll be back by four o'clock."

*   *   *

The back garden was divided from the Travers home by a
tall wooden fence fronted by a thick barrier of overgrown
ivy. A terrace led off the back door to a scruffy lawn and
was connected to the side walkway by a crumbling concrete path. A rusted metal washbasin and broken wash-
board were propped against the back wall of the house
along with two broken lanterns and a stack of broken crock-
ery. Halfway down the lawn was a tall line of bamboo that
cut the garden neatly in half. A ramshackle gray structure
that had once been a folly stood behind the bamboo.

"Do you think *that* was what Durant was referring to
when she called this place her sanctuary?" Barnes pointed
at the tiny, decrepit building.

"I think it must be." Witherspoon's lip curled as he surveyed the dilapidated area. "Gracious, when Constable
Griffiths searched out here and said it was a bit of a mess,
he wasn't joking."

"He's not given to exaggeration," Barnes muttered. "This
is the most unwelcoming garden I've ever seen. There's not
so much as a stool or a wooden bench, let alone a flower or
shade tree. She must have done that deliberately, sir." He
went toward the hedge. "It would be one way of making
sure that neither her tenants nor her servants wanted to hang
about here. Shall I start in the, uh, folly?"

"Mind you, be careful, Constable, the thing looks like it
could collapse any moment. I'll start around the side of the
house at the walkway and we'll meet near the bamboo."

They worked diligently for the next two hours; Barnes
wasn't sure what they were looking for, but he suspected
he'd know when and if he found it . . . and then he did.

"Here, sir." He waved at Witherspoon, who, having worked his way down the side of the house, was now at the far end of the ivy bed. "I've found something."

Witherspoon groaned as he straightened up. He moved as fast as his aching back and legs would let him, grimacing in pain as he reached the spot where the constable knelt. He hoped he could see whatever it was without having to get on his knees or bend over too far. "What is it, Constable? What have you found?"

"The reason Edith Durant threatened her neighbor." Barnes pushed a huge clump of ivy to one side, revealing a large hole. A dark green oilcloth was crumpled on one side next to an open wooden box. "I think this was where she hid her treasure."

"She had something buried here." Witherspoon clenched his teeth and knelt down to have a closer look. He pulled out the oilcloth first. "She used this to keep the box from rotting." He put it to one side and picked up the box. It was made of a dark wood with brass hinges on the back and a broken brass lock on the front. "It's about twelve inches long and eight inches wide," he estimated. "But it's a good seven inches deep. Big enough to hold a substantial sum of money in either notes or coins."

"Hello, sir." Constable Griffiths and Constable Shearing suddenly appeared from the side of the house.

Witherspoon waved them forward. "Constable Griffiths, did you and the other lads search this area thoroughly?"

Griffith's eyes narrowed as he saw the gaping hole. "We did, sir. We searched every bit of it and there was nothing like that. I personally examined the ivy bed and the ground was good and solid."

"I'm sure you and the lads did an excellent job, Constable," Witherspoon said. "We're trying to ascertain when this might have been dug up."

"If it was after the search, it means the victim didn't do it," Barnes commented.

"But someone did." Witherspoon's knees creaked as he stood up. "What did you find out at the Plough Inn?" he asked Griffiths.

"Mr. Redley was there at the time of the murder," he reported. "The lady wasn't the only one to verify it. The other barmaid who has a room upstairs next to the owner's quarters saw Redley come up the stairs just before nine, and he didn't leave until after eleven that morning."

"What was your impression, Constable? Do you believe both the lady and the barmaid are telling the truth?"

"I do, sir."

Witherspoon turned to Shearing. "And how did you do, Constable? Find out anything useful at the baths?"

"Mr. Erskine was there, sir." Shearing glanced at Barnes, who had moved onto his knees again and was pushing the ivy surrounding the hole out of his way. "Patrons have to sign in and his signature was there. Also, he's a regular and the clerk knows him by sight. He confirmed that Mr. Erskine was present from eight forty-five to nine forty-five on the fifteenth."

"Here, sir." Barnes pointed to the exposed earth. Two half crowns and a five-pound note lay in the dirt about eight inches away from the hole. "Whoever dug this up must have dropped these." He picked up the five-pound note, slapped it onto his palm, and then ran his fingers across the surface. "It's damp, sir, but not wet, and as it rained last night, that means this was dug up early this morning."

Mrs. Jeffries forced a smile as the others filed in for their afternoon meeting. She was so disappointed but she didn't want her foul mood to influence the others. This case was difficult enough without her adding to their self-doubts. "Where's Luty?" she asked as she realized that Hatchet was alone.

"Madam and I went our separate ways this morning." He frowned toward the back door. "Frankly, I'm worried. Her gun case was empty, which leads me to believe that Madam has taken her peacemaker with her."

"You mean 'er gun, 'er Colt .45?" Wiggins asked. "Cor blimey, I thought we talked 'er out of carryin' that thing. It's right dangerous."

"I, too, had assumed that Madam had ceased taking it with her." He sighed heavily. "Apparently I was wrong."

Alarmed, Mrs. Jeffries asked, "Where did she go today?"

"I've no idea. She refused to tell me." He hesitated. "But I believe her feelings were a bit hurt, because though you gave the rest of us specific tasks this morning, you didn't give her one."

Mrs. Jeffries closed her eyes for a moment. "That was foolish of me. Luty contributes more than her fair share to our investigations."

"Good." Luty stood under the archway with her hands on her hips. "But it's okay that you didn't have anything for me to do—I had plenty of investigatin' of my own." She whipped off her cloak as she spoke and tossed it on the back of the chair that Hatchet had quickly pulled out for her.

"Did you take your gun?" he demanded as he seated her.

"I did. When I'm out in the carriage on my own, I always take it. But that's not important. What's important is what my lawyers told me."

"Have your tea." Mrs. Goodge pushed a full cup to Luty's side of the table.

"Oh, Luty, I'm dreadfully sorry if I offended you. This wretched case has me at my wit's end and I simply ran out of ideas by the time I got to you this morning."

Luty waved her off impatiently. "Don't fret about it. I could tell you was graspin' at the wind this morning. But sometimes it goes that way. Not to worry, you'll sort it out. You always do."

Mrs. Jeffries blinked in surprise. She hadn't realized her concerns were so transparent. "What did you find out?"

"That Edith Durant's will is valid." She grinned. "What's more, I also found out that Carl Christopher's heirs can inherit her estate as long as the Crown can't prove that estate was obtained by fraud or any other criminal enterprise. I'm givin' you the easy version here. I had to listen to the legal boys give me a whole crock of long-winded speeches before I could git one of 'em to boil it down to candy. I tell ya, I'm right tuckered out. I had to give 'em a right complicated bunch of excuses to keep 'em from bein' suspicious about why I was askin' such questions, but don't worry, I didn't mention Edith Durant's name."

"But we don't know who Carl Christopher's heirs are," Mrs. Goodge complained.

"And if one of them murdered her, they'd have to know she lived here in London," Ruth pointed out. "I hardly think that's likely, considering that his family, if any of them are even still alive, lost what little they had paying his legal bills and bribing clergymen."

"I'm not sayin' they had anything to do with it," Luty replied, "but this mornin' Mrs. Jeffries made it clear that unless one of the tenants turns out to be the murderer, we've got to start afresh and findin' out this little bit is startin' afresh."

"Indeed it is, Luty," Mrs. Jeffries agreed. "Thank you. Your information could turn out to be very useful."

"I'm glad you found out something." Betsy gave the elderly American a warm smile. "I've found out nothing." She turned to Mrs. Jeffries. "I couldn't find anyone amongst the shopkeepers that knew anything about the tenants. They don't shop in the neighborhood."

"You're not the only one who found out nuthin'," Wiggins added. "I tried chattin' with two housemaids in the neighborhood, but neither of them knew anything except that the lodgin' 'ouse was a good place to work if you liked your liquor. One of 'em was right annoyed when Annie Linden got sacked."

"Why? Was she friends with Annie?" Phyllis asked.

"Nah, she wanted her job, but before she could get over there and chat with Mrs. Robinson, another woman had got the jump on her. But despite my poor showin' today, I'm not givin' up. Besides, when the inspector gets 'ome tonight, he might 'ave all sorts of good bits for Mrs. Jeffries."

The housekeeper smiled uncertainly. She felt like such a fraud. This morning she'd given them tasks to ascertain once and for all if it was indeed one of the tenants who had committed the murder. She'd not had a lot of hope that any of them would be successful, but she'd been at her wit's end and had done the best she could. She'd had a moment of inspiration earlier today and had gone off with high hopes and expectations. But her inspiration had turned out to be nothing more than wishful thinking. Still, she'd tried and so had they. She was proud of them. "How about you, Ruth? Any luck?"

"No, sorry," Ruth replied. "I spoke with both the ladies in my women's group who live in Highgate but neither of them knew anything."

"Not to worry." Mrs. Goodge helped herself to a slice of seedcake. "My source was useless as well. But as Mrs. Jeffries says, if it's not one of the tenants, then it's someone else, and we'll suss it out. We always do."

Mrs. Jeffries was touched by their faith in her, but she certainly didn't share it.

"My day was a bit better," Smythe announced. "My source told me that there's been five burglaries in the Islington/Highgate neighborhood in the last four weeks."

"Did your source know what was taken?" Hatchet asked.

"The usual bits and pieces: expensive stuff that 'as a decent resell value," he replied. He'd gone to Blimpey's house, not his pub, and being a smart enough fellow to listen to his wife, he'd taken Nell a huge bouquet of flowers. They'd cost the earth but had been worth it. "One of the houses was robbed just last week, and the thief got an emerald bracelet with matching earrings from the safe as well as a couple of silver goblets and a set of gold candlesticks. Toss in two small Italian paintings done by old masters for good measure and whoever did it walked away with a fortune. But the most interesting thing I found out is that all of the burglaries in the neighborhood have been done when the houses were empty."

"Lavinia Swanson," Hatchet murmured. "That woman has a lot to answer for."

"She didn't know she was passing along information to thieves," Ruth protested. "She was simply trying to earn a bit of money."

"Yeah, don't be such a snob, Hatchet." Luty cackled. "Poor woman's got to do somethin' to make ends meet."

"I didn't do so well, either," Phyllis admitted. "I managed to find Annie Linden and she wasn't all that pleased to see me. She was working at a café on the Holloway Road. I asked her about the tenants and she said she'd already told me all she knew about them. The only other thing she said was that she'd seen the woman who'd ruined her skirt going into a hotel on the Edgware Road. Annie said the woman was wearing a fancy cloak over a maid's uniform."

"When did she see her?" Mrs. Jeffries asked.

"She couldn't recall the exact day—she thinks it might have been a week or so before the murder. Like I said, Mrs. Jeffries, she wasn't all that pleased to see me and wasn't in a real chatty mood."

Mrs. Jeffries smiled absently. "You've done well, then. Anyone else?" When no one spoke up, she said, "I suppose it's my turn, then." She picked up her teacup and took a sip. Failure was never easy to admit. "I've no idea who murdered Edith Durant, and furthermore, I think I've led you all down the garden path." She ignored their protests and raised her hand for silence. "I'm not being melodramatic. I genuinely have no idea who killed that woman, and after what happened today, I'm not sure I trust my so-called inner voice, either."

Stunned into silence, they sat there until Mrs. Goodge

snorted. "Don't be ridiculous. You get melodramatic all the time and your 'inner voice' hasn't failed us yet. Now, instead of sittin' there slapping yourself up because you've not solved it yet, tell us what happened today."

Mrs. Jeffries gaped at her a moment and then burst out laughing. "Oh gracious, I needed that. Thank you, Mrs. Goodge. Alright, I'll tell all. For some reason, I got it into my head that the key to this murder was Highgate Cemetery."

"Which means that it probably is the key," Luty confirmed. "I trust that 'inner voice' of yours. As a matter of fact, I trust my own 'inner voice.' It's kept me and a few other people alive more than once in my life. But go on."

"Thank you, Luty. It's comforting when your friends have faith in you. But as I was saying, I had it in my head that the key is Highgate Cemetery, and as the evidence is now pointing to the killer being one of Edith Durant's tenants, I went there and gave the clerk in the office a rather complicated story about coming here from Australia and needing to pay my respects to my dead relatives."

"I take it those relatives had the surnames Morecomb, Redley, Teasdale, and Erskine," Hatchet said.

She nodded, her expression forlorn. "The clerk was most polite and opened his ledger. Unfortunately, there were no Morecombs, Redleys, or Teasdales buried there, and the only Erskine that has a grave in Highgate died in 1840, well before Edith Durant was born."

"That don't mean one of them tenants ain't responsible," Luty insisted. "They're crooks. We don't even know if they're using their real names."

Mrs. Jeffries stared off into space, and the others, somewhat alarmed by the misery in her expression, kept silent.

Again, it was Mrs. Goodge who spoke up. "Hepzibah, put it away for now. We'll meet again tomorrow morning after you've had a chance to hear what the inspector and Constable Barnes have to say. They must have learned something useful today."

Mrs. Jeffries' frame of mind hadn't improved very much by the time the inspector came home. As she hung up his bowler, she noticed that he didn't look all that chipper, either. "How was your day, sir?"

"I'm not sure," he admitted honestly. "We found out an enormous amount of information, but I've no idea if it puts us any closer to finding Edith Durant's killer."

She understood completely but could hardly tell him, so instead, she said, "Nonsense, sir, you know it's simply your mind doing what it always does at this point in the case. You think you're hopelessly muddled and then seemingly out of nowhere your 'inner voice' leads you to the right conclusion."

He looked at her, his expression hopeful. "Do you really think so?"

She forced herself to laugh. "Oh, sir, stop teasing me. Let's go have a Harvey's and you can tell me about your day."

"That's an excellent idea." He grinned broadly. "I always feel better when we have our sherry." He marched down the hall to the drawing room.

She came in behind him and went straight to the liquor cabinet. Pulling out a bottle of Harvey's Bristol Cream, she poured both of them a drink. "Now, sir, tell me about your day and don't tease me anymore—we both know that your 'inner voice' is guiding you in the proper direction."

"One does like to think so," he agreed. "But honestly, you've more faith in my 'inner voice' than I have."

"Don't be ridiculous, sir," she said, echoing Mrs. Goodge's words. "You're brilliant." She pulled out all the stops. "You simply must have more faith in yourself. Now, what happened today?"

"Oh, it was most extraordinary." He sipped his sherry as he told her about the events of his day.

"So of the four tenants, three of them have confirmed alibis," she clarified. "Morecomb's the only one who is unaccounted for at the time of the murder."

"Indeed, and of course, I feel somewhat annoyed with myself for not insisting he be more specific about his whereabouts when she was killed. But considering what he claimed he did for a living, selling safes and vaults, I understood that it might do real damage to his livelihood if we insisted on speaking to his customer. That was a terrible mistake."

"Because he's disappeared, sir?" she asked.

"That's right. We've got constables watching the house tonight in case he returns, but I've a feeling he's gone."

"Do you think he took whatever was in that buried box? I know you think it was money, but there could have been something else, right?"

"Oh yes, and that's one of the reasons that we've constables guarding the house: We don't want any of the others making a run for the Continent," he explained. "Morecomb went to Victoria Station, which leads me to think he planned to cross the channel. Yee gods, it's difficult to find them when they do that."

"I don't understand, sir. If the other three have alibis,

why would they make a run for the Continent? You're not going to arrest any of them for murder."

"Not murder, no, but there's a good chance Inspector Rogers will arrest one or more of them for burglary tomorrow morning." He took another sip. "After we finished searching the garden, we went to Y Division. I told him what Constable Barnes pointed out to me—mainly, that the ledger was basically an account book. Once one looked at it from that point of view, it became obvious that Edith Durant was nothing more than a very clever purveyor of stolen goods. A fence."

"Gracious, sir, that's extraordinary. How on earth did Constable Barnes and you come to that conclusion?"

"The only thing that made sense about the entries was that each one had a monetary value, a city, and a date. The names were from nursery rhymes and didn't seem to make sense at all until Constable Barnes suggested that we look at the nursery rhyme names and substitute them with the identities of the people who lodged in her house. That seemed to work. She used these silly names to keep track of who had stolen the goods. It was her own personal code."

"But surely a real name would be easier to remember."

"Not really. When we took another look at the ledger with Inspector Rogers, it became obvious the burglaries were spread over the past two years and involved a lot of thieves. She might not have wanted to use real names in case the book fell into the wrong hands, which, of course, it did. Ours. Rogers said he'd heard rumors of a large international fencing ring run by a woman, but he'd not given it any credence."

"And you think Edith Durant was the brains behind this,

uh, criminal ring?" Her spirits lifted. The constable had cleverly come up with a way to pass along their suspicions about Edith Durant and her tenants.

"Indeed we do. That's why we've constables guarding the lodging house. We don't want Gordon Redley or John Erskine stealing off in the night." He finished his sherry. "Shall we have another?"

"Of course, sir." She took both their glasses to the drinks cabinet and refilled them with sherry. "What about that Norman Teasdale, sir? Aren't you afraid he'll try and leave as well?" she asked as she gave him his drink.

"Not really. Mr. Teasdale is the one person we think might be a legitimate businessman."

That had been Hatchet's assessment as well, she remembered. "The box, sir, the one you found buried—are you fairly certain it belonged to Edith Durant?"

"Oh yes, that's why the constable and I did another search," he said. "I got to thinking about Mrs. Travers' statement, and I realized that there had to be a reason Durant got so upset when she thought she was being watched."

"Very clever, sir, and when you came home, you were convinced that you didn't know what to make of this case."

"Well, one doesn't like to count one's chickens before they hatch, and hopefully, by tomorrow, we'll have some idea as to where Andrew Morecomb has gone."

"If he left from Victoria, it was probably to the south coast," she suggested.

"That's what we thought, so Inspector Rogers immediately sent off telegrams to all the authorities in the port cities. We don't think he's left the country as yet so we're hopeful we can get our hands on the fellow."

"Will you arrest him for murder?"

"Probably, but we've got very little evidence against him. That's one of the reasons I don't quite understand this case," he admitted. "On the other hand, Morecomb was the most adamant in refusing to tell us where he was at the time of the killing."

"Do you think she was blackmailing him?" Again, something tugged at the back of her mind and then disappeared as quickly as it had come.

"That's possible, I suppose, or perhaps he simply wanted to steal the contents of the box she'd buried in the ivy. We might know more tomorrow."

"What's happening tomorrow?"

"Inspector Rogers and his men are going to search the house."

"But you've already done that," she protested.

"Not the tenants' rooms," he reminded her. "But tomorrow, Rogers and his lads are going over their quarters most carefully."

"Will you and Constable Barnes be there as well?"

"I will, but the constable has to testify at the Old Bailey on that fraud case we worked on last month. He'll come when he's finished. Inspector Rogers asked me to attend just in case they find any evidence pertaining to the murder."

Mrs. Jeffries put the last of the dinner dishes in the drying rack over the sink and wiped her hands on her apron. Outside, it was full dark, and from her vantage point on the lower ground floor of the kitchen, she watched the wheels of a carriage as it trundled past the quiet house.

Over dinner, she'd told the others what she'd found out

from Witherspoon, and she'd been surprised by how disappointed they were that their dear inspector had solved this one.

"Is this all there is, then?" Phyllis had demanded. "Our inspector just waits until Morecomb gets spotted somewhere and then gets to arrest him?"

"Well, yes, I suppose that's right," she'd replied.

"But why? Did he say why Morecomb wanted her dead?"

"No, but the police are hoping to find something tomorrow when they search his rooms that might explain his motive."

"But there's no evidence that Morecomb's guilty," Mrs. Goodge insisted. "All he did was steal what was in that box and leave. He's a thief—isn't that the sort of thing they do all the time?"

"It don't make sense that 'e did it," Wiggins muttered. "'E was right there in the 'ouse with the woman. Why would he bother lurin' 'er to a ruddy cemetery? That'd be too much like 'ard work."

Mrs. Jeffries had finally calmed them down and shooed them off to their rooms by declaring she'd do the clearing up on her own. In truth, she shared some of the same concerns they'd brought up. She unrolled her sleeves and grabbed the broom that she'd propped against the end of the sink.

Sweeping was a mindless, boring activity that left her mind free. She swept her way to the middle of the kitchen floor with long, even strokes of the broom, shepherding the dirt into a neat pile in the center. Then she went to the other end and continued. Wiggins had made an important point: Why bother luring the victim to Highgate Cemetery? That was indeed too much like hard work.

Surely, in a household where no one apparently paid attention to normal social conventions, Morecomb would have had ample opportunity to murder the woman. The other tenants were often gone, the cook spent her evenings at the pub, Etta Morgan stayed out late on her day off, and Carrie Durridge probably took advantage of the situation as well.

Mrs. Goodge had made an important point as well, she thought as she nudged one of the chairs to one side and jammed the broom under the table. They had absolutely no evidence against Andrew Morecomb. Stealing the contents of the box and running off was generally the kind of behavior one would expect of a thief, but that didn't mean he was guilty of murder.

She pushed more chairs out of the way and swept the crumbs from under the table. Phyllis, of course, had hit the nail on the head, so to speak. Why would Morecomb want Edith Durant dead? There was no honor among thieves; she knew that quite well. But when crooks fought between themselves, the battles were short, hard, and practical. Edith Durant's death was the opposite of that. It was planned and staged as if it were a Greek tragedy. She was murdered by someone who hated her and wanted her to suffer. Someone who had taken great pains to insure that her real identity would be exposed even before her body was cold.

But who?

Mrs. Jeffries finished her chores, made sure the doors were locked, and then went upstairs to her room. She was tired, depressed, and didn't know what on earth she could do about it. She undressed quickly, put on her nightdress, and stood in the darkened room, staring out the window at the lamplight across the road.

Telling the inspector Morecomb wasn't the killer wouldn't work, because there was a chance that he *had* done it. For all any of them knew, Morecomb and Durant might have had a long and convoluted history.

They could have once been lovers and perhaps she'd abandoned him just as she'd abandoned Carl Christopher. The more Mrs. Jeffries thought about it, the better she liked that idea. After all, she told herself as she pulled back her covers and climbed into bed, Durant had been strangled with a bright red cord and red did symbolize affairs of the heart.

Closing her eyes, she took deep, even breaths until she dozed off. But her sleep wasn't peaceful. Bits of conversation and strange images drifted through her half-sleeping brain.

Annie said the pub was real crowded that night and the woman next to her had jostled her arm, spilling her drink over and ruining her skirt. Phyllis' soft voice drifted in and out of her consciousness. *She admitted she went to the pub, but she claimed she'd never slept that hard before, and then it happened again the next night—that's when Edith sacked her.* Maybe this means something, she thought. Then again, maybe it doesn't. But Phyllis' soft voice kept intruding. *The only other thing she said was that she'd seen the woman who'd ruined her skirt going into a hotel on the Edgware Road. Annie said the woman was wearing a fancy cloak over a maid's uniform.*

Mrs. Jeffries rolled to her side and gave up trying to sleep. It would be impossible anyway. When her mind was in this sort of state, the only thing to do was to give in and hope that exhaustion or inspiration would eventually claim her.

Then it was Witherspoon's voice she heard. *Mrs. Travers*

wasn't even home the night that Edith Durant supposedly saw her spying over the fence. We verified she was telling the truth. Her maid had accompanied her to the train station and helped her on the train to Leeds.

So if it wasn't Mrs. Travers spying on Edith, she wondered, then who was? Perhaps the woman had simply imagined seeing someone. Mrs. Jeffries discarded that idea immediately; the victim was a cold, calculating person not given to flights of fancy or imagination. What's more, she'd been living a life outside the bounds of society and the law for a long time. She was not only used to looking over her shoulder, she was probably very proficient at spotting danger.

Suddenly, it was Mrs. Goodge's turn. *Karlotta Christopher swore vengeance when the judge sentenced her brother to hang. But we've not heard of any judges bein' murdered in the last few years.*

All she said was that the Christopher family sold the house to pay the legal bills, and there was gossip that Karlotta Christopher had used the money to bribe a clergyman to write a letter to the Home Office in an attempt to get his sentence commuted to prison rather than hanging.

Then Luty came into her mind. *I found out that Edith Durant's will is valid.*

But Edith Durant had left all her worldly goods to Carl Christopher, who was dead and buried. But even dead men had relatives, she thought. No, she concluded, it was stretching credulity a bit to think that one of Christopher's long-lost cousins could have tracked down the woman Scotland Yard had hunted for years and then lured her to a cemetery in order to kill her for her fortune. Furthermore, knowing what they knew about the victim, there was a good chance the Crown could prove that every penny of her estate was obtained through a crime.

What about Karlotta Christopher? Surely she had a motive to murder Edith. Mrs. Jeffries discarded that idea as well. No one had seen or heard of her since her brother's execution. According to the inspector, they'd sent Christopher's personal effects to her flat and they'd been returned to the police. Witherspoon had gone there personally and spoken to the porter. He said that the day after her brother died she'd simply walked out of the flat and disappeared. There was some speculation that she might have committed suicide but that was never proven.

Mrs. Jeffries shook her head. She was certain that unless Andrew Morecomb had another personal reason to murder his landlady, then someone else had done the deed. Edith hadn't been murdered for her money or her house. She'd been killed because she was hated.

CHAPTER 11

Mrs. Jeffries stifled a yawn as she slipped into her chair and picked up the tea Mrs. Goodge put in front of her. She glanced around the table, her gaze stopping at the empty spot next to Smythe. "Where's Betsy?" She put her cup down. "Isn't she coming?"

"She's home with the little one," Smythe replied. "The princess seems to be sproutin' more teeth so both of 'em 'ad a miserable night. But she told me to get 'er if she's needed."

"That won't be necessary," Mrs. Jeffries said. "I don't think we've much to do today." She'd spent half the night going over and over everything she could remember about this case, and she was almost certain that Andrew Morecomb wasn't the killer. But despite that, she simply couldn't determine who might be guilty or what they ought to do next. What was worse, she had the feeling the answer was right in front of her but she was too blind to see it.

"Didn't you find out anything useful from the inspector last night or Constable Barnes this morning?" Ruth asked.

"Constable Barnes didn't come today. He's testifying at the Old Bailey in a fraud case but I found out quite a bit from the inspector." She told them what she'd already shared with Wiggins, Mrs. Goodge, and Phyllis. "Andrew Morecomb will be arrested as soon as they find where he's gone. But in all honesty, I don't think he's guilty."

"Then who is?" Luty demanded. "We're runnin' out of suspects. If it ain't one of the tenants or some relative of Carl Christopher, then I'd like to know who else it could be."

Everyone began talking at once, agreeing with Luty or voicing their disappointment that the case might, for once, have defeated them.

"We can't give up now," Hatchet argued. "If Morecomb is innocent, then it would be a terrible miscarriage of justice if he's arrested for the murder."

"I agree," Ruth added. "Even if he is a burglar, that doesn't mean he's a killer. Besides, Durant's murder seemed very staged, as if the murderer was making a statement of some kind. Why would Morecomb bother with all that when he could have just slipped into her room and put a pillow over her face?"

"It was like a play, wasn't it?" Phyllis mused. "The murder weapon was a red cord and the newspaper clipping was left there deliberately. But why? What was the killer trying to say? That's what I don't understand."

"But if it's not Morecomb, who is it?" Smythe argued. "Unless it's some long-lost relation of Carl Christopher wanting either Edith Durant's fortune or a bit of vengeance on 'er for leavin' 'im to hang, then Luty's right and we're out of suspects."

Mrs. Jeffries went perfectly still for a moment as she realized precisely what her "inner voice" had been trying to tell her last night. "My gracious, I've been such a fool. Of course she disappeared—that's the only way she could achieve her goal."

Everyone stopped talking and turned their attention to the housekeeper.

Her face was a mask of concentration as she stared off into space. "I can see where I went wrong," she finally muttered. "We don't know that the two women ever met, which means she could easily have slipped past Durant's usual defenses."

"I do hope you're goin' to be sharin' whatever it is you're muttering about with the rest of us," Luty said.

"She's figured it out." Mrs. Goodge beamed proudly. "I knew she would."

Mrs. Jeffries gave her head a small shake. "Wiggins, can you get to the Old Bailey? Find Constable Barnes and get him to the lodging house as soon as he's free. He might have been planning on going there in any case, but don't let him hang about the court—get him moving quickly. Tell him to keep a close eye on our inspector."

Wiggins was already on his feet and moving toward the coat tree. "Should I take a hansom? That's the fastest."

"It'll be even faster if I take ya in the carriage." Luty shoved back her chair. But Mrs. Jeffries waved her back in her seat.

"No, Luty, I need you to do something else," Mrs. Jeffries

instructed. "Wiggins can take a cab." The footman nodded in understanding and headed for the back door. She turned back to the American. "I need you to go to Highgate Cemetery. I can't believe I was there yesterday and I stupidly asked about the wrong people. The clerk has already seen me, and this time, I don't think he'll bother to pretend to believe me."

"What do ya want me to do?"

"Find out if the Christopher family has a mausoleum or a crypt."

"That's all?" Luty stared at her suspiciously.

"Don't look at me like that," Mrs. Jeffries protested. "I'm not just sending you off to get you out of the way. We really need this information."

"But wouldn't Carl Christopher be buried at Newgate Prison?" Mrs. Goodge asked. "That's where he was hung."

"That's right, but it makes no difference if my idea is right." She stopped. "Well, it might, but it shouldn't. Oh gracious, it's hideously complicated and I might be leading all of you down the garden path."

"Stop yer frettin'." Luty hung on to her fur muff as she got up and went around the table toward the coat tree. "I'll do it."

Hatchet leapt up and grabbed her cloak. He draped it around her shoulders. "Stop at the house and pick up young Jon. I don't like you out and about on your own."

"I can take care of myself. I don't need that young pup doggin' my heels." She started for the back door but Hatchet moved to block her.

"Unless you give me your word of honor that you'll take Jon, I'll accompany you myself."

She glared at him and scurried to the right. "Oh, alright, you stiff-necked old woman. I'll take him with me."

"And mind you, leave that ridiculous gun of yours at home," he called as she stalked off.

Luty didn't dignify that with an answer; she simply gave the door a nice slam on her way out.

Hatchet smiled apologetically as he came back to the table. "I take it you have something in mind for me to do?"

"I've something for all of us to do," Mrs. Jeffries replied.

Two constables guarded the open doors of the drawing room. Inside, the inspector could see Gordon Redley sitting on the settee, staring forlornly at the floor while John Erskine paced back and forth in front of the fireplace. Erskine stopped when he saw the inspector. "You've no right to do this," he spluttered. "You'll be hearing from my solicitor."

Inspector Witherspoon turned as he heard footsteps coming down the stairs. Inspector Rogers grinned broadly. Behind him came two constables. One carried a large black canvas bag and the other carried a paper-wrapped bundle. "Constable Jones," he called, "ask Mr. Erskine to step out here. We'd like him to explain how these items came to be in his room."

Witherspoon stepped back out of the way as Erskine raced into the foyer and then began howling that he'd never seen those things before. Five minutes later, Erskine was in handcuffs and being led out of the house to the police station.

Rogers turned to Witherspoon. "We owe you, Inspector. Without your information we'd never have solved these burglaries. There was a coin collection, a small painting, and a pair of gold candlesticks in Erskine's room, and I imagine we'll find some equally interesting bits and pieces in Redley's quarters."

"You owe me nothing, Inspector," Witherspoon said. "I was merely doing my duty as any officer would do. I'm pleased to have been able to help. I don't suppose you found anything up there that's connected to the murder?" That was his whole reason for being at the lodging house while Y Division searched the premises. He was to take charge of any evidence pertaining to the Durant murder. But thus far they'd found nothing.

"Sorry," Rogers said. "Nothing yet. But we've still got two more rooms to do as well as the box room. Something might turn up."

"Where are the servants?" Witherspoon asked.

"They've all gone." Rogers glanced up the staircase. "I thought it best to keep them out of the way in case there was any trouble with Erskine or Redley. The cook's gone to the pub and the little scullery maid went to visit her family. As to the other lady, I've no idea where she went."

There was a scraping noise and a series of thumps from overhead and then a shout. "We've found something, sir." A constable appeared on the landing. "You'd best come see, sir."

"Keep an eye on that one, Constable." Rogers pointed to Redley as he sprinted up the staircase.

"Will do, sir," the constable by the drawing room replied. A moment later, he frowned. "Hey, Mickey, who let you in here?"

Witherspoon turned around to see a young lad standing in the doorway. Pale faced, black haired, and wearing a thin gray jacket that was two inches too short in the sleeves, he looked to be one of the boys that hung around the streets earning a few bob running errands or delivering messages.

"The constable outside said I could come in. I've got a message for Inspector Witherspoon." He held up a cream-colored envelope.

"Well, give it to him, then, and take yourself off," the constable ordered.

"I've got to take 'im somewhere," the lad looked at Witherspoon. "You the inspector?"

"I am indeed. What's your name?"

"Mickey Bales." He gave him the envelope.

Witherspoon ripped it open, pulled out a piece of matching stationery, and read the note.

Inspector Witherspoon,

You're the only person I dare trust. Please help me.
I know who killed Edith Durant and I'm afraid I'm going to be next.
I beg you, if you value my life, tell no one. Just follow the boy, he'll bring you to me.
Carrie Durridge

"Can we go now?" Mickey looked worriedly at the door. "She told me to bring you right quick if I wanted the other half of my money."

Witherspoon hesitated and then made up his mind. Inspector Rogers didn't know where Carrie Durridge was so she might genuinely be in danger. He couldn't take the risk.

"Everything alright, sir?" the constable on the door asked.

"Yes, yes, I've just got to go with this young man right now. Tell Inspector Rogers I'll be back as soon as I can, and if Constable Barnes arrives, ask him to wait for me."

"Let's go," he said to the lad.

"I think we've come the long way around, madam," Jon, Luty's tall young footman, commented as he pushed back a clump of overgrown brush and held it so she could step past him.

"Don't matter which way we've come as long as we git there." Luty stopped and took a deep breath. She stared at the narrow path leading to a row of crypts.

"Should we take a closer look, madam?" Jon asked. He, like everyone who worked for Luty, adored her. She'd taken him in years ago and supposedly he was her footman, but in truth, she'd seen that he had a fine education, and next year, she was paying for him to go to Harvard.

Luty opened her mouth and then just as quickly clamped it shut.

"What's wrong?" he began, but she shushed him.

"What in the name of blue blazes is goin on here?" she whispered as she stepped backward, almost shoving Jon into the shrubbery. He grabbed her arm as he stumbled, pulling them both back behind the overgrown bush.

Luty yanked hard on his hand, bringing both of them down onto the path. "Stay down. Somethin' ain't right here. I can feel it."

She straightened up and took another peek at the path.

Jon, being a foot taller, only had to crane his neck to get

a good view. "Hell's bells, isn't that Inspector Witherspoon?" he muttered. "And does that woman have a gun to his back?"

"She does," Luty whispered. She knew what she had to do. "You still a fast runner, Jon?"

Jon nodded and then caught himself. "I ain't bloomin' leavin' ya," he hissed. Despite his fancy education, he reverted to his previous speech patterns and accent when upset. "You're goin' to try and 'elp the inspector and that woman's got a great big gun."

Luty smiled craftily. "If you insist on stayin', you'll git us all killed. I know what I'm doin'. Now, git. Sneak down this back path and out to the road. There's a fixed point constable on the high street. Run like the wind and git us some help."

Scared that he'd never see her again, he hesitated, but she gave his a hard shove and he knew he had no choice. He turned and kept low, racing down the path and out of sight.

Luty risked standing up so she could see. Witherspoon and the woman were now close enough for her to hear them. The woman poked the inspector in the back with her gun. "Step lively, Inspector, we've not much time. It's not much farther. Turn in there, please." With her free hand, she pointed to a narrow path in front of the center crypt.

Witherspoon stopped and whirled around to face her. "Why are you doing this? You'll never get away with it. The police know that lad you sent to fetch me by name. When I don't return, they'll question him."

"I don't care, Inspector. I don't care if they send two hundred policemen here to get me, because by then, you'll be dead. Now get moving or I'll do it right here on the path."

Chills shot up Luty's spine and she straightened to her full height. The woman, whoever the devil she was, was crazier than a coot. She glanced over to where Jon had disappeared and tried to estimate how far from the gate they were and how long it might take him to bring back help. But even before she finished calculating time and distance, she knew it was futile. He'd not get back in time.

"Take a look at the name over the door," the woman ordered.

Luty turned back toward them. They stood in a frozen tableau outside the iron gates of the crypt. Witherspoon's spectacles slid back up his nose as he read the inscription carved into the stone.

"Christopher." He shook his head in disbelief. "What is this?"

"And you call yourself a detective." She laughed again, reached around him, and shoved open the iron gate. "It's my family's burial crypt, the place where my brother would be resting peacefully if you'd done your job right. Now get inside."

Luty knew she had to act; she picked up her muff and shoved her right hand inside it. She stepped out from behind the bush and waited, wanting to time it just right.

"Your brother? You mean Carl Christopher was your brother?" Witherspoon exclaimed.

"Lord, it took you long enough." She sneered. "Yes, he was my brother and I've waited years to avenge his death." She poked him again with the gun. "Now get inside. I don't want the police showing up before we're finished here. That could get very awkward."

"You killed Edith Durant," he cried. "But how can that be? You'd been working for her. Didn't she know who you were?"

"We never met." She put the gun to the back of his head. "I lived in Italy when my brother married into that wretched family, and we both know that family ties weren't all that important to Edith. The selfish cow couldn't stand her own family let alone Carl's. Now move."

"Yoo hoo, Inspector Witherspoon, is that you?" Luty waved cheerfully. "Gracious me, I thought that was you. Who's your friend? I was drivin' past when I saw you come in here and I've been followin' you all over the danged place. It'll save me a trip to your house today." She kept her smile firmly in place and the words flowing as she hurried as fast as she dared across the space separating her from the crypt.

Surprised, the woman's jaw dropped but she recovered fast. She swiveled and aimed the gun at Luty. "I don't know who you are, old lady, but you're going to have to join my little party."

"Please, let her go. She's nothing to do with this," Witherspoon pleaded.

The woman ignored him and waved her gun toward the crypt door. "Get over here, old woman."

"Hold your danged horses. I'm moving as fast as I can." She eased her fingers around the handle of the Colt in her muff.

"Get inside," she ordered as Luty reached them.

"Oh dear God, Luty, I'm so sorry," Witherspoon muttered. "This shouldn't be happening."

Luty ignored him as she stepped onto the stone stairs

leading down into the crypt. With her back now to the lunatic with the gun, she concentrated on moving her fingers into place so that when she had her chance, she could use her own gun.

Witherspoon and the woman came down the steps behind her.

"Get over to the other side," she ordered Luty, jutting her chin toward the opposite side of the structure.

The woman must have been here earlier, because a lantern burned in the far corner, and with the daylight seeping in from the door, Luty could see to make her away across the floor. Three of the four walls consisted of vaults neatly stacked in rows of three, and most had names and dates engraved in their centers. But the crypt was neglected; cobwebs hung from the corners, dirt dusted the floor, and the smell of damp and mildew was so strong it was almost overpowering.

Luty wanted to buy some time. "Why you doin' this, lady?"

"Why don't you ask him?" She shoved the inspector toward the brightly lighted corner.

"She's Karlotta Christopher, Carl Christopher's sister," he said. He looked at the woman whom he used to know as Carrie Durridge. "Please allow Mrs. Crookshank to leave. She's innocent in this matter and has nothing to do with your vendetta. You obviously don't care if you get caught and hung."

"You mean the way my brother was hung," she interrupted. "No, I don't care and what's more I don't care how many people I take with me."

"Knowin' who the blazes you are don't tell me why you're doin' it." Luty snorted. "Or are ya dumb as well as mean?"

"Do I have to spell it out for you?" Karlotta Christopher waved her weapon toward Witherspoon. "He arrested my brother but let the witch who planned it all get away. What's more, he didn't have the brains to catch her once she'd given him the slip."

"Then you must be right smart if you was able to find her after all this time." Inside the muff, Luty forced her stiff fingers to relax.

"I am smart, or at least, I'm more clever than the police, because unlike them, I never stopped looking."

"Neither did we," Witherspoon protested.

"Oh please, she was right under your nose and you didn't see her," Karlotta scoffed. "But luckily for me, I spotted her at King's Cross right before Christmas when she came back from Scotland. I followed her home, saw where she lived, and then set about laying my trap. It was dead easy."

"Easy how?" Luty wiggled her fingers inside the thick fur and prayed her arthritis wouldn't kick in when she had her chance. "Uh, I mean, what did ya do?"

"I did lots of things." Karlotta giggled. "Edith was greedy and cheap. All it took was for me to manipulate her into sacking one of her maids and then hiring me. After that, it was child's play."

"So you worked for this woman?" Luty cast another quick look toward the doorway but saw no help coming from that quarter.

"For several months." Karlotta laughed again, an ugly braying sound that echoed off the walls. "And despite her being able to outwit the police, she didn't have the brains to outwit me."

"If you hated her so much, why'd you wait so long to

kill her?" Luty hoped the inspector would figure out she was trying her best to buy them time.

"Why do you think? I wanted to make her suffer. I wanted to pay her back for all those years she kept me from my brother. She was jealous of me, you know, even though she didn't know me. She couldn't stand the thought of sharing Carl with anyone." Her lips compressed in a flat, harsh line and the hand holding the gun began to tremble. "I wanted her to pay for that." She suddenly grinned. "At first it was just petty vengeance, but it was fun. She thought she was so smart, but before I even moved into the lodging house, I managed to steal her mail three times, and once I was inside, it was even easier. She kept her bedroom door locked, but I saw where she hid her spare key."

Desperate for more time, Luty blurted, "Where was that? Where'd she hide it?"

"In that ugly cactus on the table outside her door. She shoved it under the soil at the edge of the pot and thought she was safe because no one would want to risk getting pricked by the plant. But I was willing to risk it and found that the key opened more than just her bedroom door." She chuckled. "It was literally the key to watching her go mad with worry. It caused all sorts of problems, but seems to me her lodgers should have been used to trouble—they're a bunch of thieves." She broke off and turned to the inspector. "But you know that, don't you? That's why you sent us away this morning, so those other policemen could search the house."

"That's true," he agreed. "Please, let Mrs. . . ."

"Oh, give it a rest. I'm not letting anyone go," she snapped.

"Why'd you decide to kill her when you did?" Luty asked. "Why then?"

"I had to. She'd sacked me the night before and I couldn't stay there anymore. Besides, I was afraid she was going to make another run for it. So I set her up to meet me here the next morning, waited for her, and killed her. It was very satisfying and very easy. All I had to do was slip a note under her door with her real name on it. 'Dear Edith Durant, If you don't want the police to know where you are, you'd best meet me . . .' et cetera, et cetera, et cetera . . . and then, once I'd killed her, I went back to the house and pretended I'd been there all along, working upstairs in the box room."

"That was a pretty big risk." Luty began easing the gun out of the muff. "Weren't you scared she'd have told someone she let you go?"

Karlotta shook her head. "It was a risk I was willing to take. Besides, knowing her character as I did, I was fairly sure she'd not said anything to anyone. Edith didn't like explaining her actions. But time's getting on, which, of course, brings me to the end of my sad little tale." She turned slightly and moved toward the inspector, with the gun pointing toward this heart. "Sorry, Inspector, but you're as guilty as she was."

He squeezed his eyes shut just as a shot rang out. It took several seconds before he realized he wasn't hit, and when he opened his eyes, he saw Karlotta Christopher drop her weapon as she flopped onto her knees and then crumpled onto the floor. Luty stood like a stone statue, holding a Colt .45.

"Get the gun, Inspector," Luty ordered. "She ain't hit,

but her hair's not going to be the same for a good while, and as irritatin' as this woman is, I'd rather let the law deal with her than have to kill her." On the floor, Karlotta had just realized she wasn't shot. She sat up and scrambled across the stone floor for the weapon. But Witherspoon beat her to it.

"You should have seen her, Mrs. Jeffries, she was ravin' like a banshee and it took three constables to drag her to the police wagon," Smythe reported as he helped himself to a slice of seedcake.

"She was in a terrible state," Hatchet added. "And luckily, both Madam and the inspector appeared to be unharmed."

Following Mrs. Jeffries' instructions from their morning meeting, Smythe and Hatchet had gone to the lodging house just in time to see Barnes, Inspector Rogers, and three other constables racing off. They'd followed them and arrived just as two police constables escorted Luty Belle, the inspector, and a bedraggled woman they now knew was Karlotta Christopher from the Christopher crypt. Keeping out of sight, they again followed them, this time to Y Division headquarters. They'd hung about until Barnes, guessing they might be close by, had slipped outside and told them what had happened.

They raced back to Upper Edmonton Gardens with the news only to discover that Mrs. Jeffries had already deduced the identity of the killer.

"Humph, Madam's going to be ridiculously difficult to live with now," Hatchet complained. "She's at the police station right now being preened over as if she were the

Queen. I'll never hear the end of this." Once he'd learned what had happened, he'd sent up half a dozen silent prayers of thanks that Luty hadn't been hurt. "And it could have ended very badly. Both of them might have gotten killed."

"We should all just be thankful she got there in time to save the inspector," Ruth said firmly. "I, for one, am forever in her debt. I would be so upset if anything happened to my dear Gerald."

"Nothing is going to happen to me, I promise." They all turned to see dear Gerald and a grinning Luty standing in the archway. Jon, who'd insisted on staying with Luty, stood on her other side.

"I am not goin' to be impossible to live with," Luty announced as the group advanced into the kitchen. "Like I was tellin' the inspector here, I just happened to see him goin' into the cemetery, and then Jon and I took after him to invite him and Lady Cannonberry to supper tomorrow night."

"But I got us lost," Jon said, taking up the narrative, "and when we finally found them again, we saw that woman holding a gun on Inspector Witherspoon."

Hatchet pulled out Luty's chair as she came around the table while Witherspoon motioned for Mrs. Jeffries to stay seated. He slipped into the empty spot next to Ruth.

"But luckily, Jon's as fast as the wind," Luty continued. "And I had my peacemaker with me. Mind you"—she gave Witherspoon an admiring glance—"it was right smart of the inspector to keep that crazy woman talking so long. It gave Jon time to get us help."

"You're too modest, Luty." Witherspoon smiled gratefully at the elderly woman. "If you'd not been there with your weapon, I'd be dead. She meant to kill me. And, by the way, you were the one who had the good sense to keep her talking."

"Nonsense, we both did our part."

"What'd ya say to her?" Wiggins asked.

"I jist asked a couple of questions, and she started braggin' about how smart she was and how she made Edith Durant's life miserable."

"You were very clever, Luty," Witherspoon declared. "And thanks to you, by the time Barnes and Inspector Rogers arrived, Karlotta Christopher was disarmed and we had everything under control," he added. He glanced at Smythe and then at Hatchet. "How did you two know something untoward had happened?"

"I sent 'em a message," Jon said. He stood behind Luty's chair. "When you was takin' Mrs. Crookshank's statement, I slipped out and sent a street lad with a note to Mr. Hatchet. I knew he'd be here, we were to meet Mrs. Crookshank here so she could invite you to supper tomorrow night."

This was a blatant lie, of course, but none of them minded. What's more, it seemed to do the trick.

"It must have been quite a detailed note." Witherspoon laughed. "They knew that dear Mrs. Crookshank had saved my life."

"That's really all I wrote," Jon said quickly. "Just that there'd been trouble and Mrs. Crookshank and her gun had kept you from being shot by that crazy woman."

"Tell us what happened, Gerald." Ruth patted his arm. "I got here just as Jon's note arrived, and once I knew you'd been in danger, I couldn't leave until I saw you with my own eyes."

"Now, now, my dear, I'm fine. But I will admit, it's been a very trying day," he replied. "The maid at the lodging house, Carrie Durridge, is really Karlotta Christopher, Carl Christopher's sister."

"She's the one who murdered Edith Durant," Mrs. Goodge exclaimed.

"She was. She admitted it to Luty and me when she had us in the crypt. But I get ahead of myself. I went with Inspector Rogers and his constables when they searched the tenants' rooms, and they found evidence linking Gordon Redley and John Erskine to the burglaries. They're both under arrest." He told them about the note he'd received from Carrie Durridge. "I went along with the lad to the main gate of the West Cemetery at Highgate and he led me deep inside the grounds. Finally, just as I was going to ask him if this was some sort of odd joke, I saw her. She gave the lad a shilling and he left. I turned my head for a moment, and when I turned back to her, she was pointing a gun at me. She insisted that I come with her and she led me to the Christopher crypt."

"Why there, sir?" Mrs. Jeffries asked.

"That's where Carl Christopher would have been laid to rest if he'd not been hung," Luty interjected. "Leastways, that's what she said. Mind you, I think the woman was just crazy as a coot and wantin' to shoot someone."

"But how did she know where Edith Durant was?" Hatchet asked.

"She's been tracking her for years without much success and then saw her at King's Cross Station." Witherspoon told them everything that had transpired in the crypt. "Then, just when I was sure I was going to meet my

Maker, Mrs. Crookshank came to my rescue." He smiled at her. "That was an incredible shot. You're an amazing marksman."

Luty chuckled. "I've had a lot of practice."

Hatchet snorted but held his tongue.

Witherspoon smiled faintly and angled his head to one side as he studied the elderly American. "Between the burglars being arrested and my attempted murder, there was so much confusion at the station that I don't recall anyone asking why you had a gun with you."

"That was my fault, sir," Jon interjected. "I kept begging Mrs. Crookshank to show me how to fire it. She's sending me to college in America next year, and from what I understand, everyone there can shoot. I nagged her into letting me see how it works. We were on our way out to the country so she could show me when we saw you and that lad going into Highgate."

Luty gave him a grateful smile. "I tried to tell Jon that he's not goin' to the Wild West for his schoolin', but he reads all them lurid novels and thinks everyone carries a six-shooter."

"You've had a very trying day, Gerald." Ruth ran her hand along his arm. "Why don't you walk me home and stay for dinner?"

"That would be lovely, Ruth," he replied.

A few minutes later, they were bundled in their coats. Ruth looked over her shoulder and nodded at Mrs. Jeffries as they left—her signal that she expected them to tell her any details she'd missed.

Luty looked at Jon. "That was fast thinkin', Jon, thank ya."

"I didn't want you to get into trouble," he admitted. "People don't understand that when Hatchet's not with you, you feel safer with your peacemaker."

"You're a good lad, Jon. Can you do me another favor? McGregor's out front with the carriage, but he's not had a break all day. There's a nice pub around the corner, so why don't the two of you go git yourself a quick one while I finish up here. Hatchet and I'll meet you at the carriage in a half hour or so."

"Thanks, madam." Jon grinned broadly, waved a quick good-bye, and raced for the door.

"He's afraid you'll change your mind," Hatchet said dryly. "Madam doesn't normally send the lad off to drink."

"After what he's been through today, he deserves one." She turned to Mrs. Jeffries. "Do you understand what in tarnation went on today? I know that Carrie Durridge was actually Karlotta Christopher, and she told me herself about how she pulled off her tricks and the actual killing, but I'm still confused about a few things."

"We all are," Smythe muttered.

"Mrs. Jeffries had already figured out Carrie was Karlotta," Mrs. Goodge said, "but she didn't reckon on the crazy woman trying to kill the inspector today."

"No, and if Luty hadn't been there with her gun, my stupidity would have cost the inspector his life."

"But he ain't dead," Luty said firmly. "Now, come on, tell us how you figured it out."

"There were two items that bothered me." She took a sip of tea. "One, there was no logical reason for Andrew Morecomb to have lured Edith all the way to Highgate just to kill her. He was a cold, pragmatic criminal who wouldn't have bothered with such a staged situation. Secondly, the newspaper clipping was planted in her hand for a reason, and last night I realized the reason wasn't just so the body could be identified quickly. The clipping was planted as a way to lure Inspector Witherspoon into the case."

"You were right about that," Luty agreed. "The inspector hedged just a bit when he was tellin' what happened in the crypt. Karlotta Christopher held him as responsible for her brother's death as she did Edith Durant."

"I couldn't sleep last night. I kept thinking about who it could possibly be if it wasn't Morecomb. Then I remembered what Annie Linden had told Phyllis: that a woman had jostled her arm, spilled her drink, and then given Annie a bottle of gin to make up for it. It was that very night that Annie slept so hard she didn't hear the bell ringing, and the same thing happened the next night. Annie ended up getting sacked and Carrie Durridge got her job."

"Was there something in the gin?" Hatchet asked.

"I think so," Mrs. Jeffries said. "A bit of laudanum or some other opiate combined with gin would certainly do the trick."

"And Annie claimed she'd never slept as hard before," Phyllis said. "She also had a terrible headache when she woke up."

"Was that your only reason?" Luty pressed. "Just because Annie Linden got her arm jostled you were able to suss out who the killer was?"

"It wasn't just that," Mrs. Jeffries said. "Edith Durant claimed someone was spying on her, yet her neighbor wasn't home. But she had it in her mind that the spy was a woman because it was Mrs. Travers she accused. So I asked myself, what other woman could it possibly be? When Phyllis said that Annie had seen the woman from the pub going into a hotel on the Edgware Road wearing a fancy cloak over a maid's uniform, I just knew it was her."

"You're right about that, too." Luty gave a quick nod of her head. "Carrie Durridge lived there. They found her room key in her cloak pocket and the inspector sent Constable Jones over to search the place. I imagine he'll find more evidence there."

"You mean, like the rent money she stole," Phyllis suggested.

"Probably." Luty yawned.

"Madam, we need to get you home." Hatchet started to get up, but she waved him back to his seat.

"Not yet. I still want to understand a few things about how she pulled it off." She looked at Mrs. Jeffries. "From what I can piece together, Karlotta Christopher had been tracking Edith Durant ever since her brother was hung."

"Yes. From what we know, she simply walked out of her flat and was never seen again," Mrs. Jeffries agreed.

"So she spots Edith at King's Cross, follows her home, and decides to make her life miserable for a few months until it's time to kill her," Luty said.

"She must have been the woman who was in the neighborhood asking questions about Edith," Mrs. Goodge added. "That's how she found out about the household and the servants goin' to the pub in the evenings."

"After that, it was easy to doctor a bottle of gin and feed it to some unsuspecting young woman so she could get her job." Mrs. Jeffries nodded in satisfaction.

"Then she started playing tricks on Edith," Phyllis said.

"And gettin' a bit of lolly along the way." Smythe laughed. "She took the rent envelopes and stole from the tenants to get Edith in trouble."

"Cor blimey." Wiggins made a face. "But she was Carl's sister. How could Edith Durant not recognize her? She must 'ave seen her at 'er brother's wedding."

"Carl Christopher didn't marry Edith," Mrs. Jeffries reminded them. "He married her twin, Hilda. We don't know that Edith even attended the nuptials. Even back then, she was the black sheep of the family."

"Karlotta said she'd never met Edith," Luty said. "She was living in Italy when he married into the family, and once Edith entered the picture, she made sure he kept his family away."

"Back to the murder." Phyllis desperately wanted to understand the sequence of events. "The night before it happened, Edith caught Carrie/Karlotta snooping in her bedroom, right?"

"That's what she said at the station," Luty confirmed. "Edith told her to get out and not come back. Karlotta went up to the box room and got her carpetbag. Then she went downstairs to the foyer and got one of the rent envelopes and wrote Edith a note telling her to meet her at Highgate Cemetery or she'd go to the police. Edith did as she was told. Karlotta wrapped a cord around her neck, killed her, and tucked the clipping into her hand. Then she slipped back into the lodging house and pretended she'd been cleaning up the box room all along."

"What did the red cord mean?" Phyllis asked.

"I don't know," Luty admitted. "Maybe the inspector

will be able to find that out, but it's got to mean something." She yawned again, and this time she didn't protest when Hatchet insisted on taking her home.

But it wasn't until the next day that they found out why Karlotta Christopher had used the red cord as a murder weapon.

"Her brother had been hanged," Witherspoon explained to Mrs. Jeffries over a glass of sherry, "and Karlotta wanted to make sure that Edith suffered the way her brother had, so she used the red cord from the curtains in her room at the Edgware Hotel and squeezed the life out of her."

"The same way the life had been squeezed out of her brother by the hangman's noose. But why didn't she just use a gun?" Mrs. Jeffries murmured. "Surely that would have been more practical. We know she had one—she used it to threaten you and Luty."

"Because she wanted more than vengeance. She wanted Edith Durant to suffer. Also, she didn't have it then." He shrugged. "She stole that one from Andrew Morecomb. Took it out of his bag when he went out to flag down a hansom cab. By the way, they caught him at Dover. He's been arrested as well."

"How do you feel, sir? You finally caught the one who got away." She watched him carefully as she asked the question.

He thought for a moment. "I'm not certain," he admitted. "I'm hoping that once it settles down in my mind, I'll have some sense that the case is finally closed."

"You closed more than the old case, sir," she reminded

him. "You also closed her murder case and caught a ring of thieves."

"Inspector Rogers is being credited with solving the burglary cases." He smiled. "He didn't want to, but it's only proper, as he and his lads did most of the work."

"What will they do with her, sir?" Mrs. Jeffries took another sip.

"I don't think she'll be hung," he replied. "I'm not a medical man but I do believe that woman is out of her mind. She's not responsible for her actions. I expect she'll spend the rest of her life in prison."

"But she tried to kill you, sir," Mrs. Jeffries protested. "She knew exactly what she was doing when she lured you to that terrible crypt. She must be punished."

Witherspoon smiled sadly. "She may have known what she was doing, but I don't think she was capable of stopping herself. Since her brother died, she's spent every moment of her life wanting vengeance. That's a miserable way to live. Isn't that punishment enough?"

Mrs. Jeffries started to argue the point but then thought better of it. She was quiet for a moment, and finally she said, "Inspector Gerald Witherspoon, you have an incredibly generous heart and soul."

He looked at her and laughed.